AT DUSK

An Alex Troutt Thriller

Book 5

By
John W. Mefford

AT DUSK
Copyright © 2016 by John W. Mefford
All rights reserved.

Second Edition

Sugar Hill Publishing

ISBN-10: 1-943774-18-8
ISBN-13: 978-1-943774-18-0

Interior book design by
Bob Houston eBook Formatting

To stay updated on John's latest releases, visit:
JohnWMefford.com

One

Thirty years ago

Unable to suppress his excitement, he raced across the yard, his breathing pumping in short bursts.

He swung open the screen door until it smacked against the cracked siding on the old home and barreled into the kitchen, eager to share what he'd found in the backyard. He was only ten years old, but he'd always been perceptive enough to recognize an opportunity, especially one that showcased one of his many talents.

Darting into the living room, he found his mother cutting out coupons, one of her daily routines to save the family a buck or two. Her brow was furrowed over her dark eyes as she went about her task. She looked up at him, and her smooth, almost pasty-white complexion coiled into a prune as she swatted her hand in front of her face. "Take that thing out to the garage. It smells to high heaven."

He held the dead squirrel by its tail, its gray and brown carcass already stiffening. "You said the next time I found one, you'd let me do my artwork." He knew he sounded like a whiner, but she'd promised.

"I never said you couldn't practice your new skills, Junior."
She placed her scissors on the coffee table and folded her hands
on her lap. "You know how much I've encouraged you to learn
new things. You've mastered so much already. Come on, let me
hear it," she said with a smile that had always been able to cajole
him into anything.

"La meilleure mère au monde."

She brought her hands to her mouth, her grimace quickly
replaced by an expression of pride and gratitude, given he'd told
her she was the best mother in the world. "Such flattery," she
said, even though he'd said the same phrase to her for the last
two years. "Now, go put that stinky thing in the garage. After you
practice your piano for thirty minutes, then I'll help you get
started on your new project."

He thought about debating the order of the tasks, but he knew
it would do no good. He had another plan, a backup he'd used
countless other times. Scooting outside, he tossed his new friend
over by the tree. Then he scampered back into the house and
made his way into what his mother affectionately called the
music room. He peered over the top of the piano to ensure all
was clear, then he opened the piano bench, shuffled sheet music
to the side, and pulled out a tape recorder. He set it on the bench,
rewound the cassette, then punched the play button. A Chopin
number he'd recorded a week earlier bounced off the walls. It
was called "Ballade No. 1 in G Minor," and he knew it would
calm his always-anxious mother. He couldn't help but smile, not
only at his talent but also his *ingenuity*. His mother had taught
him that word, along with a host of other words and phrases
outside of his regular schoolwork. Anything to make him more
learned and worldly, she often said.

He quietly slipped through the back door, picked up his dead
squirrel, and took it into the garage, where a table was set up for

his craft. His tools were holstered in a leather pouch that clung to a hook on the side of the table. Reaching above his head, he pulled a string to turn on a single lightbulb just above his workstation. He popped his knuckles and then rummaged through the tool pouch, searching for just the right instrument. He picked up an X-Acto blade and twirled it between his fingers, a spear of light gleaming off the clean, flat surface. Then he went to work, pulling skin and tissue away from muscle, ligaments, and bone. He worked meticulously, ensuring the layers of skin weren't damaged. He could envision himself a few years from now performing surgery on a human, as one of the world's renowned open-heart surgeons. But for now, he'd hone his skills on animals.

"Junior."

His breath caught in his throat. He froze, the blade still clinging to the squirrel's exposed skin.

For the next ten minutes, his mother chided him for lying. He stood like a statue, looking straight ahead, but occasionally peeking at his work of art. As her voice droned on forever, it took everything in his power not to rush back and continue his work— what he realized had become more of his passion.

Finally, the endless speech about how to act like a gentleman ceased. And as usual, she leaned over, stared him in the eyes, and then pinched his cheek. "I can't stay mad at my boy long. You're just too good, too smart. Let me watch you perform your work. And remember, it's all about mastering whatever you do. You have the aptitude to do great things, to be the best the world has ever seen. You must think and behave like a winner—a boy who will grow to be one of the great leaders of his generation."

"Yes, Mother," he said graciously. Then he popped his knuckles and went back to work.

He'd studied under some of the most experienced

taxidermists in the tri-state area, and there was no uncertainty in his movements. He had no problem asking his mother to help. He knew he just had to act in a cordial manner, and she would gladly take on the role of his assistant, following his instructions with each precise task.

Among the many instruments at his disposal, he used a sharpened spoon to scoop out the brains and a #15 scalpel blade to carefully sever each of the six muscles holding each eyeball in its socket, ensuring the delicate eyelids would not be damaged. All very important steps, and all necessary to create a believable final product.

Two hours later he'd finished his work, at least the portion he could complete without taking a trip with his mother. His heart ticked faster in anticipation of the conclusive step of the process. "You said you'd take me to the taxidermy to shop for a pair of eyes, right?"

"Wash up, and I'll take you there," she said.

An hour later, the boy was transfixed on deer and buffalo mounted to the walls of the shop. Mr. Trimble, the owner of the shop, stood behind the counter, pointing out various options of eyes. "Those over there, they are the most authentic. It will seem like your little squirrel friend is alive. His eyes will appear to follow you across the room."

"Wow," the boy said. He knew he had to have that pair. He looked at his mother. Her lips were pinched together as she stared at the white price tag taped to the counter.

"Junior, I can teach you how to sew in a pair of old buttons."

"But you said I could get eyes for my squirrel," he said as his blood boiled warmer under his skin.

She took in a measured breath, glanced again at the price tag, and then pinched the boy's cheek. "I'm sorry, but it's not something we can afford right now. It will be okay. Some day you will be a real surgeon, and then you can use the finest instruments to save lives."

They went home, and she taught Junior how to sew. At the end of their session, she asked if he was ready to attempt the exercise on his squirrel.

"No thanks. I'll wait. Maybe another day."

"Suit yourself," she said, picking up her pair of scissors to restart her coupon-cutting campaign. "By the way, where did you find the squirrel? I'm wondering if you have other specimens you could work on."

He pondered the question. "Found him near the edge of the woods out back. I guess he just died of natural causes."

The boy thought about the feeling of crushing the throat of the small animal. It had been euphoric. And he knew, above all else, that particular thrill would never leave him.

Two

Present day

There was no way in hell I'd let this guy get away.

Just between the thick foliage, I spotted flashes of blue, and my heart momentarily redlined. I had him in my sights.

I motored up the incline and whipped around the dirt embankment, taking a high angle to maintain top speed, my legs chugging as hard as they could go on my off-road bike. Looking more like a jockey than a weekend workout warrior, I lifted my butt off the seat to absorb the quick drop back to the path, the deep-tread tires spitting up gravel and dirt.

A scream from up ahead. Instinctively, I pushed up to a standing position on my pedals. The voice echoed off the trees. It was Brad, playfully mocking me for not being able to keep up.

We'd been going at it for a good ten miles, and up until the last cross street, I'd kept him within four bike lengths. But when a Great Dane broke free from its owner and galloped right in front of my path, I had to take evasive action—clamping down on the rear brake and leaving rubber on the concrete. My front tire came within an inch of ramming him, but the dog barely turned its head as slobber sprayed off its wagging tongue. I somehow stayed upright. After glancing over his shoulder to ensure I was okay, Brad started chuckling as he pulled away.

My colleague at the Boston FBI office and the man of my affection was dead meat.

I approached the area I called Slalom City, a series of quick curves marked by giant trees, where a miscalculation could destroy a bike and break a few bones. I used it to make up time. Leaning into the first bend, I never stopped pumping the pedals, and I hit the next turn two seconds later, moving at nearly an uncontrollable speed. But I knew my limits, and I knew this course like the back of my hand.

I zigged in and out of turns three and four, then gripped the handlebars with everything I had as the bike rumbled over a series of five stumps. Safely out of Slalom City, yellow spears of sunlight bounced off branches and leaves, peppering my sights. Brad wasn't far ahead. I could practically smell him.

Around one more bend, and I hit the final stretch. I could see his blue jersey near the top. I'd closed the gap, but he was still a good fifty feet in front of me. He disappeared over the ridge as I hit the halfway point up the hill. Not letting up for a moment, the legs on my five-six frame churned like pistons on an engine. I was moving so fast when I hit the top, the bike went airborne for a split second.

My weight fell forward as the front tire came back to earth. Looking ahead, I saw Brad zipping out of the woods and gliding across the street. On the other side, he spun around to face me. I could see his smug but very cute dimples from twenty yards. Still motoring at breakneck speed coming down the final hill, I planned on flying right by him, just to show him how lucky he was the Great Dane had saved him from humiliation.

As I released a smile, his eyes popped out of his head. He flapped his arms and screamed something.

For a split second, I didn't know what he was saying or doing.

I began to turn my head, just a few feet before my front tire hit pavement.

It was too late. A black SUV that looked to be the size of a tank was barreling down the road, headed right for me. I crunched the brakes and started to skid. Another two seconds and I was going to be a grease spot under the SUV's giant wheels. I did the only thing I could do—I bailed.

I jumped off the bike and threw my arms in front of me to stop the forward motion of my body. But I didn't slow. The pavement came up and ripped me to shreds as I bounced off the unforgiving surface. I smelled something awful at the exact moment I heard tires screeching.

Still tumbling across the ground, I squeezed my eyes shut, bracing for two tons of metal to send me to another world.

When my body finally stopped, I realized I hadn't been hit. I opened my eyes to see a grill about three inches in front of my face. Brad came running up, shouting all sorts of expletives at the driver.

"I stopped my momentum, Brad," was all I could think of saying, though I wondered if I was still whole.

"Jesus, Alex, you scared the shit out of me. Are you okay?" He touched my forehead as a look of concern cut across his face. He then saw the palm of my hand, and his eyes got wide.

"We're going to the ER." He pulled out his phone and made a call as the driver approached me.

"Shit, lady, I'm glad you're okay. Well, I guess you're okay, right?" he said as he eyeballed me. "But what the hell were you thinking, the way you were flying on that bike? Damn, you almost gave me a heart attack."

Needle-like pains shot throughout my body. I didn't know

what to say. I just held up my hand about a foot from the man's face.

His eyes rolled to the back of his head, and then he fainted.

Three

I studied the black etching on the gray, plastic background of the name tag with as much intensity as I could muster.

"I realize the local anesthesia sometimes doesn't work very well," the doctor said, pausing for a second while he shifted a metal instrument inside the cavity of my hand, ostensibly to remove a number of small pebbles and pavement fragments.

My eyes were now practically boring holes through his name, Dr. Bruce Kim.

"I can see your jaw muscles flinching." He continued to stare at me while the instrument remained beneath the surface of my skin.

"Finish. The. Job." My lips barely opened. I didn't want to budge until he removed the metal instrument.

He must have seen a desperate but determined Alex Troutt. Dr. Kim went back to work, and a moment later I heard an object *ping* against a metal plate.

Another pause and then I could feel his stare. "Do you want a towel to bite down on?"

Laughter sounded from the other side of the curtain. Shifting my eyes above Dr. Kim's shoulder to the crack where two curtains came together, I spotted Brad's dimpled face laughing hysterically with some woman—a beautiful woman with a river of black curls spilling across her back. Even in blue scrubs, her figure could have been the template for an hourglass. I swallowed, trying not to let a hint of jealousy enter my mind while I sat there and let Dr. Kim perform surgery on me without the benefit of sedation.

"I'll take that towel," I said.

The doctor handed it to me, and I shoved it in my mouth just before Brad peeked his head inside our ER bay. "Doing okay?" He was no longer laughing, his tone caring and sincere. I tried to speak, but it came out as more of a growl.

He walked inside and gently touched my elbow. "I'm sorry about not being right here for you. I just—"

"Stay still," the doctor said to me.

For the next minute I forgot to breathe. I heard two more clinks in the tray, and then he said, "I think we're finally done." He poured an iodine solution into the palm of my hand, then pressed gauze pads on top of the wound before pulling off his rubber gloves. "Sorry if that hurt. Really no other option. Didn't think you wanted us to schedule surgery to remove a few pieces of rock."

I removed the towel and gave it to Brad. "I'm good." It felt like a jackhammer had done a number on my spine and neck, and I began to reach over my back to rub it.

"Here, let me," Brad said.

I exhaled. "So, who were you talking to?"

"Oh, that was Sophie. I used to go to high school with her younger sister. Just catching up a little."

The hot nurse—the one who looked to be at least eight years my junior—had a *younger* sister. Then again, I was dating a man who was eleven years younger than I was. Well, some might argue the term "dating." We'd spent a lot of time working out together, doing things with my two teenage kids, and we'd been able to sneak out to see a couple of movies in the two months since the kids and I had returned from summer vacation. While we were still moving at a snail's pace—I'd somehow found the willpower to avoid tripping into the sack with my younger, athletic half—the relationship was just what a doctor would have ordered. Brad was a caring, gentle soul with the body of a Greek god.

So, what was I afraid of?

"You need to make sure you keep this wound clean and out of any type of dirty water. Infection is my main concern." The doctor used the toe of his shoe to tap open the metal trash bin, tossing in his rubber gloves. "We'll bandage you up, but you'll need to change it every couple of days."

"No problem," Brad said. "But why don't you go ahead and sew her up?"

"Can't. Needs to breathe," Dr. Kim said as Sophie entered our space.

Did she just...? I know she just winked at Brad.

"Doctor, you're needed upstairs. I can take care of dressing Miss Troutt's wound."

Miss Troutt...as if I were her dear old mother's friend.

I felt Brad's hand on my back, gently kneading a couple of knots just below my shoulder blade. I looked up at his penetrating, blueish-gray eyes, and he gave me a reassuring smile. It was obvious that he could sense my anxiety, brought on in part by my brush with death, but mostly because of the swimsuit model and, yes, my renewed sense of inadequacy for being over a decade older than the man I...cared about.

"Thanks," I said quietly, then I drained my lungs and tried to let my shoulders relax.

Sophie patched up my hand as we talked casually. Turned out

she was married with three kids and, frankly, couldn't stop going on about her husband. How that body had produced three kids, I had no idea, but I tried to ignore her most obvious traits and take her for who she was.

"You're a lucky woman, Miss Troutt."

"Alex, please."

"Of course, Alex," she said with an affable smirk. "Turns out your boyfriend has always been quite the charmer. Did he tell you he used to read poems to my little sister?"

Brad's face went flush as he shrugged his shoulders. "What can I say? I'm not a great writer, so I turned to the next best thing. Walt Whitman."

His embarrassment was endearing, allowing me to recall that he was just as human and flawed as I was. Well, maybe not that flawed.

"So what's your sister up to now?" I was genuinely a curious person, which probably helped me with my job as an FBI special agent in the Violent Crimes squad.

"Oh, Sara…let's see now. I think her latest adventure with the Peace Corps has her in Africa…Kenya, I think. She's working to help create water wells for communities with very little water."

"Very cool," Brad said. "She always had that desire to help mankind. I'm sure she's getting a lot out of the experience."

Sophie nodded once and gave him a tight-lipped smile. Was there something she wasn't telling us?

She began to clean up the mess as Brad's cell phone started ringing. He pointed at it. "It's the office."

"On a Sunday?"

"Says the woman who works in seventy-two-hour shifts." He winked, then leaned over and kissed my cheek. I could feel a tingle in my stomach. We typically avoided public displays of affection, but that felt nice—normal in a way that made me think I didn't really care what people thought. He put the cell phone to his ear, a finger in the opposite one, and meandered outside of the curtain to take the call.

"He's the one who got away," Sophie said with her back to me over at the sink.

"You're talking to me?"

She flipped around and leaned her perfect derriere against the counter while using a paper towel to dry off her hands.

"Brad. He's…" Her almond-shaped eyes drifted toward the corner. "I'm not sure I really want to go down memory lane."

An awkward silence engulfed our space as I considered her little tease. Should I take the bait?

"What's on your mind, Sophie?"

She cleared her throat, as if she suddenly needed a drink of water, then she released an audible breath. "I was just going to say…you know, girl to girl, that he was the one who got away." She looked longingly at the curtain, as if she were picturing the ghost of Brad standing right there.

I still couldn't get a bead on what she was trying to say. "Sara…was she the one who actually had a case of puppy love for Brad back in the day, or was it you?"

"You can see it in my eyes?"

"And then some." I arched an eyebrow.

Another couple of ticks of silence.

"It's actually much more complicated than just puppy love," she said as tears pooled in her eyes. She brushed a thumb under one eye, ensuring her mascara didn't smear.

I didn't say a word, knowing she was about to tell me everything.

"I always admired Brad. He treated Sara with respect, as an equal. Not like some of those hunky athletes in high school who demand everyone, including their girlfriends, build up their egos. Brad was different. Very different."

I really didn't know a lot about Brad's younger life, other than he was raised solely by his mother. His dad had taken off when he was too young to recall, never to return. I also knew he played sports, but he never talked much about those days. So much of our relationship had been about me coming to terms with who I was—my past relationship with my cheating husband, the hunt for his killer, and then the aftermath, including how my kids were dealing with not having a father around. Perhaps I'd been too selfish, always talking about me.

"Brad's a good guy. I can see it when he interacts with my kids."

Sophie's lips drew a straight line. She had more to unload, and I happened to be the one standing right there.

"It all happened one night when I came back from college. Sara was going to drag Brad to one of her youth leadership meetings." She paused, probably wondering if I was going to stop her. I kept a good poker face, although with Brad being involved somehow, I could also feel my gut beginning to tighten.

"I convinced her to let Brad come with me to one of my friend's parties."

"A college party."

"One of those, yes." She glanced at the curtain again.

I wondered if she wished Brad would walk back into our space, allowing her to end the soul-searching.

"My friend put together a wicked brew of Trash Can Punch. It was the best and the worst at the same time." Another pause. "Brad wasn't much of a drinker, but I convinced him to have a cup. And then another. I did the same thing. A few hours later, after multiple cups of punch, I woke up in bed with him. We were both undressed. And yes, we had done…you know."

She obviously wasn't trying to become my best friend. Ten years ago or not, this wasn't really something I wanted to hear. I turned on the gurney and picked up my phone.

"I had seduced him, I guess because he was the forbidden fruit, or maybe because I thought I could teach him something. Or maybe I had some type of odd jealousy with my sister. But it happened, and I felt like shit."

"Sorry." I was ready to move on, so I tried to flex my injured hand. A sharp pain screamed from the middle of my palm.

"That was just the beginning of the worst night of Sara's life. Mine too." She exhaled, and I could see her jaw quivering. She had my attention.

"Sara had gone to her meeting with her best friend, Annie. It was a meeting of the Future Leaders of the World, the FLW, where they focused on trying to aid people who had the least in the world. Sara and Annie were pretty inseparable throughout high school. In fact, Annie was often the third wheel with Sara and Brad, but he never seemed to mind."

"And?"

"After the regular meeting ended, Sara had to stay late, since she was an officer. Annie needed to get home. Her parents had a pretty strict curfew. So she insisted on walking home. Sara had told her to wait for her, and, apparently, she even offered to skip the officers' meeting and take her home. But Annie insisted on walking home. She was too nice."

I could feel the hairs on my neck start to stand. "What happened?"

"Annie was killed by a car. A hit-and-run."

"Oh no," I said. "And Sara felt guilty."

"She was devastated. But I think Brad felt even worse."

"Why?"

"Two-fold. First, while all of this was going on, he was

having sex with me, the evil older sister. Second, they all knew that if Brad had been there, he would have given Annie a ride home. He always did things like that, because he's such a nice guy."

I could feel my heart sink for the man in my life, the pain in my hand all but a distant memory.

"In the middle of Sara's grief, Brad told her everything. He felt it was the right thing to do, to be honest. It destroyed her, and him too. They eventually moved on, but it was difficult for everyone."

I would have never guessed that Brad had endured such pain and remorse. Sophie began to gasp, and tears spilled down her beautiful face. I waved her over and gave her a warm hug.

"Even after all this time, it still hurts. I hate myself for it," she said as she tried to suppress her sobs.

She pulled back up and snagged a couple of tissues off the counter just as Brad walked around the curtain. He stopped for a second and gave us both a look. I was pretty sure he knew what we had just shared.

"That was Jerry on the phone," he said, walking to my side. "I'm being put on TDY—temporary duty yonder."

"I need to get your paperwork ready," Sophie said to me as she slinked between the curtains and disappeared.

Brad had a stellar reputation in the office as an intelligence analyst, and he was a natural leader of men and women. My respect for his professional side couldn't be any higher. But as I'd grown closer to "Brad the person," his professional persona didn't mean much to me. I realized that Brad the man was far more impressive than Brad the IA.

"Not surprising. If we had a draft for IAs, you'd probably be the first player chosen."

"Thanks, but this temporary assignment isn't in our office."

My back stiffened. "What?"

"It's in New York City. They need a lead IA on a high-profile case. Their top analyst just had a baby, so she's out of commission for a while."

I could feel a wave of sadness wash over me. "How long?"

"Hard to say. He's guessing one to two weeks, but it could be longer." He gave me a wink and put his arm around my shoulder. "I'll miss you. Maybe you can come visit me on the weekend?"

I tilted my head back, and he gave me a soft smooch, pressing our lips together for a few seconds. "Thanks," I said, rubbing my good hand across his chest. "I might take you up on your offer."

"I guess you and Sophie talked." He took a single step back.

"She still carries a lot of guilt."

"It was tough, especially on her sister. But I guess it's part of life. Impossible to predict."

I reached over and took his hand in mine, my good one. "You and I spend too much time talking about all of my drama. I want to know more about your life."

"I think you just heard it, at least the most dramatic parts."

My phone rang, and I raised a finger. "Now Jerry's calling me? I guess he still hasn't figured out that we're together," I said with a wry smile.

I took the call and listened to Jerry for a good five minutes before I could get a word in. When he had to take another call from his boss, I punched the line dead and set the phone down on the medical table.

"Jerry must have a hundred things going on at once," Brad said, running his fingers through his thick mane of dirty-blond hair.

"This one is big. You know that cold case I've been looking into for the last few weeks? Somerville cops found a dead girl overnight with the same MO. Ten years later, we might have a lead. Looks like it's time for both of us to get to work."

I scooted off the table and was met by Brad's lips. He pressed his body against mine. His pecs nudged my breasts, and his biceps held me tightly. Our tongues danced for a good minute until we both came up for air.

"I..." Brad's sentence trailed off, unfinished, his eyes boring holes into my soul.

"Yeah?" My heart fluttered inside my chest.

"Be safe. And I can't wait to see you again."

I went straight home and took a cold shower—while ensuring my wound stayed dry—then I dove into the dirty work.

Four

$\mathbf{A}$ blueberry slipped through Nick's fingers. When he swatted his hand to catch it, missing by a whisker, I threw up my good hand and snatched it out of the air.

"Damn, Alex, you're a regular Rob Gronkowski."

I gave him the eye, not that fond of being compared to the beast of a man who formerly played tight end for the Patriots.

"I meant that you have the *hands* of Gronkowski. Obviously, your body types are different." He chuckled twice, his cheeks instantly glowing as the early morning sun penetrated through a thin veil of fog and bounced off my partner's face. Or were his cheekbones just more pronounced because of all the weight he had lost?

"Thanks," I said with a wink, and then I popped the blueberry in my mouth. An outsider might say our relationship seemed a little on the flirtatious side, but if there was anyone in the squad I could joke with, it was Nick Radowski.

For starters, we'd worked together for more years than we'd like to admit. And he was gay. So it was kind of like working with a girlfriend, at least in how we rated any good-looking guys we came across. Nick, though, had been living with the same guy since I joined the FBI. For me, the white-picket dream was still quite elusive, although I couldn't complain these days, with Brad serving as my other half. But something was missing, something that would take our relationship to the next level. It wasn't our ability to connect emotionally—we did fine there. We had fun with each other, and there was mutual respect. All of that was great. Given my dream the previous night, I thought I knew what was needed to cement our relationship and allow us to finally share our bond with the world. S-E-X.

We circled Nick's FBI-issued Impala and made our way toward the outline of yellow police tape.

"That's probably the healthiest thing you've had to eat in the last week," Nick said.

"Screw you. Last night I had a granola bar."

"If it came out of a package, it's still processed food. Have you thought about having some flax for breakfast, along with fresh fruit from an organic farm?"

While I was plenty happy for Nick to take control of his life and get himself in shape, he'd become quite the food snob. On top of that, he now thought he could kick my ass in any type of athletic endeavor.

"I know I need to eat better, Nick, or should I call you Dad?"

"That stings," he said as he lowered himself under the tape.

A few cops milled about the crime scene, despite the fact that the body had been bagged and taken to the Middlesex County medical examiner's office for an autopsy. I wasn't as familiar with the civil servants in Middlesex County. Normally, we worked hand in hand with Suffolk County, which lined the coast, and the Boston Police Department. We always appreciated a law enforcement agency that had a lot of resources, since Uncle Sam typically pinched pennies within the FBI.

I waved my bandaged hand at one of the uniforms. "I'm looking for a Detective Askew. Know where I can find him?"

He chuckled while sticking his thumbs inside his belt loop. "Her. Detective Askew is a woman."

"Didn't know. Sorry."

"No problem. She's down by the river working with the crime scene investigators."

I gave him a courteous nod, and we followed the dirt path down a hill, through a cluster of dense trees that spilled onto a small inlet that served as a shore. I spotted the only female in the mud and rocks. Wearing rubber boots over what looked like a teal pantsuit, she was speaking to a pot-bellied man who had "Crime Scene Investigation" written in small white letters on the back of his windbreaker.

It took a moment, but she noticed us and made her way over. As we shook hands, I noticed her grip was firm, but her hands quite soft. We finished the rudimentary introductions, and I asked if she'd seen the body. She turned her head back to the shore, and the wind blew a lock of chestnut hair across her face. While she was probably close to my age, I couldn't spot a flaw on her face. In fact, she was drop-dead gorgeous—in a girl-next-door kind of way.

"I saw it, the body, before it was taken away," she said, hesitating as she looked out across Mystic River, a few remaining puffs of fog clinging to the water. Miniature swells gently lapped over the smooth stones behind the detective.

I waited a good ten seconds or so, then, "Care to share what you saw, Detective?"

"Terri," she said, turning back to me, hands now in her pockets. "Just call me Terri. I've only been a detective for five years, a patrol cop just two years before that. But I've never seen anything like this, nor have I even seen pictures of anything like this."

I could tell she was in shock, trying to make sense of how

one person could kill another. We'd all been there, and every new case brought back that same feeling, one I knew all too well. It was as if I had a perpetual case of acid reflux—the taste of my own vomit just another murder away.

I motioned with my hand for her to continue. "Sorry. When I got here, the ME took me right to the body. He pulled back her eyelids—she had no eyes. Someone had cut out her fucking eyes." Terri raked her long fingers through her hair. Even in stress, there was something about her that seemed graceful and radiant at the same time.

Shaking her head, she added, "The officer who was first on the scene has already asked for a leave of absence. A sick bastard did this. A very sick bastard."

Nick and I exchanged a knowing glance. I guessed that we both wondered if the little Somerville PD had the resources to take point on this investigation, even if we were riding shotgun.

"Those images stay with you long after the investigation ends. Maybe you need to talk to someone," I said, knowing just about every department kept at least one shrink on retainer.

"I'm okay. It's just a job, right?" She smirked, then leaned down and picked up a piece of paper that had blown near her foot.

"Evidence?" I asked.

She held the wrinkled paper closer to her face, squinting her eyes to read it. "Probably not. It's a receipt from a 7-Eleven dated two years ago, but we'll bag it just in case." She whistled at the same cop from earlier, who came over and carefully placed the piece of paper in an evidence bag.

I took another view of the river. In addition to a bunch of trash that had gathered along the shoreline, I couldn't see six inches deep into the water. It had a sludgy look, as if an oil tanker had just ruptured in the vicinity.

"Damn, when are they ever going to clean up this filth?" Nick said, beating me to it. He waved a hand in front of his face. "Smells like dead fish too."

"Some plant keeps dumping sewage into the river, and no one does anything about it," Terri said. "You know how it is, lots of government agencies pointing the finger...cities, water districts, everyone. No one wants to pick up the bill. So we're stuck in inertia."

Knowing we weren't about to solve a government throw-down, I took our focus back to the case. Actually, two cases.

"Not sure if you're aware, but we were recently assigned a cold case, now about ten years old. The vic also had her eyeballs cut out."

Terri shook her head, her deep-set eyes narrowing. "How many perps can have the same MO? It's got to be the same guy, right?"

"Guy, girl, who knows? But your vic got our attention, that's for certain. What do you know about her?"

"Listen, Agent Troutt—"

"If I can call you Terri, you can call me Alex."

"I know I'm not exactly exuding a ton of confidence right now, but I have passion for my job. I love it and hate it at the same time. So, I guess I'm saying that I'll be happy to share with you what we know, but we need professional courtesy extended back to us as well. The media and public will be all over us, and we'll need the extra help."

"I don't think so, at least not for the reasons you think," I said, shifting my feet.

She tilted her head, a quizzical expression on her face.

"The details for cause of death were never released. In fact, the body of Gloria Lopez was never claimed by any family or friends."

Terri raised an eyebrow.

"My thoughts exactly," Nick said.

"So the body your officer found…was it dumped here or did it wash ashore?" I asked.

"Our divers who know the waters, and all the sludge included, are certain the body had drifted downstream."

I took a step around Nick and scanned the area. I'd missed it when we walked up, but while we were technically next to the Mystic River, we were actually at the connecting point where the northerly Malden River dumped into the Mystic.

"Do we know which branch she came from?"

"Given where her body landed and the currents, the divers think she floated down from the Mystic. How far, no one knows."

"Unless it was made to look like it came from the Mystic, not the Malden River," Nick added.

I slapped my partner on the arm and nodded. "Can't rule it out."

"We've got two teams scanning the shoreline. My Somerville team is walking the shore up to about a half mile on the south side, and the Medford department is scanning both sides of the river up to two miles."

"Everyone is marking their territory," I said.

"We all want to find out who did this," Terri said, sounding a bit annoyed at my jaded perspective.

The CSI person called Terri over, while Nick and I stayed back and compared notes.

"We're dealing with amateurs," Nick said in a hushed tone.

I smacked his arm again. "Too far."

"Okay, we're dealing with professionals who couldn't find their asses with both hands. That any better?"

As the T train rumbled across the tracks behind me, I

released a smirk and turned my sights westward, up the Mystic River. I recalled the movie of the same name, the story of three boys who were forever jaded by a horrific childhood incident. If memory served me correctly, Sean Penn and Tim Robbins both won Oscars that year. The movie was based on Dennis Lehane's novel. As usual, the book was better. It was fiction, but there was something about this river that made my stomach turn. Was it the movie alone? Could it be the disgusting water and how it seemed like everyone was afraid to make it better? Maybe. It was almost as if the river carried some type of curse on those who dared to bring it under control.

Terri joined us. "They found a five-dollar bill floating near a rock."

"I guess anyone could have dropped that," I said.

"Well, the ME found another five-dollar bill stuck in the vic's bra."

I nodded, thinking through the facts she'd shared. "Had she been sexually assaulted?"

"Early examination showed nothing pointing to that. He's doing a more thorough examination today."

"What else have you learned about the vic?"

"She actually had a driver's license in the back pocket of her denim skirt. Name is Emma Katic, spelled K-A-T-I-C. Age thirty-two."

"Russian last name. Recent immigrant?" Nick asked.

"We don't know that much about her yet. We just now received the opening kickoff."

A sports analogy. It worked, really. That was exactly what the start of an investigation was like, if you could imagine playing a football blindfolded. "We know she was employed at a local bar in Malden—Lenny's Pub. Sending a team over there this morning to start interviews and do background checks."

Sounded like a task we should handle, but I let it rest for now.

"You're thinking something," Nick said to me.

"Just doing a little comparison to our cold-case vic."

"Do share," Terri said.

"Two notable differences. First, our vic was only twenty-one. Much younger," I said. "Second, she was a prostitute. All these years we've been wondering if it was one of her customers who had killed her."

They both nodded as another T train plowed across the bridge, drowning out all sound around us. I counted ten times that the stressed track grunted in protest.

"What was the actual cause of death?" Terri asked.

"Blunt force trauma to the back of her skull. The ME report says they found tiny splinters of wood in her hair."

"How about Emma?" Nick asked.

"Single gun-shot-wound to the head."

We further compared the vics. In addition to the differences in age, profession, and actual cause of death, my cold-case vic had jet-black hair and a tan complexion.

"Doesn't add up," Terri said, running her fingers through her hair again. And I thought *I* played with my hair a lot. That appeared to be Terri's go-to move, whether she was stressed or just pontificating.

"Any way we could be looking at a copycat killer?" Terri asked.

"But the public—" Nick started.

Terri held up a hand to interrupt him. "I know, your cold case was never made public. But a few people knew. The agents working the case, maybe the local detectives at least had awareness. And then, of course, the perp himself."

"A family member or close friend of the perp. That could be

an angle to think about," I said.

"Don't discount the idea of a former agent. You hinted earlier how this job can send you to the nuthouse. Maybe one of the good guys went over the deep end and started mimicking an old case."

As much as I didn't want to believe it, I knew Terri had every reason to throw that theory into the mix.

"Good instincts. We'll definitely start digging on that one, if for no other reason than to rule it out."

We exchanged phone numbers and agreed to touch base daily, if not more often, as both teams gathered intel and our suspect pool became clearer—assuming we could actually create a list of legitimate suspects.

Nick and I walked up the path and got back in the car. He started the engine, and I said, "I'm calling Gretchen to let her know we need her in the war room when we get back. We're running short-handed without Brad, but we'll have to make do."

Nick gave me the eye, and then a grin cracked his face.

"What?" Was he about to admit he knew about me and Brad?

My phone rang. It was Terri. I punched the line while looking for her out my window.

"You break the case in just the last minute?" I joked.

"Maybe. We just got a tip about a guy who threatened Emma, and he's got a violent past. We've got a team on the way to the guy's employer."

I spotted her jogging out from the canopy of trees.

"I see you. We'll pick you up and drive together."

Within seconds, Terri slid into the backseat, and Nick hit the gas before she could shut the door.

Five

My hand hit the roof as Nick leaned the Impala into a tight turn. Not only did the tires squeal like stuck pigs, but the steering wheel trembled.

"What the fuck is going on?" he belted, his voice sounding like an automatic weapon from the incessant jittering.

For a moment, he lifted his hands from the wheel. "Don't do that," Terri and I screamed at the same time, as the Impala fishtailed into oncoming traffic.

He slammed his hands back on the wheel, swerved to miss a garbage truck, then scooted by the median's light pole with only inches to spare.

"Woo! Damn, that felt good," he said, bouncing in his seat like a little kid who'd just finished his first-ever trip on a roller coaster.

Taking in a deep breath to gain control of my heartbeat, I just stared at him, wondering what the hell happened to my old partner. He'd gone from a sloth to a vegan, and now he was a thrill-seeker. Nothing too dangerous for Captain America.

I peeked over my shoulder to check on Terri. She'd forgotten to buckle her seatbelt and had been tossed to the other side of the car, her hair scattered across her face. Somehow she still looked

like a million bucks. Her phone rang, and she grabbed the back
of my seat, pulled up, and answered it just as Nick punched the
horn.

"Watch out!" I said, slapping the center console as Nick cut
into oncoming traffic to pass a slower car.

"Asswipe," he yelled out.

Horns blared from all angles, and Nick stuck his hand out the
door and gave them the one-finger salute.

"Jesus, Nick, you're on quite a roll. Is this burst of energy
from one of your organic fruits?"

"Yep."

"Maybe they mixed it with something just as natural, like
'shrooms."

"Funny," he said, suddenly slamming his foot on the brake.
"You said 214 Carter Street, right, Terri?" He glanced at the
rearview mirror.

No answer, so I quickly flipped my sights over my shoulder.
She was nodding at us, while talking intensely into the phone.

Nick cut across traffic amidst another horn assault and
headed north on Alford. A moment later, we sped across the
Mystic River. I glanced up the river for a quick second, but I
didn't have long enough to take in a full view.

"I thought I told you not to approach the business until we
got there." Terri's voice had an edge to it. "What do you mean,
you didn't hear me?"

I pulled down the visor and saw she'd taken the phone away
from her ear and was mumbling under her breath, her eyes
closed.

"Everything okay?"

She covered the phone with her hand. "Hell no. Two
dumbass detectives are circumventing my authority."

"I'm sure they're just eager to get the collar," I said as Nick plowed the Impala straight ahead. I could see the bridge behind us in the visor's mirror, but I kept my eyes on Terri. "What's going on now?" She had the phone back up to her ear. Another pause. I shifted my eyes from my mirror to the road up ahead, trying to keep track of both scenarios—Nick's driving and Terri's freak-out.

Terri covered the phone again and said, "One of the guys is laughing. He thinks I'm just some broad who can't keep her emotions in check."

It was odd seeing another woman go through a similar experience from my work life. Hell, it was odd seeing another woman in any position of authority. Maybe we could commiserate later over a glass of wine. Damn, I sounded like such a girl.

I shrugged my shoulders, and she went back to her conversation, trying to get her detectives back on track. "You let the foreman leave the office to get the suspect, without anyone accompanying him? Are you fucking crazy?" I could now tell she was from Boston. Her anger had whipped up a wicked accent. "This guy threatened the life of our victim…the girl who was murdered last night. Dammit, Meyers and Longfellow!"

Nick glanced at me and said, "Longfellow?" He tried not to smirk, but that was exactly what he did.

"Not the right time." I looked at the road ahead and saw nothing but brake lights. I jammed my foot into the floorboard. "Nick!"

"On it," he said. The tires screeched, and we slowed to a more sane thirty miles per hour. I took in a deep breath, exhaled, then looked in the mirror again.

"Is he back yet?" Terri asked into the phone. Then she nodded. "It's been three minutes, and he's still not back. You don't think there's a chance that he's covering for this Vince

Tripuka?"

For the first time since I'd met her, her cheeks were flush. I could almost picture steam coming from her nostrils. I could relate to the troops not following instructions, although my current team was as good as it got—Brad's tight ass notwithstanding.

"Crap, Nick, can't you move any faster?" Terri pleaded from the back. "We might have a runner on our hands while Meyers and Longfellow are playing rock-paper-scissors in the foreman's office."

He punched the gas and edged half the car into oncoming traffic so he could pass a slower car, the engine straining as the speed accelerated faster and faster.

"Roundabout dead ahead," I said with a pinched voice.

Nick's foot never touched the brake. Tires squealed as the Impala leaned into the first curve off Broadway. We were easily going three times faster than any other vehicle. He hugged the inside of the roundabout for a third of the circle, then took a quick glance over his shoulder and jerked the wheel to the right.

Another symphony of horns as we rumbled onto Main Street.

"What's the foreman telling you?" Terri asked into the phone.

"We're a minute out," Nick said.

"He's doing what? Taking a break? That's a bunch of bullshit, Longfellow. He's feeding you a line to give Tripuka a head start. Go find him!"

Nick hung a quick left onto Carter, an area of wall-to-wall industrial buildings and warehouses. Quite a few had broken windowpanes.

"Front or back, Terri?" I asked.

"Back. Meyers and Longfellow entered the office through the front office."

Nick stabbed the brake and flipped a quick left down a side

street. I think the sign said Cross Street, but it came and went too quickly.

"Terri, do you have a mug shot of this guy?" I asked.

"Hold on." A moment later, she shoved her phone across the seat, just as the car bounced in and out of a pothole. The phone clanked off my head.

"Sorry," she said.

"No problem." I could hear Nick snicker as I looked at the screenshot of Vince Tripuka. He had a mullet—long hair down the back and spiked hair on top. I also noticed a tattoo of a boob on his neck.

"Must have lost a bet on that one," I said, handing Terri back her phone.

"Need to assume he's armed and desperate," she said, pulling a Sig Sauer out of her purse. I did the same with my Glock, knowing it was in perfect working condition. That was the first thing I did before I started my shift each morning.

Nick pulled around a warehouse and right into the middle of a jumble of eighteen-wheelers.

"Crap," he banged the steering wheel with the palm of his hand. "We'll never get through this maze." He slid the gear into reverse, then quickly hit the brake and looked in his rearview. "We're trapped in here."

"Time for exercise, Nick." I opened the door and started jogging. I could hear doors open behind me, and I assumed Terri and Nick were on my heels. I dodged and weaved around the enormous trucks, looking inside the cabins as I passed each one. I turned and shuffled backward for a moment. As I expected, Terri was about thirty feet behind me, not quite as swift in her rubber boots. But no sign of Nick.

"Any update from Meyers and Longfellow?" I yelled over the drone of the trucks hulking on either side of us.

She still had the phone to her ear as she approached. "They can't find him. Everyone is giving them the runaround. Big surprise, huh?"

I flipped back around and got beyond the trucks and their putrid diesel-fuel smell. Just ahead, maybe a hundred feet, a man in a blue jumpsuit exited a garage. He looked the opposite way and then toward us. His body became rigid.

"Hands up." I raised my gun while I jogged.

He paused for a second, then spun around and hauled ass back inside the garage.

Six

"**F**uck! Tell Meyers and Longfellow he's coming back their way." Pumping my arms, I hit full stride and ate up the distance to the garage in no time. Just before the opening, I skidded to a stop on the rocky pavement and peered around the edge into the garage, seeing no one. I looked again and then slowly stepped inside, keeping close to the wall. I walked heel to toe, with both hands locked on the grip of my gun. I turned forty-five degrees in both directions as I took each step. The space was enormous, filled with delivery trucks, barrels and barrels of... Did I see a beer sign?

A squeaky door opened on a platform to my right, and I quickly swung my gun around. Two men wearing caps and holding clipboards came out, talking to each other. The shorter guy saw me first, and he nudged his colleague.

"FBI. Have you seen Vince Tripuka?"

They stared at the gun.

"I don't have time to screw around. Have you seen Tripuka in the last five minutes? Did he just pass you inside?"

They shook their heads.

"Get back inside and don't tell him you saw me, unless you both want to go to jail for obstructing justice." They hightailed it back through the door in no time flat.

A pitter-patter of shoes clipping the concrete sounded just behind me. I looked over my shoulder and saw Terri pulling to a stop.

"I chased him in here," I said. "He might be hiding somewhere, or he might have slipped out."

Terri darted up the ramp, curling her fingers around the metal railing, and put a hand on the metal door.

"Don't trust anyone," I said.

"I don't even trust my own detectives." And then she disappeared.

A glance over my shoulder, thinking Nick would be right behind her. No sign of him or anyone else, only the distant growl of engines. *He must be close*, I thought, so I started to methodically search the garage area. I shifted left, while inching forward, my head on a swivel. I swung around a concrete column, fully prepared for an attack, but I found only a small tool belt resting on the floor.

I wondered what kind of weapon, if any, Tripuka was carrying. I doubted he brought a gun to work. Then again, if he *had* murdered the girl, for him to be at work the next day took some balls. But if he could pull it off, acting like it was just another day would only help his cause.

I shuffled forward, moving deeper into the garage. I passed a delivery truck and finally took notice of the company logo painted on the side. It showed three draft beers, an overflow of suds, sitting next to a keg. I peeked inside the cab and found it empty. Another scan of the facility showed very little light farther in. I could see three floors of crates, maybe seventy feet high in total.

A beeping sound from outside. A truck was backing up. While it was difficult to pinpoint an exact location, it didn't sound like it was heading into the garage.

A click.

I swung my sights back inside the garage, looking for any movement, any additional sounds. I could smell beer in the musty air. I swallowed, forcing a dry patch down my throat. I got the feeling I was being watched, so I dropped to my knees and scanned the garage floor, looking under the trucks for Tripuka, or his legs or shoes. Nothing.

Back to my feet, I continued my search.

Where's Nick, dammit?

I approached a bay where two trucks sat, one with the hood up. To the left were three other bays, one next to the other. As far as I could see, each bay stored at least two trucks. In the bay closest to me, there was a small forklift. The arms were stopped halfway up, with a keg sitting on them. *Maybe Tripuka had been working that forklift when he got word that the cops wanted to talk to him.*

As a line of perspiration formed on my back, I made a note to personally admonish the team of Meyers and Longfellow. Those guys really fucked this up.

A quick glance over my shoulder and still no sign of my partner. Was this some type of setup? I blinked twice, thinking the notion was preposterous.

I glanced inside the one truck with its hood closed in the first bay and then started to move to my left to inspect the other bays. Nick was on his way, I reminded myself. They'd have to shoot him in the leg to keep him from coming. He was that reliable.

In the blink of an eye, an engine roared to life and tires the size of me lurched forward. I stumbled, tripping over some type of tire iron, and tumbled to the slick concrete floor. The truck came at me like a demonic freight train. I scrambled to get to my feet, the engine growling so loudly it vibrated my gut. It was practically on top of me, the tires just inches from crushing my torso.

The sole of my shoe finally caught a grip on the floor, and I dove straight into a workbench just as the frame of the truck clipped my foot, further propelling me into a rack of tools that sent metal shit flying everywhere. As I hit the floor, I realized my gun was still in my hand. I swung around on my back just as the truck barreled out of the garage. I held my breath for a second, took aim, and fired two shots into the left front tire. It was the same truck from before—the one with its hood up. Within two seconds, the truck veered left and rammed into a concrete support column. The truck growled extra loudly, and steam coiled into the air.

I exhaled, my heart still peppering my chest. A second later, Tripuka kicked open the dented front door, hopped out, and took one look at me. Blood trickled down his forehead. Before I could shout or point my gun, he darted around the column and out into the alley.

Dammit! Where's Nick? I scrambled to my feet and started running after Tripuka. I rounded the column and the truck, and that was when I saw Tripuka—airborne. He landed on his back with a heavy thud. Nick stood over him.

"Sorry I'm late to the party," Nick said, wrenching his shoulder while hobbling on one leg at the same time.

I glanced at Tripuka, who was writhing in pain on the ground, then walked toward Nick.

"Did you get mugged between here and the car?" I tossed a thumb over my shoulder.

"Not even a thanks for saving your ass and catching a killer?"

"You're right. Thanks."

He tried to put weight on his right leg, then winced and

gripped his lower leg. "Don't say a thing about my injury. It has nothing to do with my age. There's a story here. Just give me a minute to work the kink out of my shoulder."

Lots of stories would need to be told to sort through this arrest, not the least of which would be coming from Tripuka. I just hoped he would stick with nonfiction.

Seven

Twenty-five years ago

The kid inspected his face in the mirror in search of his first whisker. *Ninth grade isn't so bad*, he thought. With his adept ability to read people, he'd stayed out of the crosshairs of the upperclassmen bullies. In fact, on more than one occasion, they had actually included Junior in some of their fun and games. He played along, assuming the role of the young kid learning the ways of the pranking world from his older and wiser schoolmates.

But to Junior, while the pranks gave him a laugh or two, they seemed rather childish at times. He knew he was put on this earth to accomplish so much more than shooting fireworks into people's homes or scrawling obscene pictures on brick walls around town. He felt like a young colt, ready to burst out and really show the world what he was all about.

His mother, while an overbearing pain in the ass throughout his childhood, had repeatedly shared her opinion on what was in store for his life. "There aren't many people put on this earth who can truly make a difference. But with your intellect, you will impact the entire world. You have that special something. My son, they will speak of you in the same breath as Gandhi."

He ran a brush through his thick hair, momentarily pondering the idea of adding a bit of gel to make him stand out more, thinking one of the junior or senior girls might take notice. As his mother often said, if the girls don't like him for who he really is, then they're not worthy of his affection.

His mother drove him to the fall dance at the high school, and as if on cue, she reminded him about some of the temptations of a being a teenage boy. "Your father always treated me with respect, and I expect you to do the same whenever you're courting a young lady."

"Mom, no one uses the term courting anymore. We date." A few seconds of a clip played in his mind, a recent encounter with one of the young ladies in town. She'd introduced a few things to him that at first seemed so unnatural, but now he craved a repeat performance. And this time, he would choose his mate.

"Junior, you will not talk back to your mother. It's rude and disrespectful. I know it's been a while, but I'm sure you remember spending a few cold nights in that hall closet, alone in the dark, yes?"

Images swept through his mind as his hands got sweaty. He didn't like the feeling of being enclosed, of not being able to see a thing three inches from his face. Perhaps his mom had known that when she set out his punishment. But she'd said it was to teach him a lesson.

"Sorry," he said with as much conviction as he could muster, picking at a loose piece of plastic on the back of the headrest.

She adjusted the rearview and offered one of her patented smiles. "We all make mistakes, Junior. But how we grow from those mistakes is what sets us apart from animals. Don't forget that, especially as you start looking ahead and setting your goals in life."

He nodded, letting a few mixed thoughts comingle.

She dropped him off by the tennis courts, on the other side of the school from the gymnasium where the dance was taking place. He'd told her that he was responsible for sweeping off the courts, which allowed him to go to the dance for free. Both were fabrications, but he knew his mom could only handle so much.

Once he snuck inside, he hung out with a few of the brainiacs, anything to nudge the mental stimulation needle at least a tad. Some kid was pontificating about various theories in physics, acting as if he had more knowledge than the forefathers in that field of study. After about ten minutes, Junior could take no more.

"You might as well have diarrhea of the mouth, Samuel," Junior said, standing upright. "The fact is you're nothing but a fucking blowhard who loves to hear himself talk. The fathers of modern physics were brilliant. Sir Isaac Newton formulated three laws of motion and the law of universal gravitation. At age nineteen—yes, just a few years older than your sorry ass— Galileo discovered the isochronal nature of the pendulum and developed the first theories about properties of space and time outside three-dimensional geometry. And then we have Albert Einstein, who proclaimed that the speed of light was constant in all inertial reference frames and that electromagnetic laws should remain valid, independent of reference frame. This later became known as the theory of relativity."

By the time he took a breath, Samuel had slouched in his chair, his chubby chin resting on his chest. But something else happened. Something wonderful.

"You are absolutely brilliant. What is your name?"

He turned around and looked up at Vanessa, the most beautiful girl in the school, with eyes that practically made his heart melt.

She took him by the hand and guided him to the dance floor. A slow song had started playing through the speakers. He rested his face against her breast and swayed back and forth for what seemed like an eternity. Urges came over him, and he found his hands moving down her backside. Just before reaching paradise, he felt the grip of God around his wrist.

"This punk thinks he's going to score with my girlfriend."

It was the school bad boy, Will.

Junior swallowed once, wondering how this would play out.

Like a dog on a leash, Junior was dragged by Will to an area near the bleachers, where a couple of Will's ogre buddies were hanging out. They provided cover as Will raised his fist.

Junior quickly said, "You ever thought about making straight A's? I can make it happen."

"Did you just talk back to me, punk?"

Junior just stood there, refusing to raise an arm to defend himself. "Let me ask it another way. What kind of job do you want when you get out of here? Something that pays a lot of money, I bet."

He could see the boy with more facial hair than a thirty-year-old man ponder the question. "I don't need school. But I do need to kick your ass for touching my girl." He cocked back his fist.

But Junior only crossed his arms and pondered the Neanderthal further. The bully didn't throw the punch. He appeared distracted, like a little kid, then he started to roll up his sleeves.

"You know you need that diploma if you're going to get any type of job that will pay for you and your girl," Junior said.

"What's it to you, you little punk-ass brat?"

"Clearly you haven't learned about bartering."

"Bartending? I've watched my old man make a stiff drink." He laughed and shoved one of his buddies for the hell of it.

Junior continued to keep his cool, waiting for this kid with no future to finally get the point.

Will waited a few seconds, looked around again, then finally said, "Okay, I give. What the hell is this bar...?"

"Bartering. It goes something like this: I perform a service for you in trade for you doing something for me."

"I've got something you can service right here, bitch," he said, grabbing his crotch.

"Isn't that why you're with your beautiful girlfriend?"

Will sniffed, and Junior wondered if that might ignite a coherent thought.

"I see where you're going with this. You don't want me to beat your face in. So you want to offer me something. Right?"

"You got it. It's how small businesses operate in the real world."

This meathead probably thinks I'm talking about the show on MTV, Real World. What a fucking moron.

Will scratched his skin. "So, I spare you from the beating of your life. How do you plan on getting me a diploma?"

Junior rubbed his hands together. "I was hoping you'd ask me that."

With the ogre and his buddies providing cover, Junior sneaked into the administrative offices, hacked into the simplistic computer system, and changed Will's grades just enough so that no one would notice, but high enough so that he'd graduate in the spring, as long as he didn't blow off every single class.

Leisurely walking back to the gymnasium, he found Will in the hallway making out with his girl. Junior tried not to look, but he could see her eyes following him as he tiptoed past them. But he wasn't quiet enough. Will turned around and clocked him right in the nose. Tears pooled as he tried to push himself up off the floor. With blurry vision, he could see another younger girl had entered the hallway. She looked just like Will, only a rounder version. It was Will's sister, Lora. She started laughing uncontrollably, and then her brother joined in. She laughed so hard her belly jiggled. The three of them left Junior in the hallway, where he wiped away his tears and then decided to leave. He walked home and thought about the humiliation he had just suffered.

A month later, he was riding his skateboard down the street— while wearing a mother-mandated helmet—and he passed Lora and her friend. Lora pointed a chubby finger at him and snickered. He flipped around, picked up his skateboard, and just stared at their backs. He waited to see if it would happen.

Not a moment later, a four-legged creature darted out of the bushes. Running like its life was at stake, it crossed just in front of Lora and her friend. Lora called out, "Come here, Buttons." The cat reached the street before it stopped and released a howl that was more coyote than feline, its tail as fat as a tree trunk. Lora leaned down as Buttons turned his head in her direction. Blood poured from the sockets that once held its eyes, and Lora screamed like she'd been stabbed in the heart.

Junior's family put their house on the market and moved out of the area in less than a month. It was their fifth move in the last seven years. And it wasn't because his father was taking a different job. Junior was learning from his mistakes—like his mother told him he should.

Eight

I stared through a two-way mirror into the Somerville Police Department interview room where Vince Tripuka sat with his hands folded, his facial expression as calm as someone waiting to board the T train. Up close, he didn't look anything like the mug shot Terri had shown me. His hair was parted on the side and had a natural wave to it. The neck tattoo? Not to be found—he'd probably had it removed. Good call. From the neck up, he could have been a high school teacher or a professional golfer.

He was handcuffed to a steel railing built into the side of the metal table, which was bolted to the concrete floor. He wasn't going anywhere, at least no place of his choosing. So far, we had him on a probation violation and attempted assault on a law enforcement officer, which meant no more than probably a year back in the state pen, maybe a little more if we could actually get the attempted assault charge to stick. But I knew if we could pin the murder on him, maybe even both murders, then he would instantly become a lifer.

Terri stuck her head in the side room. "You ready?" she asked, a manila folder wedged between her fingers.

"Chomping at the bit."

I followed her out the door and could see Nick sitting at a

detective's desk, his injured leg propped on top.

"What are you still doing here? You need to get to the ER," I said, a few feet behind Terri.

He was on the phone. He shrugged, then held the phone against his chest. "Antonio is picking me up. Can I join you guys for the questioning?"

He'd probably trip and fall on the suspect, who would then turn around and sue the city and the federal government for brutality. "Dude, you're a mess, and I mean that in the most caring way possible."

He tilted his head and gave me one of those looks.

"Get your ankle x-rayed, and while they're at it, they can check your shoulder." He happened to be shifting his arm at the same time I made the comment. I raised an eyebrow, and he went back to the phone.

Terri and I entered the interview room and introduced ourselves. Apparently, the quantity card didn't intimidate Tripuka. We were clerks in a candy store to him, it seemed. "Nice to meet you," he said as if we'd just met for the first time.

"I guess you don't remember me at the warehouse. I was the person you tried to run over," I said. Terri had taken a seat. I was more of walker-and-talker.

He gave me an "aw-shucks" nod. "Sorry about that. Sometimes the human brain is so unpredictable in stressful situations." He tried to raise his hands, but his cuffs rattled against the steel, restraining his movement. Still, his facial expression remained indifferent.

Terri opened his file. "So why were you so stressed out, Mr. Tripuka?"

"Oh, please call me Vince. I'm a casual kind of guy."

"Right. Vince." Terri had a hand against her temple. When we had finally reconnected after apprehending the suspect, I wasn't sure who had ticked her off more—Vince Tripuka or the detectives on her own team, Meyers and Longfellow.

As I walked to the other side of the room, Terri interlaced her long fingers in front of her body as she leaned her chest against the desk. She may not have realized she'd created an overflow of cleavage. I watched his eyes, and they never once looked down. Even though he was staring at a murder charge, Vince had self-control. Or at least he wanted us to think as much.

"So, back to your stress. While I can set up a meeting with you and one of our psychiatrists to help you work through your...issues..." She dropped her sights to the folder in front of her, then lifted her eyes back in his direction, apparently wondering if he would respond in some manner. He just sat there, passively listening. "Can you—"

"Look, I don't mean to interrupt, but I was scared, like any man would be if he heard detectives had shown up at his work looking for him. I knew I'd missed a couple of my meetings with my parole officer. I admit it. The reality is, I didn't commit a crime, whatever you think you're investigating."

Terri released an audible breath. "Do you know how tired I am of hearing people like you say that? It literally makes me want to vomit."

"I don't expect you to believe me. It took me a while, but I've learned that life isn't fair. I can't undo—"

"The violent assault on a teenage kid at a fast-food restaurant, Vince. That's what you did, and you can't slither or lie your way out of it. Eyewitnesses saw the whole thing go down," Terri said, thumping her forefinger against the file. "Don't start blowing smoke up our asses with your calm, cool, and collected act, as if you're Mr. Mature."

Tripuka closed his eyes for a moment, appearing to gather himself. "Not to belabor the point, but if you do the research into the case and read the trial transcript, you'll see the eyewitnesses showed up *after* the altercation began. They assumed it was me who had started it because I was bigger and older."

Shaking her head, Terri said, "You never stop, do you…with your subtle innuendos. It's amazing." She shoved the chair back, got up, and walked to the far corner. Damn, she was wound tight. I walked back to the other side of the table, picked up the folder, and quickly scanned his background.

"Where were you last night between ten p.m. and midnight?" I asked. That was the estimated time of death, according to the initial report by the Middlesex County medical examiner. I closed the folder, set it back on the table, and waited.

He glanced over at Terri, then back at me, a slight twitch in his brow. "So that's what this is about? You think I committed some godawful crime last night?"

I didn't respond. I wanted to see how he handled the question.

"Well, I was doing what most Americans were doing. Watching TV, lying in bed."

"What were you watching?"

He tried again to hold up his hands, but his metal cuffs rattled against the restraint. "Jimmy Fallon, of course. Hands down, he's the best late-night comedian. Last night he did that 'thank you card' bit. It's true genius, I tell you. And I don't throw that term around lightly," he said with a slight chuckle. His answer was so casual, we could have been interacting at a cocktail party.

"We'll check that out," I said, knowing he could have just repeated one of Fallon's many often-played routines.

"Feel free. I think his funniest 'thank you card' was the one he wrote to Tom Brady, you know, for having what every man could ever dream of." He raised an eyebrow.

This guy acting so debonair, it was difficult for my mind to balance that against his record.

"To reiterate, you were at home last night, correct?"

He held up two fingers. "Scout's honor."

"You live in Malden? Home, apartment, what?"

"I'm sure you know this answer, but to pacify you, I live in a garage apartment on the property of a very sweet lady, Miss Lucille. She's got plenty of spunk, just had some rough times lately."

He was trying to bait us into another tangent. I knew we could talk to Miss Lucille to find out if she knew whether Tripuka was in his apartment last night.

Terri walked back to the table, picked up the folder, and flipped a page. Showing me the page, she put a finger next to another offense from his past and gave me a knowing nod.

"Mr. Tripuka—" she started.

He laughed. "Please, call me Vince. The only person I knew as Mr. Tripuka passed away several years ago. He's probably looking down on this, none too pleased that I'm in this pickle. That was the term he always used...'in a pickle.' Helluva guy, though. I miss that old coot."

His lips drew into a straight line.

Terri took in a deep breath. "Vince, are you dating anyone at the time?"

"Me? No. Not many women want to date a convicted felon. I don't try to bullshit the women. No offense with my language."

"Did you try to bullshit your way with Susan Miller?"

He didn't snap back with a quick reply. He just sat there and studied his nails.

"No response to your rape conviction, Vince?" Terri smacked the folder onto the table, her adrenaline back to an open spigot.

"It was..." He paused, but she didn't give him any wiggle room.

"R-A-P-E. We spell that rape. That's what it was, Vince. You can't deny that one. They had real evidence on that one."

For the first time in our interview, he seemed stressed, dejected even. I could see a green vein protruding from his temple, and the bags under his eyes appeared more pronounced.

"Vince, you hearing me on this one?" Terri snapped her fingers. "You fucking raped a sixteen-year-old girl and you've got nothing to say?"

He finally lifted his sights, his eyes suddenly moist. "What do you want me to say?"

"I want you to admit that you *enjoy* the control you have over women. You *enjoy* that feeling of power when you have your way with them."

"I don't know why you're using such generalizations, but, honestly, the charge was statutory rape because she was a week before her seventeenth birthday."

Terri planted both hands at her hips. "You raped this girl. She just happened to be a week from being seventeen. She could have been nineteen or twenty, but maybe you found it too tempting to impose your will on a naïve, young girl."

He shook his head and scooted higher in his metal chair. "You've got it all wrong. Susan..." He paused, bringing a fist to his mouth. "We cared about each other."

"Woo-hoo!" Terri yelled, throwing her arms to the ceiling. "Now you're saying you two were in love. Damn, Vince, you really know how to spin a story after the fact. What do you think, Alex? You think Vince is the biggest bullshitter in all of Boston?"

I nodded, wondering if she were truly losing it or if she somehow thought this was going to get him to talk. I couldn't see it working, so I took the opening and ran with it.

"How long had you known Susan before you were arrested for..." I purposely redacted the term so he would think I was giving him a chance. And maybe I was, if nothing else but to learn more about his motivations and what made him tick.

"We'd been seeing each other for about three months."

Out of the corner of my eye, Terri opened her mouth, but I beat her to the punch. "Where did you meet?" I asked, pulling my hands to my back and walking a few steps to my left.

"We met at a Star Wars convention. We were both sci-fi nerds. She was dressed like Princess Leia and I was dressed like Han Solo." He chuckled and momentarily glanced away. "We hit it off right away. I guess I was a little immature for my age, and she looked older."

"What was the age difference?" I glanced at the folder, but I didn't immediately see the data.

"Seven years. As you know, she was sixteen, I was twenty-three. How many sixteen-year-old girls show up at a convention all alone? I figured she was at least nineteen or twenty. She certainly didn't look like any sixteen-year-old I'd seen."

Terri placed two hands on the back of the chair, her face pinched as much as she could make it. She was ready to pounce.

"Was she mesmerized by the fact you were older, maybe wiser?" I asked.

"Eh, I don't like to brag." A smile escaped his lips. "She did seem a bit impressed with a few things I'd learned over the years. I read a lot from many different sources. Everything from white papers on the economic impact of the perpetual civil wars that have plagued Africa, to science books, paleontology, astronomy, history, and even some poetry."

I hesitated for a second. If this guy wasn't completely lying, I was again seeing a side of him that didn't match his rap sheet.

"What poem did you read to her the night you stole her virginity?" Terri shot lasers with her eyes.

"I didn't steal anything. She actually wasn't a virgin. That folder doesn't tell you everything, does it?"

Terri looked down and ran a finger across the page.

"She'd dated an older guy before me. He was actually twenty-seven. So, I was considered young by her standards."

"But the fact of the matter, Vince, is that you had sex with a minor. And she went on record that it was against her consent. That's rape in anybody's definition."

He laid his palms flat on the table and huffed out a breath. "That wasn't easy for me. Honestly, it broke my heart."

"You're fucking sick!" Terri barked, then she flipped around and faced the wall, arms crossed in front of her.

She was becoming unhinged, and I worried that she would completely lose it and blow our chance at cornering this Casanova. But I also wondered what had her so wound up, even beyond the normal shit we had to deal with each and every day. This seemed personal on some level for her.

"Vince, your caring nature is bit too much for us to believe…*honestly.*" My arms were now crossed as well.

"Fine. What can I do about it now? It's history. I have to live with it."

He paused and glanced over at Terri, who still had her back to us. She was pressing her fingers to the bridge of her nose.

"I'm really trying to understand what kind of girls you like. Only young, naïve girls who think you're the smartest guy in the room? Or perhaps you now like them a little older?" I was subtly referencing the victim from last night who was thirty-two.

"No idea what you're trying to rope me into, but Susan and I genuinely cared for each other."

Terri flipped around and stabbed a finger in his direction. "You're full of shit!"

"Doubt me all you want. You'll have to stand in line though."

Now this guy was throwing a pity party. It seemed out of

nature, given his overconfident demeanor earlier.

"According to your file, Vince, they took a rape kit on Susan. Doesn't sound like true love to me," I said.

"Her father made her. She told me that she loved me and that it tore her apart to accuse me of the crime. But her father told her if she didn't say it was rape—not just sex with a minor, but actual forced rape—then she would be cut off from the family, and from any inheritance."

It sounded plausible, and provable. I glanced at Terri, wondering if this information was learned after the trial or before. If it was before and his defense attorney knew about it...

"We've rehashed your record, Vince. You can twist the facts, but the record speaks for itself. Two felonies, two times in prison, and a number of misdemeanors," I said. "We can and will check out your alibi from last night, but I want to know one more thing before we walk out of here."

"Anything, I'm an open book. If you haven't noticed, I haven't even lawyered up. I realize I haven't been the perfect citizen. I've tried to do everything in my power to improve my reputation."

I paused at that comment. Reputation. *Reputation?* That was far different than actual behavior.

"If you're so worried about your reputation, then why did you skip your meeting with your parole officer, not just once but twice?"

"On the first time, I had to work late. My employer, Three Craft Beers, has been extra cool, and I was in the middle of my route. I couldn't just ditch the truck to go to my parole-officer meeting."

"And you never thought about calling and trying to reschedule?"

"I did, but it rolled straight to voicemail."

"You would think he'd have noted that in your record."

"Yeah, you would. But he's got a job just like everyone else. And he had to put the blame on someone other than himself. It's how the system works. It's one of the many challenges of being a convicted felon. The odds are stacked against us."

I expected Terri to chop him off at the knees, but when I glanced at her, she once again had her hands on the back of the chair, her knuckles white, her face even paler. She looked spent.

"On the second time, I overslept. Lame excuse, I know. But I owned up to it."

I nodded, while pressing the loose edges of my bandage back onto my hand, then got to my real question. "You seem to be a pretty smart guy, Vince. You know how the world works, how people are perceived. If we were to look at some generic guy who was obsessed with girls in a really sick way—like, where he would want to murder them, even rape them—would you say it would be in his best interest to show that he was actually a very thoughtful, compassionate person who seemed to be transparent about his faults and eager to prove he was a good man?"

He licked his lips, as if he were suddenly parched, and then he swallowed once.

"No need to answer just yet. Think about that a bit. We'll be back to talk to you after we've had a chance to verify your answers."

Terri didn't say a word. She pushed off the back of the chair and led us into the hallway.

"What do you think?" she said, kneading her temple.

"Either he really has turned the corner and matured, or he's a professional bullshit artist."

"I've got my opinion," she said.

"Let's get the facts and see where that takes us."

Nine

Thumbing mindlessly through a worn magazine which contained about a thousand stories on so-called exclusive Hollywood gossip news, I was kicking my leg like I'd downed about four energy drinks. I pulled my gaze away from the magazine and saw an attractive man—streaks of gray in his hair and clothing that didn't contain a single wrinkle—sitting against the opposite wall. He was also perusing a magazine. *Contemporary Art?* I thought that might have been what the title was.

I quickly set my magazine on the chair next to me. Besides us, the only other person in Dr. Dave Dunn's waiting room was a young receptionist, who had her head buried in a book. She chomped her gum and twirled a lock of hair around her finger as she read.

"I'll let you have the magazine after I finish reading this article." The man was looking at me, his eyes a mahogany brown that sparkled off the canned lighting from the ceiling.

Obviously, he'd caught me looking at his magazine—and him. "Oh, I'm fine." I started to rummage through my purse to find my cell phone.

Out of my peripheral vision, I saw him bring the magazine

down as he leaned his elbows on his knees. "We both know that Dr. Dunn has time-management issues. It goes with the unpredictability of his job, I guess," he said in a hushed tone.

I nodded and offered a courteous smile, thinking it felt odd delving into this kind of conversation in my psychiatrist's waiting room. Up until a couple of months back, I thought only mentally unstable people visited a psychiatrist. The gentleman seemed nice enough, even had a regal look about him, with his well-coifed appearance, strong chin. And those eyes...

The door by the receptionist's desk opened. "Oh, that's a hoot, Mrs. Carano. It's always great to hear stories about your two cats. I'll be laughing all afternoon." Even under a bushy, white mustache, I could see Dr. Dunn's genuine smile split his leathery face.

An elderly woman clutching a pair of fur gloves gave her psychiatrist a kiss on the cheek, then patted it, as if she were saying goodbye to a son. "It's always a pleasure, doctor. We just have the best conversations," she said, giggling as if someone had just tickled her.

He glanced in our direction. "You know how I look forward to our sessions. Same time next week?"

"Wouldn't miss it for the world."

"Wonderful. Ashling will make sure you're on the schedule." He gestured toward the receptionist, who was still reading, chomping, and twirling, then he patted his patient on the arm and took a step back through the door.

"But what do I do about you-know-what?" She cupped her hand to the side of her mouth, and I was practically blinded from the twinkling diamonds on her hand and wrist.

He gave her a quizzical look.

"You know," she said under her breath, but still loud enough so that I could easily hear her. "S-E-X."

Was this woman for real? I tried not to stare, but I sure did. Dr. Dunn furrowed his brow briefly, then rested his hand at her elbow. "Love is a strange thing, Mrs. Carano. And very unpredictable. Give it time, and I'm sure something will happen." He gave her a warm smile, and she seemed appreciative of his advice.

She turned around to speak to Ashling. "I'd like to set up my next appointment," she said, shifting her gloves into her opposite hand.

With an elbow still planted on the desk, the curly-headed brunette blew a bubble until it popped. She removed her gum and attempted to wipe the gum remnants off her lips and mouth. "Do we really need to go to the trouble, Mrs. Carano? You've been seeing Dr. Dunn on the same day at the same time every week for something like seventy-five weeks. You're more consistent than my period."

Mrs. Carano's mouth dropped. "Well," she huffed, lifting her chin higher by two inches. "It seems you have no consideration for those of us who like to lead an orderly life. I guess I'll mark it down in my little black book."

She flipped over her shoulder to give the doctor one last look.

He simply waved and said, "Black book it is. Have a good day."

She marched out of the office, and then Ashling said, "Good riddance, bitch."

Dr. Dunn leaned toward the desk and mumbled something to his assistant.

"Okay, whatever. But she's the one who's got a pole stuck up her ass."

He paused a second, then must have thought better of getting into a debate about Mrs. Carano with Ashling. "Give me one minute," he said, holding up a finger in my direction.

I looked over at the gentleman, who shifted his eyes from Dr. Dunn back to me. I spoke first. "Are you up first? I thought I had the four o'clock."

"Honestly, I can't recall if I had the four or the five," he said, pulling his phone from his front coat pocket. The color of his charcoal sport coat blended nicely with his full head of hair and those penetrating eyes.

"My calendar isn't syncing," Dr. Dunn said, shrugging his shoulders.

A beat later. "Oops. Did I schedule you both at the same time?" Dr. Dunn asked from the doorway. He slowly turned his head toward Ashling, who had resumed the position of practically lounging on the desk, a new bubble emerging from her mouth.

She would be of no help, apparently.

"Go ahead," the man said. "I've got time in my schedule. I took off early for the day."

"Are you sure?" I said, standing up. "I don't want you to think that you have to give me the earlier time because I'm a woman."

He smiled. "It's absolutely because you're a woman," he said with a wink. "But I can see in your eyes that you're a good person. Please go ahead. It will finally give me a chance to catch up on some reading." He held up the magazine.

"Thank you. I appreciate your offer. I do have a lot going on." I walked toward the door, and Dr. Dunn extended a hand into the hallway beyond. I caught another quick glimpse of the polite, distinguished man, and then headed into the hallway.

I led the way into Dr. Dunn's office and immediately gazed out the windows that lined one wall. I took my usual spot on the couch next to the armrest. I'd seen Dr. Dunn only a handful of times, something I'd never planned. He came highly recommended by one of Nick's friends, whose kids had lost two of their siblings in a car crash. Coming off a summer vacation where my kids had witnessed the murder of one of my old high school friends as well as a fatal drive-by shooting, I knew I couldn't pretend they'd be okay. Also, earlier in the year, they had lost their father. It broke my heart to see them hurt, even if they didn't show any real signs of depression or anger. They needed professional help, and Dr. Dunn had been just the right person.

About three weeks ago, the doctor said he felt like the kids had talked through all of their issues, were well adjusted, and had positive outlooks on life. At first, I'd chuckled. "My fifteen-year-old daughter? Are you sure we're talking about the same person?"

"Teenagers aren't easy, Alex. Girls and their moms especially have their challenges, but I think Erin is as well-adjusted as anyone."

I'd felt a tinge of pride bubble inside, which was quickly replaced with guilt when the doctor spoke about the kids' biggest ongoing concern.

"Concern? Well, I knew something would come from this." I released a prolonged exhale, then bounced my hand off the armrest. "Okay, doc, hit me."

He pointed a finger in my direction.

And then I responded by pointing a finger at my chest.

He countered that with a nod.

"I can't deal with all this non-verbal shit. Oh, sorry."

"It's okay to cuss in here, Alex. But yes, their biggest concern is you."

After debating the merits of therapy, I'd reluctantly agreed to see the good doctor a few times, if for no other reason than to be able to show the kids we were in this together.

By now, Dr. Dunn probably thought he'd bitten off more than he could chew.

"Would you like a bottled water, Alex?"

"Sure. That's another thing I forgot to do today...drink water," I said with a brief smile.

He pulled a plastic bottle from his mini fridge and handed it to me, then he took his regular spot in his high-back office chair. It creaked loudly as he settled in and picked up his pipe. He always had a pipe nearby, even if it wasn't lit. It reminded me that even the guards watching the asylum were normal people with normal issues.

"So why did you forget to drink water? Sounds like a pretty fundamental thing to do for yourself." He rocked the chair back until his legs dangled off the edge.

"Well, it's not like I shit myself or anything. I just got busy. Remember, I don't exactly work a typical nine-to-five office job. Life-altering events take place every day, and sometimes a few minutes here or there, or even a few seconds, can mean the difference between catching a cold-blooded killer or losing him so he can murder again. I can't have that on my conscience."

He nodded and studied me further. I was used to it. The room was cozy, but not restrictive. Books, mostly from his profession, lined numerous bookshelves and every spare inch of his desk. The furniture was circa 1995, with oranges and browns mixed in with occasional blacks and grays. I could see a layer of dust on the blinds, but it was the tranquil setting outside his window that drew my attention. A cluster of trees with yellow flowers. Thick shrubbery outlining the vignette. A birdfeeder hanging from one of the tree branches. Occasionally, I'd see a blue jay or a cardinal.

"So..." He teetered forward until his feet hit the floor. With his white hair, pipe, and oversized gray sweater, he appeared to be comfortable with who he was. To me, he looked like one of my old professors from law school. Oh yeah, that was another area he wanted to cover—my apparent distaste for everyone in the legal profession. As he paused, I cracked the cap off the bottle and chugged until I needed a breath. I glanced at the bottle.

"Okay, I guess I should take time to drink water."

"That would be a healthy choice."

"Healthy choice" was a term he used a lot.

"I'm one-for-one today," I joked.

He smiled. "Have you thought about Mark in the last week?"

My deceased husband, the man who had been screwing everything that walked, talked, and chewed gum during our marriage, including our busty nanny. I'd ushered that nanny straight out the door right about the time of Mark's funeral. Thankfully, our previous nanny, Ezzy, had agreed to come back—which was a miracle, considering Mark had threatened to deport her.

"Well, I still think he's the biggest lying piece of shit I've ever met. I just don't know how I didn't see it way back when."

"Do you think he was the same when the two of you met in law school?"

I tapped my finger on the water bottle. "I've thought about that a bit here and there. Should I have seen the signs of him being such a tool, or did he only evolve into a tool while we were married?"

"Good questions. Have you come to a conclusion?"

I smirked. "Depends on the day, I suppose."

"How about today, at this moment?"

I didn't really enjoy being put on the spot, not about my innermost thoughts. But maybe that was what I needed in these sessions with Dr. Dunn. I released an audible breath. "It's probably a little of both. He showed some signs early on, but I ignored them because I told myself I needed to see the good in people, not the bad. And then I think he took advantage of my naiveté. Let's just say we weren't a good pairing."

"Sounds like it."

"The only good things that came out of our relationship are Erin and Luke. I don't really know how to resolve that."

"You don't have to put so much pressure on yourself to have every little thought or historical fact from your life perfectly aligned. We're all imperfect. Dare to be average, Alex."

Average. Growing up, as I poured every ounce of myself into being the best at everything, from school to tennis, the use of that word would have pissed me off. I wasn't average at anything.

"I can see you don't like that word." Apparently Dunn was a mind reader as well as a doctor. Or was I just that transparent? "You're an overachiever and you have a lot to be proud of, but I think you're taking the idea of 'daring to be average' in a different way than I mean it."

"How so?" I crossed my legs and started kicking.

"Putting focus and effort into doing something well, especially if it's a passion of yours, or even simply an action that does some good—and that includes for yourself, not just others—is a good thing. A fulfilling thing. But I only mean that you need to be able to cut yourself a break. Do you feel a heavy burden and guilt from your husband dying on the case you were assigned to investigate?"

I picked at one of the orange buttons sewn into the couch's fabric. "Maybe."

"That's natural, at least early on during the grieving process. But you've been able to move forward in so many ways—and by the way, I'm really proud of you for that—but keeping that guilt on you, that's probably what Erin and Luke see and feel from their mother."

I nodded and took in a deep breath. "For the first few months, I guess I tried to fake it a little. I was just trying to keep it together."

"But you've made great strides here recently. Are you still seeing your colleague...Brad, isn't it?"

"Yes." It was hard not to smile when I thought about him, about us.

"Are you starting to accept him for who he is? You can't change his age no matter how long you wait."

I chuckled. "I'm getting there. I was burned by Mark, and...you know."

"I do know. Going slow is probably smart. But realize you're a grown woman, and this is the twenty-first century, so you're fully within your right to do whatever the hell you want to do."

He raised an eyebrow, then leaned back in his chair and put his pipe in his mouth.

"I just don't want the kids to be hurt. And there's also work and what people there might think."

"Screw the people at work. Spread your wings, Alex, and let it all out. You can't love someone unless you open yourself up."

"But what if—"

"That's life, isn't it? You can either answer the what-if question or just sit on the sideline and bitch about it until you're ninety-eight years old."

"I like your style, Dr. Dunn."

"Just offering my opinion. That and a couple of bucks will buy you a cup of coffee, my Jewish mother always says."

His rate was much higher than a couple of bucks, but I got his point.

"The kids think Brad is great, by the way. And that only deepens my feelings for him. I wouldn't do anything to hurt them. Ever."

"You're a great mother, Alex."

"I'm not trying to fish for compliments. You have kids. You know how they can shoot you down just hours after you think you've made a real difference in their lives."

"Indeed. Kids often don't realize how their decisions, their actions, their words, impact the people around them. Usually, after growing a bit, gaining more life experiences, these youngsters will see their ways and mature—and then they have kids. That's the cycle of life, I suppose."

I drank another mouthful of water, letting his words resonate a bit. My mind actually veered in a different direction.

"You've studied all sorts of psychology, I'm assuming."

He smiled. "Yes."

"I deal with people lying every day, but every once in a while, I run into a person who truly makes me wonder if I'd assumed the worst when I shouldn't have."

"One of your cases. Are you sure you want to take up your time talking about work? That's a four-letter word, you know."

I was already there. "Do you have a way of telling truth from fiction when a patient speaks?"

"There are methods, some of which you probably learned in your FBI training. And of course there are the unreliable lie-detector tests. The bigger question is really what makes a person a liar."

"A pathological liar?"

"That term can be used, depending on the characteristics of the lying, yes. I could go on and on about the topic. You've happened to touch on a topic that really intrigues me. Perhaps we could spend some time off the clock talking about it, if you're really interested."

Was the doctor asking me out on a date? Certainly not, right? I could feel my face flush, but I tried to steer us back to my reason for asking.

"Is it possible for someone to be so convincing that they actually believe the lies they are saying? Almost like some type of split personality?"

"There are extreme cases of split personality, bipolar disorder, and then, of course, external stimulants and depressants playing a role. But I think you might be describing something called false memory syndrome, where the person actually believes their own version of the truth, when it's nothing more than pure fantasy."

Picture frames on one of the walls rattled. I put my hand on the couch. "Did you just feel that?"

"Dear God, tell me it's not—" He tried to push out of the chair, but it took a second for his feet to hit the ground.

I jumped up. "It's not what?"

"Ashling's ex-boyfriend."

I threw open Dr. Dunn's office door and ran down the hall, just as I heard someone or something pounding against a wall. "Stop it, you sonofabitch!" Ashling screamed as I opened the door to the waiting room. She wasn't at her desk. To my left, a hulking man covered in tattoos pressed his forearm into the throat of the nice man from earlier. Ashling was on the floor, rubbing the side of her red face, tears flowing everywhere. Then I saw something silver and in motion.

"He's got a knife!" I yelled as I ran in that direction.

I dove for the arm that wielded the knife. The guy must have been close to six-five because I could barely reach his hand. His grip on the knife didn't waver, but I knocked him off balance, and his forearm dropped from the nice man's neck. He gagged, grabbing at his throat.

Meanwhile, Tattoo Man growled like a wild beast as he turned his back—with me holding on for dear life—and rammed me into the chairs and wall. The impact stole all remaining air from my lungs, and for a moment, the edges of my vision turned dark. He quickly regained his balance.

"This is all your fault, Ashling...if you would just give me another chance, baby!" he spat, using the knife to punctuate his words in the air.

"Fuck you, Spike! You're nothing but a lying, cheating bully. And you just assaulted an FBI agent, asshole."

He shut his pie hole, apparently processing what Ashling had just said. A second later, I plowed into him a second time. I felt his rib crack when my shoulder hit him. I drove his chiseled body into the ground and made sure my knees connected with his groin on impact. He howled, but still didn't let go of the knife.

He rolled onto his side. As I reached for the knife, the nice man put his shoe on Spike's wrist. A second later, his hand released the knife. And then we heard an enormous boom, followed by white dust spraying around the waiting room.

We all looked over to the desk, where Dr. Dunn stood with a shotgun pointed at the ceiling.

"The great equalizer," he said as his pipe dangled off his lips. "Now call the cops and put this piece of shit in jail."

Ten

Deep in a dream that included me, Brad, and a steamy hot tub in the middle of the French Alps, I felt thin fingers pushing against my shoulder. I fought to stay in my happy place, but it began to fade away. Something cold slid down my cheek. Drool.

"Mom, are you awake?"

I opened my eyes to see my daughter Erin leaning over me like a mother hen. "I am now."

"Ooh, what is all that white crap in your hair?"

I brought a hand to my hair, but a sharp pain in my shoulder altered my motion. It was the same shoulder that had tackled the piece of granite—Spike, a.k.a. George Schallot—twice in a span of a minute the previous evening. My fingers felt small granules along my scalp.

"Oh, that's the remnants of the ceiling from Dr. Dunn's office."

"Is he okay?"

"He's fine. He was the one who fired the shotgun. But he wanted me to tell you that's not the best way to solve a problem." He didn't really say that, but I couldn't let her think that her former shrink had stored a shotgun in case one of his more unstable patients fell off the rails. I brought myself to my elbows, then pushed up from there to lean against the headboard. I tapped the bed. "Sit down for a second, sweetie."

"I've got to go to school, Mom."

"Just a quick moment."

She sat, her arms crossed. She had on a halter top, one of the many pieces of gear from her stint on the Salem High School tennis team. I could actually see nice definition in her shoulder and triceps. She was my daughter.

"You're old enough to hear this. Dr. Dunn's assistant, Ashling..."

"Yeah, I remember her. She could blow a wicked bubble."

"Well, as I learned after the incident, her boyfriend has been abusing her for the last year. She put up with it and didn't tell anyone. He would always promise to change, but he kept drinking or whatever, and it only got worse. All hot air and no change."

She didn't respond instantly, which was a good sign. "Is she okay? You know, not just physically, but up here?" She pointed at her head.

"I think she will be, after a good amount of therapy. The reason I'm telling you is because no one would have guessed that Ashling was dealing with those issues. She seems like a free spirit, no cares in the world. She's smart, reads a lot, and is a fun person to be around. But she hid a dark secret because she was ashamed. And once it started, she didn't feel comfortable telling anyone."

Erin's shoulders dropped a couple of inches as a wrinkle formed between her pretty brown eyes.

"I just want you to know that it can happen to anyone— fooling yourself into the thinking this big, protective guy is good for you, but when the doors shut, he turns on you and beats you."

A tear pooled in her eye. "That's so sad, Mom. I wish she

would have asked for help."

"That's why I'm telling you. Please don't let yourself get involved with boys like that. And if you do and something happens, please know that you can tell any adult about it, and we'll put a stop to it. Start with me first, please."

She nodded. "What about Brad?"

"Yeah, he's good too."

"Good, because he's younger and he can probably kick anyone's ass."

She ran off as I rolled out of bed and shuffled down the steps at half her speed, thinking more about her comment. I was glad she felt comfortable in looking at Brad as someone who would have her back, but damn…that age issue always seemed to creep back up. Even my kids could see a major difference between me and the man I'd been dreaming about just moments ago.

And what a dream it had been.

I made a mental note to call or text Brad today as I waltzed into the kitchen and saw Luke fixing his own lunch, Ezzy at the sink cutting fresh vegetables.

"Looks like you've got the troops stepping up and taking some extra responsibility this school year."

She looked over at me and winked. "Luke is growing up. He said he needed to accept more responsibility. He wants to be team captain on his basketball squad this year."

"Cool. Luke's the man," I said.

"That's kind of lame, Mom." Then he ran over and gave me a tight hug. I kissed the top of his head. He was a sweet kid, but at twelve years of age, I'd already been able to pick up signs of his teenage alter ego, the cynical, glass-half-empty side.

He'd yet to hit a major growth spurt, so he angled his head to look up at me, big, brown eyes reminding me of those times when he was my snuggle bear as a toddler. I rustled his thick

AT DUSK73

mane of hair.

"You need a haircut."

He flipped his head to the side.

"Are you trying to grow Bieber hair?" his sister asked from across the kitchen.

"Hell no. But Bieber is old anyway."

"Cussing before it's eight a.m.?"

He ignored me. "You've got a little something," he said, pointing to the side of his lips.

I reached up and felt the dried saliva that was left over from my slumber. I tried to wipe it off.

"Dr. Alex, do you actually think you'll join us for dinner tonight?" Ezzy asked as she shaved carrots in the sink.

"I should, why?"

"Just fixing an old family stew recipe. It will knock your socks off."

I waddled over to the coffeepot, working out the kink in my shoulder. As the coffee brewed, I pulled out my phone and saw a text from Nick.

Can't pick u up, but meeting at 8 w/Gretchen. Will u be there?

"Crap," I said, quickly moving back over to the coffee.

"Work calls again," Ezzy guessed, her tone flat.

"Right. We've just got this crazy case where we think we can crack this ten-year-old murder based on a guy we picked up for a murder that took place two nights ago. But if we don't start putting holes in his stories, then he might walk. Then again, I'm not sold that we have the right guy. Whatever, I'm late."

I felt a hand on my back. "Dr. Alex, there is always a big case. While I know it's important, don't forget the kids would like to see you around every once in a while." She raised her silver eyebrows and gave me one of those Ezzy looks—the kind that served as a gentle reminder to heed her words.

"Yes, work-life-health balance. I'll repeat that ten times on my way out the door."

She actually laughed at my response. Cupping the mug of hot coffee, I turned back around just before exiting the kitchen. Erin walked by just then and tossed an orange in the air on her way to where she was packing up her lunch and snacks for her daily tennis workout. I snatched the orange out of her hand, then held it up so everyone could see. "This is proof that I will eat breakfast. A healthy one at that."

I left the house to a string of *I love you*s. And that made my heart sing all the way to the office.

Eleven

Gretchen blew her nose into the tissue, which she then tossed onto the pile at her feet. The mound of used tissues reached her knees, and I was beginning to wonder if she might suffocate in her own snot. It was a little gross, but it also made me feel badly for the woman, whose string of bad luck lately was now punctuated with some type of allergy/cold combination she just couldn't shake.

"Can I get you anything?" I asked.

"No." Her nose actually honked when she spoke. "I think I have everything I need right here." She glanced around her section of the worktable in the same war room we'd used for a number of other high-profile cases. Three boxes of tissues were stacked off to her left, along with bottles of ibuprofen, allergy medicine, three types of cold medicine, and some leftover chicken soup that Nick had ordered for her from the diner down the street from our office at One Federal Plaza in Boston's West End.

A metal rattling sound brought my attention to the other side of the room. Nick had just wedged his way through the frosted glass door while maintaining his balance on two crutches. The ER doctor said he'd suffered a grade 3 sprain in his ankle. He had a look of determination on his red-blotched face, but he stopped every few shuffled steps and twisted his shoulder a few times.

"Need any help?" I asked as I propped my legs on the chair next to me and rocked a bit.

"Something about this just doesn't feel right. I go a few steps and...I don't know. Probably just getting used to this new mode of travel."

I sat up and took another look at the asymmetry of how he was hobbling along. When he finally reached the table, he fell into a chair, and I took his crutches and did a quick inspection.

"I see the problem." I turned one crutch upside down.

"What?"

"You're five-ten, right?"

"Yep."

"Not sure if you saw this, but your crutches have different levels for each inch of height. This one here is set to five-eight." I pulled out the metal two more inches until it clicked into place, then I rested it next to the other one on the floor.

"Thanks. I thought my workout regimen was getting me in good shape. But this one-legged mode is kicking my ass. And this really puts a damper on me qualifying for the Boston Marathon."

My partner had made a remarkable life change in the last few months, committing himself to eating healthy, working out like a maniac. He had lost forty or fifty pounds while adding definition and muscle. He looked five years younger and seemed to have the energy of two kids. Plus, his general attitude had improved. I was really impressed. Well, I was impressed with everything up to the point when he sprained his ankle.

"How'd you do it?" Gretchen said in the nasally tone, her sinuses so clogged it was difficult to distinguish individual words.

"It's all because of that asshole locked up in the Somerville jail."

"All because of him?" I asked with a wink.

"He started it." He paused. "Okay, I know I sound like one of your kids."

I held my thumb and finger close together. "Just a wee bit."

He turned to Gretchen, who grabbed a handful of tissues, brought them to her mouth, and sneezed. "Bless you." Nick and I said in unison.

"Thanks. Your ankle?" she asked, shifting her red-rimmed eyes to Nick.

"My first step out of the car and my damn shoe got wedged in a grate. A few of the truck drivers saw me struggling to get out, so they decided to help. They were all pulling me in different directions. Then I heard a pop. My ankle swelled up to the size of a cantaloupe within about ten minutes."

"This all happened while I was in the garage looking for Tripuka," I said to Gretchen. "Then that maniac tried to run me over. He crashed when I shot out the tire, and then Nick showed up just in time to clothesline the guy."

Nick and I both twisted our shoulders while glancing at each other, but neither of us said a word. I was tired of dwelling on his or my ailments.

"Tripuka tried to act like the model citizen during our first formal interrogation. He had an answer for everything."

"They all do. In fact, the smoother they are, the higher likelihood they're guilty," Nick said.

"Gotta admit, he's convincing. Given his crime résumé, I wasn't expecting Mr. Smooth. But that's exactly what we got. He actually sounded...authentic."

"I know I wasn't there, but you're not going to fall for that crap, are you?"

"Falling isn't how I operate, Nick. You know that. But we need something to charge him with."

"He threatened the vic. Someone overheard him. Start with that."

The war room door opened. "We will."

It was Terri, wearing a visitor's badge on top of another well-tailored pantsuit, this one gray with thin, black pinstripes. But I was really salivating over her purse.

"Michael Kors?"

She smirked. "It was a gift to myself."

"Celebrating something big?"

"It was a Friday night, and I was sitting at home eating a tub of ice cream. I told myself to stop, which I did, and so I bought this as a reward."

"Very strange how the female mind works," Nick said with a shake of his head.

Terri and I exchanged a smile. I looked over at Gretchen, whose veins were popping out of her neck as she put everything she had into her nose-blowing effort.

Terri grimaced. "You might want to sit over there." I pointed at the far end of the table.

"Okay, just for a quick moment," Terri said. "We've got an appointment in thirty minutes with the guy who overheard Tripuka. Works at Lenny's Pub, where Emma used to work."

"Great. I was about to tell the team that Tripuka is likely to lawyer up soon."

"Maybe twenty-four hours, if not sooner, I'm guessing," Terri said.

"When that happens, we'd better have solid evidence of his connection to either or both murders—Emma Katic from two nights ago, or our cold case, Gloria Lopez. Otherwise, the lawyer will demand bail, and Tripuka will be walking the streets. He could either drop off the radar, or—

"He might have the balls to strike again," Nick said.

"Neither is a good option. We have to find the evidence. I won't take anything less." Terri poked her finger into the table, her emotional spigot nearly fully open again. Something about Tripuka or this crime lit a fire inside the detective. Then again, I'd just met her, so maybe she was this emotional about every case.

"For now, Nick, given your mobility issues, I think we'll be more efficient if Terri and I work the field on this one. You can be the lead back here at the office, working with Gretchen."

"I don't like sitting on the sideline, but it's the only way I'll heal. I think we need to focus on where Tripuka was ten years ago. See if we can connect him to Gloria Lopez. While the idea of two people with the same warped desires and skill sets to carry out these murders seems hard to fathom, maybe Tripuka met someone in prison and developed some type of twisted mentor relationship with the original killer, then got his jollies by mimicking the same act ten years later."

A stunned silence filled our space, three pairs of eyes staring at Nick.

"That's a brilliant theory." Terri nodded repeatedly, her eyes never leaving Nick.

"Uh, thanks."

I could tell he was starting to feel a bit uncomfortable. "Double that, Nick. I think you and Gretchen just added to your task list. While digging into Tripuka's full history—and somehow verifying that history—find out who his contacts were in prison, and then work it from there."

"But how do we go about finding cellmates, other people he might have come in contact with in prison? They call it prison for a reason," Gretchen said with a tissue at her nose.

I opened my mouth, about to offer some guidance.

"Between this..." Nick held up his cell phone. "This..." He rested a hand on his laptop. "And this..." He put a finger to his head. "...I think we'll be able to piece together something. If it's there, we'll do everything we can to find it."

"We need a warrant to search Tripuka's garage apartment. Nick, think you can—"

"My guys are working on that right now," Terri said.

"Meyers and Longfellow. The same two who—"

"I'm giving them a chance at redemption. Shouldn't be difficult." She twisted her lips, obviously thinking about something. "Nick, if you don't mind, can you follow up with them and make sure they don't, you know..."

"Fuck it up?"

"Right. That."

"Good," I said. "It's a lot faster at the local level than at the federal level anyway. We should get the search warrant today."

I was then distracted by a text from my daughter Erin.

Mom, need your help with a class project. Can u give me some time after school?

She never asked for help, so I knew I couldn't ignore her.

I typed a quick response.

No problem. Mom and daughter time.:)

As soon as I punched send, I regretted adding the last sentence. It only took her a few seconds for a new message to pop.

Ok. Just need help on a project, nothing big.

That was Erin. She didn't like to think anything was forced or pre-planned. I had to take my moments in ten-second intervals when I least expected them.

I set my phone on the table.

"Nick, Gretchen, keep in touch with both Terri and me. Who knows how many hours we have until the attorney vultures start hovering over the Somerville Police Department?"

I turned my head to Terri to ask if she needed to make a pit stop before we headed out, but she was already out of her chair and walking toward the door.

"We'll be late if we don't hustle," she said with a hand on the door handle.

I picked up my purse and phone, wondering if this was how others felt when working with me.

Twelve

Skip Binion thumbed through several pages of crumpled paper on his clipboard. Even with bottles clanging together while being stacked around the bar in Lenny's Pub, I could hear his slithering wheeze. My son would probably offer up a Darth Vader analogy, but Skip's appearance said Mad Max. He had a bleached-blond spike for a goatee, which matched the bed of white thorns on his head. I counted six piercings in his right ear, seven in his left, three more in his nose, two in his lip, and a single hoop attached to his right eyebrow. He wore enough eyeliner to make a raccoon jealous.

"You, with the vodka shipment, I need those three cases parked right over there." His voice sounded hoarse. He picked up a glass of something amber and tilted his head back until he had downed the last drop. It wasn't even noon yet, but Skip appeared to be starting the party early, in front of two law enforcement officers, no less.

Terri walked over from the jukebox while pocketing her phone. As Skip stepped back to speak to the vodka delivery guy, she leaned closer to me. "Just spoke to Miss Lucille, Tripuka's landlord, and she's distraught that her 'sweet Vince' is being held for questioning for an unspecified crime. She has her weekly bridge party in an hour. Said we could drop by before then, if we can make it. Otherwise, she's not sure how long she'll be once she starts yapping with her friends."

I nodded. "You're stacking these one right after the other. You sure you weren't an admin in a prior life?"

"Actually, I was. Did temp work, but was an executive assistant for a few years before I got the break I'd been dreaming about since I was twelve."

"From an admin to a cop. I can see the correlation of roles...kind of." I offered a brief smile.

She pressed her lips together and paused for a second. I shifted my eyes over to Skip, who was now ushering in another delivery guy. Terri continued. "Being a cop was my second career, but, frankly, my first real adult choice. It gave me a purpose to my life, and it allowed me to display my Type A personality without getting catty looks from the other girls."

Other girls. Was she a stripper?

"I won't make you guess. I was a cheerleader for the Patriots."

"So that explains the Miss America looks."

"Thank you? Not really sure that's a compliment. I've had people tell me I was pretty my entire life, so, really, it doesn't mean much. I don't know, it's probably why I gravitated to the cheerleading, dancing squads in school. And without thinking about it much, I thought the ultimate gig was being a cheerleader at the highest level. Well, it didn't take me long to figure out a few things. The pay stinks, the players and anyone who can walk and talk hit on me constantly—"

"I thought that was against NFL rules?"

"So is taking steroids, but it still happens."

"Good point."

"I think they looked at us as the forbidden fruit."

I gave a good-natured roll of my eyes. "Anyway, a few things happened, and I realized there was more to life than showing off Bert and Ernie and wondering how high I could kick my leg."

I covered my mouth, trying to stop the burst of laughter I felt coming on. It wasn't the time or place. But still...Bert and Ernie? Oh, that was good.

"You ladies got five minutes before my team of folks get to the bar to clean the whole place. It will be loud, chaotic, and there will probably be more than one broken glass. Shoot," he said, his palms flat on the table where Terri and I sat. He had tats on every finger, as well as a picture of a hula dancer on his forearm. Every time his muscle twitched, she twerked.

I tried not to stare.

"This shouldn't take long, really. Just need to clarify the conversation you overheard between your employee, Emma Katic, and Vince Tripuka."

He nodded, his eyes glaring straight ahead, and then he blew out a breath and wiped his eyes. "It's not every day that someone you know is killed. Not just dying in a car accident or something completely random, but murdered. I've been trying to not think about it, but it hit me pretty hard. Hit everyone here pretty hard."

His voice became raspier. Holding up a finger, he stepped over to the bar and leaned across to grab a bottle, the contents of which he poured into his glass. He quickly drank half the liquid, then wiped his mouth clean.

I glanced at Terri then said to him, "Drinking may not solve your problems."

"I'm not a lush. I sing in a band, and my voice is fucked. My pops told me I can't drink enough whiskey if I want to clear up an overworked voice box. In fact, if I were to drink anything for Emma, I'd have one of those fruity lemon martinis. She was a hell of a lady...just fell on hard times lately."

AT DUSK   85

He looked down at the table.

"Can you share more?"

He nodded. "Anything to catch the motherfucker who did this." He took in a couple of breaths, hissing like a snake with a nasal problem. "She's had a few issues with drugs in her life. She has two kids and always seemed to struggle to keep it together. Her old man didn't help. She was in an abusive relationship. She didn't tell us, but we saw marks all over her. It was pretty obvious. There were times when they would fight right here in the bar."

"Do you have his name?"

"Sure. Darryl Reese. But no need to look him up. He's in prison. They fought just before he turned himself in, and they hauled his slimy ass to jail. I think it was some type of drug distribution charge."

"When was this?" Terri asked.

"About three, maybe four weeks ago. It was kind of strange. She was actually upset that he was going to jail. But most of us who work with her were thinking it was a good thing for her. A damn good thing. But..." He shook his head and stroked his spiked goatee.

"But what?"

"It just got worse for her. I guess she was barely hanging on, you know, to her sobriety and all."

"How bad did it get, from what you could see?"

Another Darth Vader exhale. "I don't like dissing on the deceased, especially someone with a good heart like Emma."

"But...?"

"She had a few outbursts, even in front of customers. Lenny can't take that kind of shit. No one who owns a business can. And then one night, he caught her stealing some cash out of the register. He had no choice. He let her go right there on the spot."

"Wait, so she wasn't working when she was killed two nights ago?"

"Lenny canned her about a week ago."

"I'm a little confused on the timetable," I said, taking a momentary glance at Terri. "I was under the impression that Vince and Emma got into it the day or night she was killed."

"Sorry, but that's not what I told the detectives. I told them that Vince and Emma had a disagreement a couple of weeks back. Maybe they got weeks and days mixed up."

I could see Terri's jaw muscles flex. Another Meyers and Longfellow screw-up. I knew she would chew their asses later.

"Okay, this Vince-Emma fight was two weeks ago. What happened?" I asked.

"Vince showed up for his normal delivery. It was early afternoon on a Tuesday. It was actually pretty busy. We had deliveries, a few early customers, and a couple of contractors in here doing some work on the plumbing in the bathrooms. I was trying to juggle everything since Lenny is a late arriver, so I asked Emma if she could check the manifest to ensure we were getting everything they were delivering. Lenny's a real stickler for that kind of shit. Hates to get ripped off."

I nodded.

"Apparently, Vince got a little ticked when Emma started asking questions about his delivery. And given her situation, she was on edge, and I think she bit his head off. I heard her screaming at him from where I was inside the bathroom."

"Then what happened?" Terri said.

"I ran out into the bar area, and just as I turned the corner, I saw Emma all up in his face. He didn't push her back or anything, but he said something like, "Bitch, you better back your junk up, or I'm gonna split your head like a watermelon.""

"How did Emma take that?" I asked.

Skip's eyes got wide. "She went apeshit, that's what she did. I jumped in just as she tried to hurl a bottle of beer at the guy. I think it scared the shit out of him."

I followed with another question. "Did calmer heads prevail after that?"

"I yelled at Vince to leave and then spent the next thirty minutes calming Emma down. She was a mess. But if you've ever seen her with her kids, you know she's got something right here." He thumped his chest with his fist and then wheezed out a sigh. "It's just so damn sad to see someone fall apart. And then to get murdered. Man...hopefully she's at peace now."

He crossed himself.

As we walked out the door, Terri turned to me and said, "It's amazing how removing the middle men—Meyers and Longfellow—in the description of the fight alters my perspective of things. Vince might have a temper, but..."

"But it doesn't seem to be a predictable behavior of a killer who was obviously very methodical in how he carried it out and got rid of the body with no one noticing."

Neither of us said a word on the drive across town to where Vince Tripuka lived.

Thirteen

I paused at the edge of the pebbled sidewalk, my eyes drawn to the detached garage positioned behind the house, a pair of massive cedars on either side. Like the house, the three-car garage was painted in soft blue, but I could see some brown starting to show. It needed a new paint job. The main garage doors were also wooden, which told me the house was likely thirty years old, if not older. On the right side, opposite the house, a staircase led to a door. That was Tripuka's place. I wondered what secrets his apartment might hold.

"Any word from Meyers and Longfellow on the status of the warrant?" I kept my gaze on the garage and studied its position to the home, about fifty feet away.

Terri pulled out her phone, then huffed out a breath as she raised the phone to the mostly blue sky. "Dammit, what do these guys do every day? Sometimes I think they're screwing around just to make me look bad."

I couldn't argue the point, not from what I'd seen so far.

She banged out a text and punched send. I had a feeling her language was rather direct. I heard a ding come from my phone, and I checked for text messages. Nick was acknowledging receipt of the note I'd sent him and Gretchen—that we needed more focus on Emma's whereabouts over the last week since she was fired at Lenny's Pub, what she was doing, whom she was with.

I rang the doorbell and immediately heard a barking dog. Turning to look over my shoulder, I could see that the neighborhood was quiet and well kept. Every property was a good half acre, with manicured lawns and beds of shrubs and flowers that looked like they'd been put together by a high-end designer. Lots of trees dotted each plot, concealing a few of the homes better than others. Miss Lucille's blue house with white shutters and trim was probably one of the more understated homes in the community.

The door opened, and a yelping black and brown dog ran headfirst into my leg. I tried moving out of the way, but then I realized he was trying to bite my shins, ankles, even my shoes.

A woman appeared around the door and clapped her hands. "Stop it, Harry."

The Yorkshire terrier—at least that was my guess—growled as he dove at my ankles.

She clapped again. "Stop it, you little shit."

Terri and I exchanged a quick grin as Miss Lucille bent down and picked up Harry. She didn't have far to go. She was no taller than my shoulders, and that was with her two-inch heels. She wore a dress that looked like it might have fit about twenty pounds ago. But she had a grandmotherly look—short, permed hair, pearl earrings, and a matching pearl necklace. The lines in her face seemed to indicate she smiled a lot.

"He's such a naughty dog, but he's so much worse with strangers. Please come in and take a seat in the living room. I'll go feed Harry, which should calm him down a bit."

As she walked away, I noticed she had a little hitch in her step, as if someone might have put a penny in her shoe.

I picked up a musty smell as we found our way into the living room. Then, just as quickly, I passed through an invisible cloud of peaches, as if someone had used one of those sprays.

With a cadre of dog toys in one chair and a paperback in the other chair, Terri and I approached the couch with a purple and pink flowered print.

"Please, please have a seat," Miss Lucille said as she entered the living room from the kitchen at the back of the home, carrying a tray with a pitcher and three glasses. "I've pulled together some lemonade."

She put down the tray and noticed we were still standing. "Sit, please. Can't have a proper conversation while standing up."

I sat down, and I swore I saw a plume of dog hair hovering around me. I sank so low into the cushions my feet arched into the air. I moved to the edge of the couch.

Terri started talking even as she struggled to pull herself out of the cushion wedge. "Miss Lucille, we know you have your bridge party to get to, so we don't want to take up much of your time."

Terri's voice already carried an impatient tone, but I didn't think Miss Lucille noticed.

"That's fine. I called Marion and told her I might be a few minutes late." She lowered her center of gravity and used both hands to pick up a heavy crystal pitcher, then poured out three glasses of lemonade.

"You have a beautiful set of crystal." I knew she'd appreciate the compliment.

A smile split her face, revealing a set of teeth that looked like they'd been sawed off. "Thank you. My dearly departed husband...his mother gave this to us."

She took a sip of her lemonade. "Of course, that didn't

happen until they read her will after she died." She attempted another smile, but her cheeks didn't move. "That woman lived to a hundred and four," she said, shaking her head. "Made my life hell right up to the day she finally kicked the bucket."

I heard the pitter-patter of paws on tile, and I saw Harry meander across the kitchen floor and then slowly plod over to the chair. Looking more like a human who'd just consumed an overindulgent Thanksgiving dinner, he glanced up at Miss Lucille. It didn't appear he had the energy to jump, so Miss Lucille picked up the dog, and he quickly found his resting spot in her lap.

"I suppose you want to first know why I allowed a convicted felon to live in my garage apartment."

Terri and I sat there, slowly nodding.

"I knew Vince had been in prison. He was very honest with me about his past. But really there are two reasons I gave my consent. While my husband—Arthur was his name—was an orthodontist, he and his fellow deacons at church had worked with a number of young men at halfway homes, helping them reacclimate to the real world. Get them jobs, balance a checkbook." She stroked Harry's back as if he were a prized trophy.

They definitely had more patience with the system than I did. "Very nice of your husband. Did he meet Vince when he got out of prison?"

Miss Lucille waved a hand, and I saw some bling. "Arthur's been gone for almost two years now." She looked toward the mantle, where I saw a framed black-and-white picture of a young couple—I assumed it was Miss Lucille and Arthur—sitting next to what appeared to be an urn.

Her lips drew into a straight line, and her eyes pooled with tears. She reached over and pulled a tissue out of a box and lightly dabbed at her eyes.

My phone dinged, and I rebuked myself for forgetting to turn on the mute button. I took a quick glance. It was Brad—my heart skipped a beat.

Hey beautiful. Hope you're kicking ass without me. Just thinking about ya. I'll call you later.

I took in a deep breath, momentarily distracted by Brad's warm thoughts. Damn, he was sweet.

I sipped my lemonade to cool off a bit and wait for Miss Lucille to gather herself. She continued petting her dog, whose lazy eyes told me he had the good life.

"Harry here lost his significant other about the time that Arthur passed."

"I'm sorry."

"Yes, Hermione was run over by some teenage hooligan racing through the neighborhood in his souped-up Mustang," she said emphatically.

I nodded, telling myself I shouldn't bother mentioning that Harry Potter and Hermione never ended up together in the J.K. Rowling series.

Her story reminded me of someone, although the guy I knew was twice as old, had a helmet of curly hair, and drove a Camaro. He was also the biggest cheeseball I'd ever encountered. But I also couldn't forget that he had saved my life over the summer. Archie Woods.

I set my glass on the tray. "You said there were two reasons why you allowed Vince to live in your garage apartment?"

"I guess I thought it was clear. I needed the money, and he was the first one to respond to my ad on Craigslist. Arthur's insurance policy only left me with so much, and his stingy mother didn't give us a dime, outside of the crystal and a book full of family recipes. That woman couldn't cook worth a damn. I threw it away the moment I received it from the probate lawyer."

Terri moved another inch closer to the edge of the sofa. "We'd like to get your feedback on two nights ago."

Miss Lucille's brow furrowed with concern. "I'm really worried about Vince. Can you tell me what he's accused of doing?"

"We can't share details. I hope you understand," I said, still hoping she'd view us as allies.

"I suppose," she said, her eyes drifting to Harry for a second.

Terri didn't give her much time to think about it. "Two nights ago. Can you tell us your routine? Were you at home? What time did you go to bed?"

"Two nights ago. I always watch the news, then I open the door and let Harry do his business in the backyard one more time."

"And you did that two nights ago?"

She put a finger to her chin, which had a vertical crease up the middle. "Now that I think about it, two nights ago I actually let Harry out twice. Once before my show started and then again afterward."

"What show is that?" I asked, to get an idea of the time.

"A re-run of *Scandal*. It's about as believable as aliens landing on earth, but I love me some scandal. I didn't want Harry interrupting my show."

"And when you let Harry outside, did you happen to notice if Vince was home in his apartment?"

"Of course. His red Chevy pickup was sitting in its normal spot, and his light was on in the living room area. I can always see the light through the blinds in that front window. He's just like me. We laugh about it all the time, how he has his own routines. He's a big fan of that Jimmy Fallon."

Interesting to hear her corroborate part of his story so

quickly.

Terri jumped back in. "You watched your show, *Scandal*, then you let Harry out again."

"Well, not until after I watched the news. Lots going on in this crazy world. You've got to stay up on things. Oherwise, you'll wake up and a real nut job will be in charge, and you won't know what happened."

"Yes ma'am. I understand."

I could see Terri slowly reach up and rub her temple. She wasn't a fan of waiting for the game to come to her. In fact, she was so high-strung and hard-charging they might have to create a new personality description, maybe Type AA.

I tried to pull Miss Lucille back on track. "I'm sure you checked out the weather."

"Yes, had to do that. That's the only way I can sleep at night. Storms scare the crap out of me. If I know precisely when they're supposed to hit, then I can prepare for them. Well, me and Harry."

She smiled as she raked her fingers across his back. He yawned until his jaw popped and then rolled his eyes and fell back into his slumber.

I could sense Terri rolling her eyes.

"So the news ended and then you let Harry outside?"

"Let me think through this now. Wasn't that Monday? Yes, it was. I always have to watch Chip Moody to get the latest scoop on the Patriots."

Terri fidgeted in her seat a bit. She was like a bottle of champagne, and if Miss Lucille didn't stop screwing around, she might get a cork in the eye.

"And so then, the news finally—"

"That Bill Belichick is an absolute genius. Year in and year out, they just figure out a way to win. He is kind of an ass though." She leaned closer, as if she were about to break some big news. "Speaking of asses, do they get any finer than Tom Brady's? I know I'm old and decrepit, but Lordy, I'm still a woman."

I couldn't help but laugh at that comment, and Terri followed suit.

"But enough of that," Miss Lucille said, waving her hand. "You're here to learn about Vince." She exhaled and looked toward the corner, then she nodded and looked at both of us. "You know what? After finally walking through the events of that night, I recall letting Harry out that second time more vividly now. I remember it because he found a squirrel and chased it over to a tree and started barking. He wouldn't come in, that little rascal."

"What did you do?"

"I used every four-letter word I know, but he still paid me no attention. He only had squirrel on his mind. I had to run outside in my nightgown. The wind was howling, and there was chill in the air. I was stressed out, I tell you. Harry wouldn't stop barking, and I'm trying to wrangle him inside, then the wind catches my gown and blows it up in my face."

She was on a roll until suddenly she stopped, and her lips pressed together.

"What?" I asked, my arms splayed.

"I'm ashamed to admit it, but I was so embarrassed."

"About your gown flying up?"

She nodded. "Worse than that."

"What?" Terri asked, an edge to her voice.

"I had forgotten to put on my panties after my evening bath. So I was going commando when I went outside. Then my gown flew up. I'm pretty sure I turned so red that I was glowing in the darkness of the backyard."

"Was there someone back there? Was Vince outside?"

"Oh, no he wasn't. In fact, when I finally grabbed Mr. Troublemaker here, I glanced up at his apartment, and his light was off. I assumed he'd just gone to bed early."

I shut my eyes and recounted what I'd just heard.

Terri chimed in. "Wait, you're saying that during the time Jimmy Fallon was on, Vince wasn't there?"

She nodded.

"But what about his red pickup? Did you see it?"

Narrowing her eyes, she seemed to be replaying the scene in her mind. "I was walking back with Harry in my arms, rebuking him for his sassy behavior. My free hand was trying to make sure I didn't moon the free world again. I glanced over at the garage, didn't see the light in the living room. But then I looked down, and...wait, the spotlight under the garage was out. I didn't see the truck, because I couldn't see anything. It was pitch black. He could have been parked there, or perhaps he wasn't."

While Miss Lucille was a sweet woman, Terri and I knew when to cut and run. We had the data we came for, even if it wasn't completely clear. We walked out the front door two minutes later.

Fourteen

I'd only seen luggage push through the dirty rubber curtains on the *other* side of the wall, where the public usually stood and waited after a long flight. Terri and I stood next to a conveyer belt that angled upward at a forty-five-degree angle, one of several ramps that cut across the expansive area in the bowels of Boston's Logan International Airport.

It looked more like a maze of intersecting highways with bumper-to-bumper bags on some type of predestined journey, similar to drive-time traffic. The procession of bags, even with such variations—a clean, black Louis Vuitton bag climbed upward just in front of a bag sealed with duct tape—was a bit hypnotic, along with the drone of the machines that propelled the bags. The air smelled of rubber and oil, with a hint of exhaust.

It actually felt good to stand still for a moment. We'd been moving fast and furious ever since our early morning meeting at the office with Nick and Gretchen. The repetitive motion of the conveyor belts allowed my mind to process the data that we'd learned about Vince and Emma's altercation, more on Emma's background, and then at least the possibility that Vince wasn't at home at the time Emma was killed.

We were waiting to have a brief discussion with Kurt Miller, the father of the girl who had put Vince in jail for statutory rape eight years earlier. Gretchen had searched everywhere for Susan Miller, but the only address that came up was that of her parents. Her mom had answered the first call and cordially deferred all questions to her husband. Although Terri was in a full-on press about every aspect of the investigation, I wasn't sure how much could be gained by interviewing Kurt Miller. But Terri had insisted. He was a baggage handler at the airport, and so there we were.

She turned her bracelet watch, then started tapping her heel on the concrete. "Where is this guy? After Miss Lucille held us hostage for over an hour, we don't have time to sit around and play the waiting game. This isn't a surveillance operation where we have the luxury of drinking bad coffee and eating worse food while a suspect takes a piss in a gas station."

Type AA Terri had resurfaced. Or was it more like she had descended from the skies again, like a tornado? I tried to rein her in a bit, gently of course. I didn't want to get *too* much in the middle of the shit storm. "I don't know about you, but this kind of feels like speed dating. I love your commitment to urgency, but I don't want us to overlook a detail or a different angle just because we're trying to check all the boxes."

She nodded and forced out a breath. "You're right. I know as much as anyone that cracking a case can often come down to a piece of evidence or data point that wasn't thought through well enough early in the investigation."

I nodded, and then she cracked a smile as she looped a lock of hair around her ear.

"What?"

"Speed dating." Her eyes went from watching a bag on the conveyor belt to me. "I was actually desperate enough to do that once."

If she'd told me she actually *played* for the Patriots, I wouldn't have been more surprised.

"You can close your jaw now," she said.

"Was it that obvious?"

"It's not something I brag about, but I figured since we're basically partners on this investigation, and we're both girls, then, you know…"

Another piece of luggage caught her attention, and she followed its path.

I thought about my scrutiny of guys who'd shown interest in me since Mark died. I could also recall a few lookers before he died, not that Mark had ever noticed. His nose was apparently stuck so far up…

I blocked that thought, not wanting to retain any visuals of that nature. "How is it that you couldn't get a date?" I asked.

"It's not how I couldn't get a date, but rather how I couldn't get a date with the right guy."

"That part I get."

"I guess it all became clearer when I dated someone in the Patriots organization."

Now she really had my curiosity.

"And no, it wasn't number twelve."

Damn.

"Well, in my opinion you do have the looks to compete against Giselle. Just sayin'." I smiled, but her response was less jovial.

"It was someone in the front office. He wined and dined me. Treated me well, or so I thought. Turned out, I was just his little toy that he occasionally wanted to take for a ride and show off. He had another girlfriend who was a lawyer at one of the top firms in New York City."

"What is it with lawyers?"

"What is it with front-office assholes?" she shot back.

I arched an eyebrow.

"I found out by hearing her leave a voicemail on his home phone one evening. I put him on the spot, and after a few minutes, he finally cracked. Then he showed me what kind of person he really was. He talked about how smart and cultured she was with her law degree from Harvard, and how they had plans to marry, have kids, and start their own little dynasty."

"Must have been tough."

"It ripped out my heart, made me feel like the ugliest, most undesirable girl in New England."

I wasn't really in the mood to open up all of my old wounds. The scars were still present, but they blended in rather nicely with my skin tone. I did say, "There probably isn't a woman in the country who hasn't been belittled to some degree. But out of that, we create thicker skin, which allows us to survive in the world."

"Makes us stronger," she said.

She looked away for a second, possibly trying to spot Mr. Miller. A number of men in brown uniforms were hauling luggage on and off the conveyor belts at different points, but no one was approaching us.

"Look, I read all the blogs and articles and social media gossip, so I'm aware of what you went through with your, uh…his name was Mark, right?"

A tiny ball of anxiety sprouted deep in my gut. I did everything I could to keep it from growing. "I try not to dwell on the past. I've got two kids who are the center of my world, and they keep me on my toes."

"Sorry. Didn't mean to make you feel uncomfortable. Just wanted you to know that you've had a secret supporter out there. And I'm sure I'm not the only one."

"Thanks. Appreciate that."

An engine groaned in the distance, and we both moved a couple of steps from the nearby conveyor belt. Still no sign of Mr. Miller.

"So, if you don't mind me asking, have you gotten back in the game...you know, dated any?"

I pondered the question for a moment, but that only gave me time to feel heat at the edge of my collar. I wasn't used to being interrogated, certainly not about my private life. She was no Dr. Dunn. But what was stopping me from sharing what made me happy? When would I get over this age obsession I had?

"I'm kind of seeing someone."

She smiled. "Kind of?"

"I guess we are."

"Is he as committed as you are?"

"I hear you. It's really not him. It's me. It came out of nowhere, and then it hit me like someone dropped a brick on my head. When I'm around him, or even think about him, I get butterflies in my stomach and essentially feel like I'm floating in midair. But then I have my moments when I, uh—"

"Think it's all a mirage."

I snapped my fingers. "Exactly. It's like I'm waiting for someone to open up the curtain that exposes everything that's bad about him, and us. But when it comes down to it, I'm probably just a chickenshit at heart. Maybe I'll grow up some day."

We both laughed as a man with grease spots on his face walked up.

"I'm told you're with the FBI and want to talk to me."

I flipped a mental switch and turned serious.

Fifteen

Pulling out my creds, I introduced myself. Terri followed suit.

"The Feds and the local police department working on the same case. Amazing. Eight years ago, I couldn't get any of you guys to even make a phone call." He wiped his brow with the edge of his shirt, his face contorted with a combination of fatigue and stress.

It appeared he wasn't aware of the nature of our visit.

Terri got the ball rolling. "Mr. Miller, we just have a few questions about the incident you and your family endured eight years ago."

He ceased movement, and I could see a wave of red invade his neck and cheeks. "What do you want to bring that up for?" he asked with narrowed eyes.

"The man convicted of hurting your daughter is a suspect in a crime we're investigating."

"What did he do?"

"We're not at liberty to share that information. No offense."

With his hands planted at his waist, he glanced away for a second, his jaw twitching every few seconds.

He turned back to us. "You really know how to ruin a guy's day, you know? But okay, I'm here. What do you want to know about that maggot?"

"Are you sure you're comfortable talking about this topic out here, or do you want to find an office—"

"I got nothing to hide. Everyone knows my story."

"I'd like to verify the facts with you," Terri said.

"Facts? You should know the facts. We told the police everything. And I'm sure you have the transcript from the trial."

Terri nodded, but she seemed a bit flustered, so I jumped in.

"We reviewed that information, thank you. To get right to it, Tripuka said that...well, that it was consensual between him and your daughter."

"He's full of shit."

I waited a tick to see if he was going to offer a more detailed answer. It didn't come.

"He actually said that he and Susan were in love," I said. "And that the only reason she pressed charges was because you threatened to cut her off from her inheritance."

It just hit me that I was looking at a baggage handler—not typically a career that would make for a huge inheritance. Something didn't add up.

With eyes that welled with tears, Mr. Miller stared me down. I tried not to take it personally, since I knew this was like having open-heart surgery without anesthesia.

"Do you remember what it's like to be sixteen years old?" he asked.

"I understand teenagers, if that's what you're asking. Depending on a lot of factors, it can be a very tumultuous time."

"I'm not naïve, Agent Troutt. I know what teens do, what they *want* to do anyway." He paused, scratching gray whiskers on his leathery skin. "Susan was an adventurous type, never really satisfied with the regular things other kids her own age did. She was one of those gifted and talented kids. I think she got bored by her peers. It was rather obvious to her mother and me that she was seeking someone she could relate to intellectually, which just wasn't possible with her teenage friends."

Out of the corner of my eye, I could see Terri subtly glance my way. I guessed that we were both thinking the same thing. How well had Mr. Miller really known his daughter when she was a teen? Intellectual stimulation might have been part of the equation, but I would be shocked if she didn't have some type of thing for older guys. Or random adventure. Whatever.

"Did your daughter date another man before Tripuka...an older man?"

He crossed his arms, and I noticed a pair of dirty, blue work gloves in one of his hands. "To be honest, we didn't know about it until after everything blew up. It was almost too much to handle."

"Not to press you on this, but did you threaten to cut your daughter off from her inheritance?"

He huffed out a breath. "Vince Tripuka is a child predator. I'm convinced of it. He—"

"They met at a Star Wars convention, correct?" Terri asked.

"Yes."

"Where high school kids would not normally attend without a parent or maybe an older sibling."

"I suppose that's right."

"And I understand your daughter had a nice figure."

"What are you implying?"

"Is it possible that Tripuka thought your daughter was older than her actual age?"

"For starters, if you were to look into her face, there would be no way you could think she had been a day older than sixteen."

That sounded like a dad talking, but at least he was talking.

He added, "Okay, even if he did make that assumption initially, eventually he had to know. He knew where we lived, that she didn't have a car or a job."

Terri nodded, which allowed me a chance to get us back to what was most important.

"So, back to what you discussed with your daughter. Did you threaten to cut her off?"

Another twitch in his jaw as his eyes settled on mine. "Not in those exact words, but…yes."

"Mr. Miller, I know it's none of my business, but I have to ask…how much money are we talking about?"

"Why do you ask?"

"People are motivated by money, but they can be extra motivated to say or do certain things by the sum of money."

"Ha!" His chuckle echoed off the cavernous ceiling. "You think because I haul luggage all day I wouldn't have any type of nest egg?"

"It's my job to ask questions. I don't mean to offend you."

"We owned some farmland out in western Pennsylvania. Me and the wife expected to retire there some day. But some big company came in and wanted to build a plant. So we sold it. They agreed to pay us fifty thousand dollars."

"That's a nice sum of money," Terri said.

He shook his head. "Let me clarify. Fifty thousand a year for twenty years."

My eyes didn't blink, and for the first time in our conversation, his lips turned up at the edges. Just as quickly, his look turned serious.

"Listen, you can think what you like, but Susan and us, we talked it out. I truly feel like she was forced to…you know. In the end, does it make much difference? Probably not, because prosecutors said they'd never be able to prove anything above statutory rape. But I looked in that man's eyes at the trial, and what I saw wasn't noble or innocent. He was out to rape my child, and I knew he'd do the same to any other young girl out there. It's just a damn shame they let him out after serving only two years. The justice system is…don't get me started."

"Can you tell us where we—"

I put a hand on Terri's arm and gave her the signal that Mr. Miller had endured enough. His chest was heaving, and he looked like he'd aged ten years during our fifteen-minute discussion.

I wrapped up the interview. "What we meant to say was that we're sorry for dredging up old memories. We appreciate your candor and your time."

Once outside of the airport, Terri said. "I realize I don't know when to stop sometimes. Thanks for jumping in."

"Sure. You're like a dog on a bone."

She giggled. "Remember, it's been a while since a guy has even held my hand. You shouldn't go there."

We both laughed this time, then my phone buzzed as we reached my car. I pulled it from my purse. A text from Erin.

School project???? Did u forget about picking me up from school????

"Crap."

I explained my predicament to Terri, and she insisted on taking Uber back to police headquarters. We agreed to talk later tonight and compare notes. I switched into mom mode and clawed my way through traffic to make my way up to Salem High School.

Sixteen

Twenty years ago

Sitting in the university president's office, the twenty-year-old young man gazed out across the stately buildings and tree-covered campus. Shades of orange, yellow, vibrant red, and even aqua blue made up the spectrum of colors as far as the eye could see. It was a sight to behold, a scene that could have been captured on the cover of an esteemed magazine or even in an art gallery. He could envision the name above the watercolor: *Shades of an American Campus.* The picturesque sight reminded him of some of the portraits he'd painted, a new passion that he'd recently taken up. Like most other new things that he tried, he'd shown a natural gift. He wasn't surprised. So many things came easy to him.

He checked his watch, remembering that the secretary had said the president was running a bit late, but that he had some very important news to share with him. He had an idea what all the fuss was about. Not only was he certain he had made the dean's list, but he thought this would be the formal announcement that he had been awarded the prestigious Rhode's Scholarship. He had worked long and hard—albeit not in the traditional manner—to achieve this goal, and he looked forward to studying at the University of Oxford. Then again, when had he ever followed the same predetermined path as everyone else? The sheep mentality at every level of the American society or academia had turned the country into a blind herd of idiots, plain and simple.

His vision drifted back to the expansive office, a virtual gallery of impressive artwork, mahogany furniture, and collectibles encased in glass. Above that was a wall filled with framed honors and degrees. The university president, who had held the office for a good ten years, was obviously quite proud of his accomplishments.

The young man could relate, although he wasn't afforded the opportunity to publicize the methods, and possibly the madness, of his brilliance. His extra-credit project that had led to this proud moment had actually infused him with an energy and vigor to succeed he had rarely experienced—at least the kind that he was willing to openly admit to the rest of the world. There were other parts of his life, of his temperament, that were manifested in ways that couldn't be labeled as normal behavior. It had taken a while, but he'd finally come to terms with the kind of person he truly was. It was all a matter of steering his energy to causes that had meaning, minimizing his extracurricular activities to when the urge couldn't be contained. And that rarely happened.

An image slowly came into focus in his mind: a sheet smeared with blood, his valuable tools piled on the side, and in the plastic container nestled in an ice chest, the precious pair of...

The office door clicked open, and his breath caught in the back of his throat. He swallowed and then exhaled, allowing him to relax. It was the president. Wearing his typical blue blazer with his gut bulging out from under the buttoned coat, the half-bald university official looked straight ahead as he attempted to rub the back of his own neck. The college senior stood up, his chest bowing out slightly, but it seemed like President Furley purposely avoided eye contact. A second later, another man walked through the door. He was younger, more athletic, and wore a long-sleeve polo shirt with the red and white university logo embroidered on the upper left side.

As the young man began to turn his sights toward President Furley, who was moving to the other side of his desk, he picked up the click of a familiar sound. Heels worn by his...*Mother*, he mouthed. And in she walked, wearing the same beige heels she wore every time she attempted to dress up.

"What?" he whispered to her. His heart dropped into his gut, his brain doused with possible theories regarding her presence. But it was as if he were being sprayed with a firehose, unable to breathe or comprehend any logical understanding as to why she'd driven two hundred miles to campus.

"Junior, not now," she murmured between her teeth. She quickly found a seat on the opposite side of the room, her knuckles white as they clutched her frayed purse.

Junior began to sit.

"You can remain standing." President Furley momentarily picked up his reading glasses and read a note on his desk. His voice seemed stressed.

Junior shuffled a few steps, then put his hands in his pockets. He couldn't help but let his thoughts run rampant, and his core temperature began to skyrocket.

"As a four-year attendee of this university, you have accomplished a great deal. In fact, up until today, I would have grouped you with just a handful of students who had truly made a positive mark on this university."

President Furley glared at the wall where all of his degrees hung, then he turned his gaze to the young man, who could feel the weight of the world slowly pressing against his chest. He attempted to breathe, but it only made the weight that much more oppressive. For a moment, it seemed like he might hyperventilate, but after a few focused breaths, the feeling subsided.

"Young man, do I have your attention?"

Of all the times for his mind to wander, Junior was astonished that he'd let the same images from earlier reappear. And for some reason, he fixated on the sheet, as if the streaks of blood were born from some type of creative stroke of the paintbrush. That was it. He'd seen the correlation between his painting and his other passion, as uncontrollable as it was.

"Young man. Are you even listening? This is your future we are talking about."

"Yes. I am listening, President Furley." He was surprised by how calm and confident his voice sounded. As usual, no one heard the whispers of self-doubt and self-loathing, his innermost demons that had steadily grown from making cameo appearances to now becoming a more regular voice, one that enjoyed sucking him into his other world. With clenched teeth, he did his best to remain still. While it felt like a steel rod had been inserted into his neck, his eyes were pulled toward his mother. She met his gaze, her lips quivering.

An audible sigh from the headmaster himself. "It has come to my attention that you have broken our code of ethics."

"Sir, I can explain. I'm sure it's not nearly as bad as it might appear."

President Furley glanced over at the other man, who still had not been introduced. He had a poker face, with no emotional response. He was clean shaven and had a definitive part in his hair. With no lines on his face, he looked to be around thirty-five or so. He gave a single nod toward the president. Junior couldn't determine what the signal actually meant.

The president replied with a similar bow of the head, and then held up a hand as if he were addressing a congregation, not one young man. "I'm sure you can offer us a bevy of explanations and stories, all of which would probably contain as much fiction as a work by Ernest Hemingway."

He cleared his throat and then put on his metal-rimmed glasses. Holding up a single piece of paper, he began to speak. "We have evidence of you breaking into the offices of four of your teachers. Once we followed the trail to see the name of the teachers who had supposedly written a letter of recognition in support of your application for a Rhode's Scholarship, we were then able to determine that you have committed the act of forgery on a scale of which we have never seen at this university."

He could feel the glare of his mother, so he decided not to shame himself further. As he remained focused on President Furley, the same, quiet whispers returned, toying with his thoughts.

Junior swallowed, but chose not to speak up.

"In addition, we have evidence that you have hacked into the computer system at this university to alter your grades, dating all the way back to your first semester on campus."

Another pause and all three of them stared at the college senior. As the searing internal heat made his head feel like it had been put into a microwave, he mentally repeated the phrase "college senior." And then another, "college graduate," and this one: "soon-to-be Rhode's scholar." That was how he had identified himself. But he knew now the use of those terms was like trying to hold sand in his hands.

"On top of that, we have worked with our colleagues across the pond and feel strongly that you have also hacked into the computer system at the University of Oxford to include your name in the prestigious list of winners this year." He removed his glasses. "I could go on further, including breaking and entering, and then there is a list of other things where we have our suspicions."

"Dear God, what now?" his mother whimpered behind a bed of tears.

"Certain objects have gone missing from the Biology Department. Once we picked up your son's fingerprints from the four teachers' offices, our head of security, Mr. Steele..." President Furley extended a hand to the silent man standing with his hands clasped behind his back. "...was able to pick up a partial print from two doors in the section where the dead animals are kept—the ones used for experimentation. We can't be certain, but we have our suspicions." The president turned his gaze back to the man. "I don't suppose you want to clear your conscience and tell us the entire *true* story?"

The young man's jaw twitched. "I have nothing to say, sir."

"Okay, well. It goes without saying that you are—"

"Sir."

Junior turned to see his mother raising a hand that held a tattered tissue.

"I can understand how troubled you might feel, in addition to feeling betrayed," the president said to her. "We all do. This, frankly, is one of the saddest days in our university's history. But we must move forward. And to do that, justice must be served."

She waved her hand. "Might I have a word with you...privately?"

President Furley glanced at his desk and moved a folder to the other side, then he lifted his eyes. "No one has ever accused me of being a dictator. I wouldn't want to gain that reputation, even in these unfortunate circumstances." He looked to Mr.

Steele. "Please accompany...*him* out into the waiting area. This shouldn't take long."

The wait was more like thirty minutes. Junior paced some, looked out a window, even skimmed through a recent edition of the school's alumni magazine. All it did was remind him of everything he would never be able to accomplish. More than that, he realized how much he had anticipated the idea of sharing his brilliant feats with his peers. He recalled thinking that the school might even raise funds to name a new library after him. That was how much impact he felt he could have on the world. His mom had told him as much ever since he remembered going to school.

And it was all gone. He'd been outed...just as he was about to begin the final leg of his journey, as fake as it was.

Two female students walked into the area and spoke to President Furley's secretary. One glanced at Junior out of the corner of her eye. The hem of her skirt had a nice long slit, the buttons on her cardigan sweater bulging from the size of her breasts. She gave him the once-over, then ran her tongue along her lips. He was intrigued, but repulsed at the same time. It was a familiar feeling. Deep within his body, his psyche possibly, he could feel an urge begin to take root—even at this defining juncture of his life, on the precipice of watching it all implode into vapor.

The urge would never go away, not until he did something about it.

The door to the office opened, and his mother walked out with President Furley right on her heels. She gave Junior a slight wink, then turned around and gave the school president a firm handshake.

"We'll take care of all the details. I think this is best for everyone involved," he said.

"I appreciate your willingness to meet me halfway." His

mother flipped on her ancient heels and headed for the exit. "Junior, let's go home."

He glanced at President Furley on his way out. He shook his head with his lips pressed together, and then he caught up to his mother.

"What happened?"

"I wrote President Furley a check. A contribution to the university."

"What? Why?"

"Because." She stopped in the hallway and put a hand on her son's broad shoulder, a hesitation in her voice. "You're a very smart young man. But you still have lessons to learn."

Later that night, Junior took one of his trophies he had confiscated from the Biology Department, laid a white sheet under his temporary workstation behind the garage, and used his tools with remarkable precision. When it was all over, he had one prevalent thought.

Playing with animals no longer fulfilled his desires. It was time to up his game. It was the only way.

Seventeen

Erin barely said a word on our drive to the Boston Museum of Fine Arts. She either stared blankly out the window or was pounding away on her phone, no doubt sharing her thoughts with her friends. I got it. She was pissed, thinking I had forgotten about her and her art history project.

It was only temporary amnesia, but it felt like I'd committed a felony.

"Okay, let's get started," I said with a good amount of energy.

Without saying a word, she walked timidly into the first gallery, her eyes wide with... What was it exactly? Fear, excitement?

"What is it, sweetie?" I asked as I sidled up next to a golden statue of a notable figure from the Chinese Song Dynasty.

She threw up her hands and then slapped them against her jeans. "I have no frickin' clue what I'm doing, what I should focus on. It's overwhelming."

I gently put an arm over her shoulder and led her around a throng of onlookers marveling at the ancient artifacts. "Does any of this interest you?" I asked.

"Not really, Mom. I guess it's cool that someone was able to recover this stuff and preserve it, but I don't really relate to any of it."

Nearing the end of a small wing, we found ourselves right in front of another sculpture, but this one stood out. It appeared to be a woman with long hair and two large hoops piercing her nipples. We slowly turned our heads toward each other, blank stares on both of our faces. The stare-down lasted about five seconds before Erin burst out laughing, and I snorted out a guffaw a moment later. Erin laughed so hard she started crying. And then so did I.

"I...I think I might have just peed my pants," I said, resting a hand on her shoulder.

"Oh, Mom." She was overcome with another round of laughter before she could utter a word, her neck and chest bright red from the exertion.

"Just wait until you have kids, Erin," I said, finally able to breathe without losing it. "I think I have a better idea of why you don't really relate to any of this." I pointed at the sculpture again. "You don't have any plans to get nipple rings, do you?"

"Mom, you just said nipple in front of me."

"You're older...we can joke around, right?"

"Sure, Mom, it's just strange to hear you saying...nipple." We both cracked up like a couple of little kids.

We started walking back to the center of the first floor, gazing at different works of art, when I felt Erin hook her arm inside mine. She smiled, resting her head against my shoulder. She was getting much taller now, maybe just a couple of inches shorter than my five-six frame. And I could feel the muscles in her arm and hand. She'd begun to excel in tennis, although she didn't like to talk about her tennis life, not to me anyway.

Erin looked at me again and batted her eyelashes. They were like mine, thin and not very long. She was a cute tomboy, sweet and innocent, and that was how I hoped she would stay until she was about thirty years old.

"Mom," she said, her cheeks glowing from grinning so hard.

I'd almost forgotten I was walking with teen Erin, not my little girl when she would just appreciate our little moment of mother-daughter time.

"I know that look. What do you want?"

"Well, I'm not really asking for anything. It's more about what I'd like to do…with your permission, of course."

She batted her eyelashes again and stretched her grin even wider.

I knew her question had nothing to do with boys or dating. Or did it? Was she about to ask if she could start dating some gangly, snot-nosed kid? Wait…what was I thinking? She was all about *Teen Wolf* and Zac Efron this and Zac Efron that. Hmm. She might have drawn the eye of the starting quarterback of the football team, and she wanted to warm me up to the idea before Mr. Charisma showed up at the house to take her out on some innocent date.

Innocent, my ass.

"Yes, Erin?" I could feel my body temperature rising with each beat of my pulse.

"I was thinking that I'd like to get my ears pierced."

"That's all?" I said casually, the tension already dropping.

"Mostly." She sucked in her lower lip and bit it.

We were now unhooked, and she was starting to take in more of the artwork around us. Apparently, we had waltzed into another section of the museum—a lot of paintings with vibrant colors.

"Mostly. That's all you're going to say?"

She turned around and flipped back her long, dark hair so I could see her ear. It was cute, just like her. "Well, I was thinking that I'd like to get multiple piercings, maybe three on this ear and four on the other?"

"You're not trying to be twenty-one again, are you?"

She knew I was referring to our summer vacation, when she just happened to make friends with some college kids on the beach.

"Mom, are you really going to bring that up? I don't want to fight. Besides, you know I was really only interested in learning more about Corey's marine biology major. Well, *mostly* anyway." She winked at me.

"You're right."

She stopped and put a hand on my arm. "Wait, did you just say I'm right?"

"Very funny. I know I'm not perfect, Erin. There isn't a blueprint on how to master parenting. But just tell me you'll keep the piercings contained to your ear."

"Totally, Mom. I just want to be able to express myself."

I nodded and smiled.

"You know, kind of like this cool painting behind me here." She swung around just as a man passed by, sipping from a bottle of water. Erin knocked the plastic bottle right into his face, spilling liquid all over his blue shirt.

"Oh my God, I am so sorry," she said with both hands at her head.

The man froze for a moment, apparently stunned by the lightning-quick jab from Erin, who reached down and picked up the bottle of water and handed it to him.

"Thank you." He slowly turned around, and I held up a finger.

"I know you."

A warm smile came over his face. "I starred in *Aquaman*."

Erin had a confused look.

"I'm just joking," he said, tugging at his soaked shirt. "At Dr.

Dunn's office, of course. Alex, right?" He leaned closer. "The FBI agent."

I nodded. "Small world," I said, once again admiring the sparkle of his dark eyes and his streaks of silver hair.

"This is kind of my home away from home."

"You work here?"

"They pay me a small stipend, but I really do it because I love being surrounded by such amazing beauty."

Erin's mouth opened as she looked at me.

"You know I'm talking about this incredible collection of artwork." He began to chuckle, then pulled out a handkerchief and blotted his shirt.

"Of course."

"Not that you and your daughter aren't...well, I'm just digging myself a hole, aren't I?" He paused and blotted his shirt again. "Don't answer that," he said with a slight wink and an unassuming smile. "So, are you guys just having a mother-daughter day out at the MFA?"

"MF...what?" Erin giggled.

He smirked. "Good one."

"Oh, this is Erin. Say hello to... I'm sorry, I didn't catch your name in the middle of the fight against Spike."

"He's the man who helped kick the gun away?" Erin asked.

"I tried telling you I'm a super hero. Today Aquaman, tomorrow the Incredible Hulk." He winked again and released a slight chuckle. He held out his hand until I shook it. "I'm Colin Brewer."

"Colin." I gave Erin the signal to also shake his hand. "We're actually here for Erin to get some information on a school project."

"Oh really? What's the topic?"

"I need to figure out something that interests me and write a paper on it and tell the teacher why," she said.

"Yes, so far, we're striking out though. She's finding it a bit difficult to relate to any of the various periods of art."

"I don't know, I kind of like this stuff," she said, swinging her finger to the art on the walls near us.

"Interesting," Colin said. "Tell you what, if you'll give me a minute to go grab a towel and dry off a bit, then I'll be happy to give you a brief tour of our Impressionism section, which actually starts right here in this very room."

"Impressionism," Erin repeated. "That could be really cool."

"You sure you have time?" I asked.

He splayed his arms. "It's what I love to do. Back in a second."

Erin and I walked around the room. Every few paintings, she would pause, and her eyes seemed to study all the different colors and brushstrokes. Colin came up with a towel in hand and saw the same thing I did: Erin was into it.

She turned around and faced Colin. "Can I ask you a question?"

"Sure. That's what I'm here for."

"Why are the paintings so…you know, not very detailed, just splotches of color?"

"Great question, Erin. That's the very definition of an Impressionist painting. In France during the late 1800s, this type of painting was considered to be nothing more than sketches by most painters and critics, something that would essentially serve as an outline, to preserve an idea so they could later come back and paint a more detailed, refined version."

Erin nodded. "So how did it become this big deal if everyone thought it sucked?"

"Let's walk and talk a bit," Colin said, clasping his hands as he strolled through the colorful gallery. "Paris was one of the centers of the artistic world in those days, and there was really just one official exhibition for artists to sell their works. It was called the Salon. But the qualification process to show your work at the Salon was arbitrary."

Erin raised part of her upper lip.

"He means random, or maybe subjective."

"Indeed, Alex. Most of these artists had been rejected by the Salon over the years, and they just didn't feel like they were getting a fair shake. So the artists pooled their money together, rented a studio, and set a date for their first collective exhibition. They called themselves the Anonymous Society of Painters, Sculptors, and Printmakers."

Erin put her hands in her skin-tight jeans. "Kind of reminds me of the movie, *Dead Poet's Society*."

"I can see that," Colin said.

"Since you have a whole gallery filled with this work, I guess it kind of caught on."

"Yes and no. Initially, they had to endure a tremendous amount of criticism."

"Who are some of the most recognized Impressionist artists?"

"Have you heard of the names Monet, Renoir, Degas?"

She smiled. "Yes. That's kind of cool."

"It's my favorite form of art, mainly because of how the artists focused on a particular moment in a scene. They typically painted outdoors to capture the appearance of light on the various forms in the scene, maybe how it shimmered against a body of water, or how clouds moved through the air, or maybe viewing a moving train through a burst of rain."

Erin's eyes gravitated back to the painting in front of her, a flowing river with the soft sun setting behind it, just before the calm water spilled into a churning ocean. She moved farther down the line of paintings, now stopping at each one.

"I think you did the unimaginable," I said to Colin with a smile on my face.

"And what is that?"

"You've made Erin interested in something from school. She's not fond of the typical subjects: math, science, English. I don't recall her being this inquisitive about a school topic since elementary school."

"I'm glad I could help ignite that fire. Growing up, I was always hungry for information, to learn everything I could. But I've learned that not everyone had the same upbringing or feels the same way, even if they had. The younger generation has so many distractions it's a wonder they learn anything of substance."

"Do you not have kids?" I asked with one eye on Erin.

"Kids...me? No. Just haven't found that one special person to share my life with."

I had noticed he wasn't wearing a ring, but that didn't mean much. A lot of guys chose not to wear their wedding bands, for one reason or another. But I was more shocked that he wasn't married or somehow attached to a woman. With his casual, approachable demeanor and focus on education, he didn't have that ladies'-man persona.

I watched a young man in baggy jeans stroll by and then stop a few feet away. It didn't take long for his eyes to give Erin the once-over. I took a step in that direction, about ready to pounce on the guy, but something stopped me. I waited. He made his move and said something to her. They began to talk for a moment, and then she nodded toward me. He quickly exited the opposite direction.

"Do you have to fend off the boys with your FBI-issued sidearm?" Colin said, chuckling.

"It really came out of nowhere. She was just a regular, little girl, and then over the summer she started to develop. And now she gets ogled everywhere we go. I'm not sure I can handle this transition. Not on top of everything else I've got going on."

"Stress at work?"

"Eh. I shouldn't complain. Everyone has their issues. But I've got two great kids. Yep, a good life, that's for certain."

"You're not married?"

"No," I said bluntly, not wanting to get into my personal life.

He pulled out his phone and tapped through a few screens, then he glanced at me again. "Hope I didn't offend you. I guess I feel like I know you a little bit after our discussion today and our near-death experience at the doctor's office."

I hadn't put a lot of thought into how the incident with Spike at Dr. Dunn's office would impact a normal citizen, someone who had probably never witnessed such rage and aggression.

"It takes a lot more than that to offend me. I have to say the incident at Dr. Dunn's office was as bizarre as it was disturbing. I might be in the FBI, but I don't live for those times. And I'm sure it wasn't easy for you to process."

"I appreciate your concern." He touched my elbow, his eyes warm with gratitude. "Well, there is one way of looking at it. I didn't have to go very far to talk through any issues."

"Then again, it was our doctor who pulled the trigger on the shotgun."

Colin nodded while offering an affable smirk. "Good point. And I have to say the gun blast nearly made me throw up my lunch. Certainly didn't expect that."

We both chuckled for a quick moment. "I just hope that Ashling understands she's worth more than being with a guy who treats her like shit. No offense."

He winked again. "Sounds like another case for Dr. Dunn. I

think we're going to keep him in business for quite a while."

Part of me wanted to ask about his issues, why he felt like he needed to see a shrink. From my limited perspective, the greatest stress he had to deal with was a spastic teenager spilling water all over his clothes. But I knew all of us had something buried deep inside.

I felt a buzz from inside my purse, and I knew I'd received a text. Erin happened to look my way and smile as she shuffled to a painting that featured a family having a picnic in a field of wild flowers. With white puffy clouds dotting the sky and a giant tree in the foreground, the sunlight cast a spindly set of shadows.

I let my eyes wander a bit, taking in more of the paintings, then the second buzz came.

"Uggh," I said, digging through my purse for my phone.

"Uncle Sam needs you?" Colin asked.

I finally felt the metal edging of my cell phone. I pulled it from my purse and saw a text from Nick.

Terri said you want to meet tonight. Good timing. Tripuka met with lawyer late today.

"Crap," I said, my intensity already on the increase.

"Something wrong?"

I waved at Erin.

"Just, uh...Uncle Sam calling, like you said."

Erin walked over, and I told her we needed to leave.

"I'm not sure I have everything I need, but I guess I can check online," she said.

"Tell you what," Colin said, patting his pockets until he pulled out a business card from his back pocket. "If you have any questions or want to learn more, feel free to call me, email me, or you can just meet me here at the MFA."

Erin took the card. "You're a bullfighter?" she asked with a slight giggle.

"Ha! I tried to make my business cards lighthearted, showing all the various things I've experienced or had a passion for."

I looked over her shoulder. Under *Bullfighter*, I read *Curator, Chef, Science Nerd,* and then *Painter.*

"So you paint as well?" I asked.

"It's another passion. What is life without a passion or two?"

After Erin thanked him for his help, we walked out. I glanced over my shoulder to take another look at the Curator, Chef, and Science Nerd. He was speaking to a couple, pointing to a painting on the wall. It was obvious he loved what he did, and it truly served the interest of the public. Besides being a good-looking man who probably was about my age, he was calm and had lived a life full of experiences. He intrigued me.

I couldn't help but wonder if my infatuation with Brad was more of a surface level relationship. Perhaps I was meant to be with a more mature person, like Colin, for instance. As Erin and I got in the car and headed home, I temporarily pushed the uncertainty of my feelings out of my mind. We had to determine if a serial killer was sitting in the Somerville jail. And now that he'd finally brought in a lawyer, we probably only had a few hours left until he would walk the streets again.

Eighteen

I picked up a handful of nuts and started eating.

"Hey, hey!" Nick said into my earbuds.

"Sorry, guys. I forgot to click mute when I started eating again."

We had just pulled everyone into a conference call and were waiting on Gretchen to join the line. I was sitting under the halo light at the kitchen bar, the kids in bed and Ezzy likely curled up with a book and Pumpkin, our oversized cat, nestled at her feet. I'd spent the evening providing feedback to Erin on the outline of her paper on Impressionism—she'd realized there were a few gaps that needed to be filled—and attempting to reach everyone on the team to get updates on any new information about the two murder cases.

I shoveled in another mouthful of nuts, trying to squelch some nervous tension, and got started with Terri and Nick.

"While we're waiting on Gretchen, do either of you—" I choked on an uneaten cashew. "Sorry." I sounded like a chain smoker. I gulped down some water.

"Okay. Take two," I said, clearing my throat. "Do we have any feedback from Tripuka's attorney?"

"Loud and clear," Terri said. "He told my lieutenant that we either need to charge him with a crime and start the booking process or release him. He gave us until noon tomorrow."

"It's what I was afraid of," I said, reaching for the water again.

"It gets worse," Terri said.

"What could be worse?" Nick asked.

"The attorney's name is Winston Wise, and he has a very litigious trigger finger."

"Meaning?"

"Does the name Gloria Gardner mean anything to you? Wise worked at her firm a few years ago. He seeks out clients whose rights might have been violated, and then he threatens to sue the city, the county, and any other agency in his crosshairs to not only get their release but to ensure they are never charged with a crime. In a few instances, it's gone all the way to a jury. He won one client eight million and another client five point five."

"I hate it when suspects who we know are guilty get smart. It makes our job twice as tough," Nick said.

"But do we really know it? We only know that he tried to run me over, and then there's his probation violation. Not sure what exact charge your DA will file, Terri, but I'm guessing they don't want to overreach. So, Winston Wise might—"

"You mean Wise Ass," Nick chimed in.

"I like it. Wise Ass could probably get Tripuka pushed through the booking process and get him out on bail before the end of the day tomorrow."

"Might not take that long. He'll scare the crap out of anyone he interacts with."

I did a search on Wise Ass and checked out his mug shot. For him, it should have been called a smug shot. His wise-ass attitude was etched on his face, arched eyebrow and all.

We were screwed unless we could find something connecting

Tripuka to Emma or to our cold case. "Terri, did you get ballistics back yet on the bullet that killed Emma?"

"Just came in. It was a .38."

"Okay, we've got something. What's the hold-up on the search warrant, Nick?"

"I tried reaching out to Meyers and Long Duck Dong…"

Terri snickered.

"And they pretty much blew me off. I guess they don't like the Feds offering any help. I get it. But they didn't fill out the forms correctly, and it got sent back. You hear anything more, Terri?"

"Hell no. They only told me that the judge was tied up until tonight." I heard a huff of air.

"Okay, let us know the second you have it. Hoping we can find something…a hair, some blood, a chipped nail…"

"I'll take the murder weapon," Nick said.

"I don't want to get greedy, but if we're asking for favors, that would be at the top of the list," I said. "Any headway on figuring out Tripuka's whereabouts ten years ago, at the time our Lopez was murdered?"

"Sketchy right now. He spent some time in Chicago that year. He actually attended Illinois State for a period of time, but didn't get a degree. Then he worked at Chicago University. Not sure of his job there, and we don't know the exact date he returned to Boston."

"Any luck finding any of his prison colleagues?"

"Working on it. Getting callbacks from prison officials to the FBI is difficult."

A sneeze erupted into the earbud, and I had to yank it out for a second.

"I think Mount Gretchen just joined us and she blew off her nose," Nick joked. "Are you okay?"

"I'm...I'm..." she huffed. A moment later, she released another powerful sneeze.

"Bless you," I said.

"Thanks."

"Have you thought about going to the doctor?"

"No time. I'm actually feeling a little better since I've been working from home this evening."

Her nasal passages sounded completely stuffed, but if she felt better, then more power to her.

"I've got my five cats sitting all around me. They're the best medicine any girl could have."

"Not sure about that," Terri said. "Wouldn't you rather have a hunk of a gentleman waiting on you, taking care of all your needs?" She actually giggled, but she didn't know Gretchen's history with men, including my man, Brad. I had to get us back on the rails.

"Gretchen, we're all exchanging notes on what we learned today."

"I know. I was on mute while I was blowing my nose. Took me about twenty tissues. But enough about me. Just before the call started, Nick, I got a call back from Emma's sister."

"And?"

"She said that Emma had confided in her that she was so strung out she'd started hooking to pay for her drugs. She was in tears when she told me this. Really sad."

Two dots just connected. "Guys, this is big. We knew Gloria Lopez had been a prostitute ten years back. And now confirmation that Emma has been in the same profession. That's another piece of evidence that shows this could be the same perp."

"I'm assuming you mean Tripuka," Nick said.

"That's my guess at this point. But we need someone to say

he knew both Gloria Lopez and Emma. The question is: where do we take it from here?"

"To Mattapan, that's where," Gretchen said. "Emma had told her sister there were a couple of rundown motels off Woodrow Avenue where most of the business took place. One where most of the hooking went down, and the other where this one guy sold drugs, mainly ice and coke. He also pretty much served as their pimp. The king of the hill, she called him."

I could hear a door slam and keys jingle. "Alex, I'm on my way to pick you up, if you're game," Terri said.

"If you hadn't offered, I would have been offended. Gretchen, do we have a name for this king of the hill?"

"The sister heard Emma use the name Crack Daddy."

The hunt for a man named Crack Daddy was on.

Nineteen

I counted eight streetlights that were out, and we'd only made it about a quarter mile down Woodrow Avenue. Through a light mist off in the distance, I could see two pairs of brake lights. Not a lot of people or movement of any kind. This area of Mattapan seemed deserted and eerily quiet. The windshield wipers scraped across the glass, interrupting the silence.

"Check it out." Terri nodded to her side of the street. A woman wearing purple stretch pants and four-inch heels came out of a shadow, sauntering toward the edge of the sidewalk. As we moved closer, I could see her swaying, and I wondered if she might topple over. She was yelling something at us. Terri punched the window down.

"Hey there." The woman waved, then shook her torso to create an avalanche of boobs, an enticement that she had probably found to work with most of her potential customers.

Terri stopped the car.

"Don't say anything, just wait for her to approach our car," I said.

The woman took a quick glance up and down the street, then hopped off the curb and stepped toward our car. Her heel-clipping echoed off the surrounded buildings.

"Hey, honey," the woman said as she approached. Up close, she looked like a clown who had applied her makeup in the dark. Purples and blues and a loud orange-red all shouted that she either had no clue what she was doing or she didn't care...or perhaps that was one of her marketing techniques. She leaned down and noticed me in the passenger seat.

"Whoa, I charge extra for a three-way. You got the cash?" She put her hands on the side of the car, peering inside. Then something clicked, and she jumped away, her eyes suddenly on high alert.

"What the fuck? You guys are cops. This is entrapment, that's what this is." She started backing away while wagging a finger that appeared crooked.

Terri held up her hand. "Hold on, we're not here to bust you. Just want to ask a quick question."

The woman kept backing away and gave us a little wave. "Say bye-bye. Candy is going to continue her evening walk now." She spoke to us like we were little kids, even splitting her red lips for a moment to grin.

I yelled from across the seat. "We'll pay you if you answer our question."

Candy's backpedal slowed to a stop. She lowered her chin, and a serious look came over her. It was obvious she was desperate for money. If Emma's sister had it right, this woman could very well be an addict, only working the streets to pay for her next fix.

"Come back over here and talk to us, and we'll pay you." I picked up my purse so she could see it. I dug for my wallet. My fingers couldn't find it, and I quickly became frustrated. I looked down for a moment, but all I saw was a cavern of junk. "Dammit, where's my wallet?" I said under my breath. Then I remembered Erin earlier asking for her allowance. She might have left my wallet out on the counter. "Terri, you have any cash?" While she dug through her purse, I called back out to Candy, "Hold on. We're getting the cash, just to prove it to you."

A moment later, Terri said, "Found it." She slid a number of bills between her fingers and held up her hand so Candy could see it.

Candy was like a dog who'd just seen hamburger meat. Her eyes fixated on Terri's hand, and after a brief pause, her heels clopped closer to the car, stopping an arm's distance away. "What am I thinking? I can't be seen with no cops."

"Then get in the car," Terri said. "Quick, before anyone notices."

Candy shuffled her feet, her face contorted. "Okay, dammit." She jumped in the backseat and shut the door. "Drive," she said.

I faced forward in my seat and allowed my fingers to brush the grip of my Glock. We hadn't searched her, so who knew if she had a weapon on her, or even a dirty needle? I noticed Terri look in her rearview mirror.

"It's okay." Terri gently pushed the gas pedal, and we started moving. Within a few seconds, we came up to a corner next to an alley and noticed three more women dressed in similar garb as Candy and looking just as desperate.

"Don't slow down," Candy said, hunkering lower in her seat. "Keep moving, or they'll see me and think I'm ratting out the whole operation."

Terri kept the Crown Vic moving, and after another two blocks, she turned left and pulled to a stop.

"Are we safe here?" Terri asked.

Candy rose up in her seat and quickly peered out the back window. "Should be." She turned back around and stuck out her hand. "Cash."

Terri handed me the wad of money, but I held it back. "Not

until you answer a few questions."

"You said one question."

"Okay, how about we give you a bill for every answer you give us?"

Candy ceased movement for a moment, apparently thinking over the new terms. This was a better deal. More questions now meant more bills. But we hadn't established the denomination of the currency.

"How much you going to give me each time? Don't be throwing those one-dollar bills my way. I ain't no cheap stripper. Candy don't play that shit."

I thumbed through the cash. A little bit of variety, but not much quantity. "How about we start with a ten, and then we'll work our way up."

She licked her lips, her eyes focused on the ten-dollar bill in my hand. "Fire away, Five-O."

"Do you know a girl who worked the streets in this area named Emma?"

She glanced out the window. I could see red veins splintering the white background of her beady brown eyes. She looked like she was hungover, hadn't slept in a while.

"Candy, did you know Emma?"

She rubbed her nose, then cleared her throat. "She called herself Pandora. She jokingly said that if someone really opened her box, everyone would be shocked with what came out. Shock and awe, that was what she said. Dare to open Pandora's box, and she'll go shock and awe on yo ass."

"Candy, are you aware that she died? Someone killed her."

She brought a hand to her face. Her nails were chipped pink. I guessed they hadn't been painted in weeks. She gasped a couple of times, and her eyes became moist. "I didn't know for sure. There was a rumor. But around here, we always assume the worst, because then you got nowhere to go but up. It helps us deal with all the shit in our lives."

Terri pulled a tissue from her purse and handed it to the broken woman in the backseat.

"How did she go?" Candy asked, her voice cracking.

"Can't get into all the details about everything that she endured, but she was shot in the head."

"Oh God." Candy rocked forward and groaned. She laid her forehead against the back of the front seat and sobbed, then dug what little nails she had into the cloth seat.

"Candy…"

Another sob, this one laced with garbled words.

"Candy, you can help us catch the person who did this."

She slowly lifted her head and sat back. Smeared makeup and tears coated her face. Terri quickly pulled out three more tissues and gave them to her.

"I'm a fucking mess," she said. "And I'm not talking about my face." She tried to laugh, but more tears squirted out.

As she wiped under her eyes and across her cheeks, the real Candy became visible. She was younger than I'd thought, although her skin had red splotches, as if she were allergic to the face paint.

She released a breath, dropping her arms into her lap. "I hate to even admit it, but I need that money you promised me."

I handed her the ten-dollar bill, and she stuffed it into her undersized sports bra.

"Next question," she said in monotone, her eyes blankly staring out the window.

Terri and I traded a quick glance. We both knew Candy was back in survival mode.

"Candy, you can help us catch the person who did this."

She jerked her head around. "What are you talking about?

I'm just a working girl, doing my thing, making my money, paying my bills. Taking care of numero uno, that's what I'm worrying about."

Terri yanked out her phone, flipped her thumb across the screen, then stuck the phone in front of Candy's face.

"You see that?"

Candy strained her neck to look ninety degrees to her left, refusing to glance at the phone.

"Candy, it's time to face reality and see what this life will do to you. Look at the picture."

Candy shook her head as more tears trailed down her face. "No. No…I can't. You can't make me."

I grabbed the package of tissues from Terri and handed a couple more back to Candy.

"We know this isn't easy. You didn't expect to deal with this tonight, but you knew it was a possibility, right?"

She sighed. "We hadn't seen her in a couple days, and then one girl said she heard she'd been capped."

Another gasp and she scrunched the tissue against her face. "Usually in the past, whenever she was gone, we knew that she'd gotten back with her boyfriend, the one who beat the shit out of her. And then, without warning, she'd show up, all strung out and needing to turn a few tricks to pay for her drugs. Anything for Pandora to take the edge off."

Terri started to bring her hand back to the front seat, but Candy quickly grabbed her wrist and focused on the picture of Emma's corpse. I could see the muscles in her jaw clamp down.

"I had to see her one last time. It's tough, but in some ways she looks more at peace than any time I can remember."

I handed her another ten-dollar bill, just so she wouldn't ask. She stored the bill inside her bra again.

Terri thumbed through more pictures, then found the one of

Tripuka.

"Have you seen this man trolling around the neighborhood, possibly one of Emma's customers?"

Candy blew her nose, then tossed the tissue on the floor. She leaned closer and studied the picture, her eyes blinking repeatedly, as if someone were shining a light in her pupils.

"Hmm. I can't say yes, but I can't say no either."

I held up another bill, this one a twenty. She snatched it from my hand.

"I wasn't really asking for more money, but if you're offering, I'm not going to turn it down."

I just nodded. "So does he look familiar? We only want to know if it's true."

She drew her lips into a straight line. "I've seen so many guys running around here, they all blend together. Nothing about this guy in your picture stands out, so I guess it's a no."

"You guess?" Terri asked, irritation in her tone.

"I don't have a photogenic mind."

Terri and I avoided the obvious correction.

"And I don't ask for IDs or get fingerprints before I do my thing."

"Okay."

"But if you got a hard copy of that photo, then I'll show it to a few people. If something comes up, I'll let you know."

Terri pulled out a copy of Tripuka's mug shot, then wrote her number on the back. "Here you go."

Candy took one more look, then stuffed it in with the cash. "I need to clean myself up before I get back out there. Do either of you have some lipstick I can borrow?" She began to fan her face.

I continued our interview. "I might have something, but I first need you to tell me everything you know about a guy who goes by the name Crack Daddy."

"Who gave you that name?"

"Emma's sister."

"Look, bringing up his name, that's nowhere you need to go." She slid closer to the door.

"Candy, hold on. This guy might know who killed Emma. He's your pimp, right?"

She rubbed her nose and looked down. "I guess. He does a lot for us." Another tear escaped her eyes, and she used a thumb to snuff it out. "And he's done a lot *to* us."

"How?"

"Do we really need to get into this now? I'm a fucking mess as it is, and I just need to get back to work and pray like hell that no one has seen me."

"What if they have?"

"What if they have?" She cocked her head. "Then you-know-who could come crack my head open. Do you want that on your conscience?"

I felt a tick in the back of my mind, and my neck grew stiff. "Candy, do you think that this Crack Daddy fella had anything to do with Emma's death?"

"Oh shit, you going there? You really going there?"

"Only if it's real, Candy. Tell me what you know, or at least what you're thinking. It will only stay between the three of us."

She smacked her thighs with both hands. "Look, you two got nothing on the line here."

"We're paying you, aren't we?" Terri said.

"Pssh. What's a few bucks to you? You'll just drive your ass out of here and go to your safe homes in your safe neighborhoods, not a care in the world."

"I get it, Candy...your life sucks," Terri said, now up on her knees. "But we want to help you. We can take you right now to a home for battered women. As long as you promise to keep clean, they'll let you stay there. They will protect you, feed you, and help you find a real job."

"And what about my babies?"

"You have kids?"

"Two. Ages ten and thirteen. Both girls. Adorable as hell."

I put a hand on the seat. "Are they with someone tonight?"

"At my sister's. Why?"

"Nothing."

She shook her head. "You think you're better than me, don't you?"

"Didn't say that. We only want to help you kick whatever drug habit you've got."

"Screw that shit. That'll never happen. Thanks for the cheap date, but I gotta get back to work." She pulled the metal door handle, and it clicked.

"Hold on," I said. "Crack Daddy. We need more information, even if you're not going to take the opportunity to get yourself fixed."

"Look, I don't know if he had anything to do with Emma's death. He's all bark and very little bite. I know he's beaten up a few girls, even threatened one with a gun right in front of me. But he knows if he crossed that line, then he'd lose his moneymakers. Us."

I nodded. "Good to know. Where can we find him? We need to ask him a few questions."

She looked through the back window. Apparently satisfied there was no one watching, she turned back around and extended her hand, palm up, wiggling her fingers. "More questions means more money, right?"

I found another twenty in the thinning stack and gave it to her.

"He's set up at the Paul Revere Motel down the street, the

one with the blinking orange sign."

"You know what room?"

"The whole west wing on the second floor. His boys have torn down a few walls and made it into his man cave. He does everything there. Runs his drug business, interviews girls, takes them on a 'test run,' as he calls it. Even lives there, when he's not driving around in a Seville." She pushed open the door, then leaned back in. "You got any makeup to spare?"

I moved a few things around in my purse, found a lipstick, and handed it to her. She shoved it in her pocket, then we looked at Terri.

"What? I don't really carry any makeup."

I smirked. "Not surprising, I guess."

"Later, Five-O." Candy slipped out of the car and shut the door.

I motioned for Terri to roll her window back down, then I leaned over and hollered, "Call that number, Candy, if you want us to help you. Don't worry about what other people think."

She waved a hand in our direction, then glanced up and down the street, appearing to ponder her next move.

"Candy, can you at least show that picture around?"

"I'll do it." Then she started jogging precariously in four-inch heels back to the main road, waving and yelling at a passing car.

Twenty

With my back pressed against a brick wall that sagged slightly and Terri to my left, I hunched down and peered into the motel office. One man stood behind the counter. He wore a sun visor, and I could see his shiny, balding head as he leaned on the counter, flipping through a magazine.

The motel was L-shaped, with the office protruding off the front section closest to the street. I nodded at Terri, and she shuffled to the rear of the small office building and looked through a covered walkway back into the teeth of the motel. On our first pass driving by, we'd seen a handful of cars, a few people going in and out of rooms, mostly in the west corner. The occupants didn't look like they were tourists. We knew we couldn't just walk up and ask for Crack Daddy's room, certainly not without some type of warning reaching our suspect before we could reach him. We needed to mitigate that risk.

"We're good," Terri whispered as she pulled up just behind me. That meant no one was heading toward the office.

Keeping my back against the wall, I whipped around the side and walked through the front doorway, which gave off a cheap chime that sounded like the batteries needed changing. Terri followed a few feet behind me.

"Can I help you?" the man asked with little enthusiasm, his eyes still scanning his magazine.

As I approached the counter, he lifted his eyes and saw the two of us. His hand subtly dropped from his chin, and he began to reach under the counter.

A split second later, my Glock was an inch from his nose. "You touch that button, and I pull the trigger."

"Hey, lady, I'm just scratching my leg. No worries, lady." He quickly brought both hands above his head, which raised his T-shirt, exposing a flabby, hairy belly.

"That's obscene. Lower your hands. Just a little."

After taking out two plastic cuffs, Terri moved behind the counter, grabbed the clerk's arms and pulled them to his back. I could hear the plastic cuff tighten with a zipper sound. She leaned down to look under the counter.

"Nice."

"What do you see?"

"A shitload of porn mags. I'm not touching those."

The man snickered, showing off a set of teeth that looked like they were covered with mold.

"What else?" I asked.

"There's a light switch with a small, clear lightbulb mounted next to it. Then there's a wire that runs out from under the plate and goes over to the wall—you can see it here, running into the ceiling." She pointed at it.

Placing my gun behind my back, I pulled my eyes away and peered through a broken, plastic blind to see a man holding a girl by the arm as he walked her up the black metal steps to the second floor. She stumbled once, then he yanked her back to her feet and they continued up the stairs.

"Need to know if Crack Daddy is here," I said, turning back to the clerk, who had a scraggily beard and looked to be no more than thirty.

He shrugged. "Never heard of him."

Terri moved to within a foot of his face. "We can shut this whole place down with one phone call."

"You think I'm stupid? This is America, last I checked. You're all hot air, just to impede on people's civil rights. So, I know you're full of shit."

He had experience at being arrested.

"You really want to call our bluff?" I asked.

"I don't own this place. I just work here."

Terri jumped in. "I bet you make some pretty good side money by feeding information to Crack Daddy and his gang, right? Or do you just sit around and whack off to your cartoon porno mags and eat Big Macs all night, completely oblivious to the drug-dealing and pimping that goes on around here?"

"Neither. I just do my job. Nothing more, nothing less." He pretended to yawn, showing off those gnarly teeth again.

I took two steps and placed my pistol on the counter, the barrel pointing at the slimy punk. "We need to talk to Crack Daddy. You can either tell us where he is, or we will call in about forty cops. Your place will be shut down, and charges could go against you for allowing this shit to go down with your knowledge."

"Eh, I'll be out by tomorrow working at another motel. That's how I roll." He chuckled again, and this time spit flew out of his mouth.

"You are fucking nasty," Terri said.

He laughed even harder.

"One more thing, clerk boy," I said. "When we find Crack Daddy, we're going to make sure he understands that you were the one who called the cops and told them to come clean the place up. You and you only."

His left eye twitched, and I could see a gulley take shape between his eyes.

"And if you don't think I'll do it, then you don't know how *I* roll."

Terri produced her phone and held her finger just above the screen. "Your call."

"Okay, okay. He's in room 225, but that opens into 224 and 223."

"Is he carrying?"

"You kidding me? Who isn't around here? What do you think this is...church?"

"How many guys are in his group?"

"It varies, depends who's out making runs. Anywhere from four to ten can be in the rooms. He keeps girls in there too."

"Good boy. For that, we're just going to keep you tied up until we're all done."

Terri grabbed his wrists, moved him against a door, and zip-tied his hands to the doorknob.

"Dammit. You really going to treat me like an animal? You know I could file charges. Where's your warrant, bitches?"

"Such a foul mouth," I said.

Terri took a bandana from her pocket, twirled it until it was taut like a rope, then pulled it tight around his mouth and head. "That should shut you up for a while."

He grunted out indecipherable words, lunging at Terri. She shoved her elbow square in his gut. His grunts became moans.

"Don't complain, dude. If Crack Daddy or one of his boys sees you tied up, then you're probably safe."

I felt a buzz in my pocket. I looked at my phone and saw a text from Gretchen.

Crack Daddy aka Jasper Finley. Two convictions for drug dealing, one for assault of a woman. See mug shot.

"Let's roll," I said to Terri.

I filled her in on Finley's background and let her take a look at his mug shot as we made our way around the back of the motel. We found three guys sleeping in a van, but the set of stairs we were hoping to use were under construction. We were left with no other option than to use the stairs on the front side. I knew we were taking a risk by not having backup, but I also believed that bringing in the cavalry might put not only a lockdown on the complex but also on everyone's ability to recall facts. Quick and bold—that was the best approach to penetrating enemy territory.

Marching around the front, I took the lead, with Terri ensuring we wouldn't be ambushed from behind. We passed a man and woman mugging down on the hood of a Monte Carlo. In normal circumstances, I would have said something. But this time, I kept my mouth shut and my eyes in scan mode.

"Ooo-wee, lookee what we have here." A man came out from an open door on the ground floor. He was shirtless, a tattoo of wings on his chest. As we moved closer to make our way to the steps, he flexed his pecs to the beat of some rap tune emanating from inside his room. Impressive, even for a thug.

I hooked my hand around the railing and ascended the stairs, taking a quick glance over my shoulder to ensure Terri was right behind me. She was, although I noticed another man in a wifebeater approaching her. He had his hands extended, as if he meant to touch her...or worse.

"You two fine crackers are just going to dis us like that? That's plain-ass rude from where I come from."

The bare-chested man also walked closer.

I stopped and stared down the two punks, then grabbed Terri by the shoulder. She moved up next to me on the fifth stair. The dude in the wifebeater stopped at the bottom of the stairs, ogling every last inch of Terri and then me. "Oh, the silent treatment. Yeah, Jerome, we're used to getting that from our bitches," the man said, his pecs pulsating like they had a mind of their own.

The other guy proved he could speak English...well, sort of. "Damn straight. We experts on knowing how to fix shit like that. That's right. Because we all know what a woman is supposed to do in this world. Know what I'm saying?"

They started chuckling, and they gave each other one of those bro handshakes. A second later, another one wearing a do-rag with a skull and crossbones on the side sauntered up, a cigarette dangling from his lips. He dragged his high-tops on the pavement, and I could only see slits for eyes. Then, five, six, seven more just like them, maybe a slightly different flavor, materialized out of rooms or from under the staircase—it was hard to say. They had multiplied like cockroaches.

Terri and I continued to back our way up the stairs. I didn't want to draw my gun, but if our lives were threatened I'd have no other choice. But I also knew we'd probably lose what little chance we had of having a sane conversation with Finley if the situation became escalated. We made it to the first landing, and I allowed myself to take in a breath.

That was too soon.

The skinny kid, Skull and Crossbones, had a sudden burst of energy, clapping his hands, shouting to the entire outdoor crew, "It's time to party everyone, and you can't throw a party with a bunch of butt munchers. Fine wine has arrived, and we need to pop the cork and start drinking." He quickly hopped up four steps.

Terri reached for her weapon, but I grabbed her wrist, then stomped down three steps and stuck my creds a foot from the face of Skull and Crossbones. "FBI, asshole. You leave us the fuck alone, or I'll throw you in federal prison where you'll be taught how to act like a real man."

His cigarette dropped from his lips, his eyes never leaving mine. I looked over his shoulder. I'd drawn the attention of everyone in the area, the music thumping in the background. I backed up one step and then another, my sights scanning the group. An arm moved, and I jerked my head to the right, where one of the roaches was pulling a phone out of his pocket.

"You, with the butt chin, put your phone back in your pocket and keep your hands where I can see them."

He complied, and then Terri and I continued our ascension. Near the top of the stairs I leaned down.

"We're going to go have a conversation, nothing more and nothing less. We don't want any trouble, and we're not trying to interrupt your lifestyle. But just know that when we're not out here ensuring you're behaving, I have two teams with eyes on you."

"Fuck you do," someone said from the group.

"I don't see shit," Pecs said.

I turned to look at the one with all the muscles. "That's the point. If you saw them, then that wouldn't help us a whole lot. But that shouldn't matter. If you're cool, then it's just a normal night. But if you cross the line, the sky will collapse on you and your lives will never be the same."

A few mumbles, but no outright dissension. We made it to the top, Terri now in the lead and me keeping an eye on the group below. They had started to move about and talk, and I didn't see any of them reaching for a weapon or phone. But I knew there were no guarantees.

"Nice bluff," Terri whispered.

"It's not my strong suit. I had to imagine they were actually out there taking aim on this group."

"Method acting. I like it."

I couldn't help but smile. She had my sense of humor.

Terri reached 225, and I took one last look over the railing. Everyone seemed to be on their best behavior.

"They could have warned Finley."

Terri put her hand on the doorknob and slowly twisted it. "I know. That's why I'm not knocking."

She pushed the door open, and we walked in, my fingers on the handle of my Glock, but still holstered. Smoke glowed from the soft lighting in the room. I knew the smell, and it wasn't cigarettes. Off in one corner, a guy and girl were rubbing all over each other, half clothed. They stopped for a moment, glanced our way, but then went back at it.

I could hear voices and more music, but this wasn't rap. I heard horns and an orchestra. As I turned to my left, I noticed a set of black, velvet curtains. I scanned our area, probably the original room 225. There were three beds—one containing the half-naked couple, and two more that were unoccupied, only a pile of white sheets on top of bare mattresses.

Bringing a hand to the edge of the curtains, I locked eyes with Terri. This time, she pulled out her sidearm, the Sig Sauer P226. I kept my Glock holstered, but my hand now had a firm hold on the grip. I mouthed a countdown...*three, two, one.* Then I threw open the curtain.

"What the fuck?" a guy said. He and another guy were sitting on a couch, hovering over a pile of blow on a coffee table. Another guy wearing a Celtics cap sat at a card table filled with stacks of cash two feet high. Off to my right, a woman had quickly covered herself. She was sitting on top of another man with a flat-top fro and one gold tooth. They were cozied up on a La-Z-Boy.

"Crack Daddy. Nice to meet you."

Twenty-One

Crack Daddy didn't scramble to pull up his jeans. Instead, he just sat in his recliner with the girl on his lap, thankfully covering just enough to not give us nightmares. He reached over to a table, picked up a bottle of what looked like champagne, and took a swig.

"What you bitches want?" He couldn't have been more relaxed if he were taking a stroll through the park.

"Quit calling me a bitch, for starters," Terri said, her gun still raised at the boys on the left side of the room.

"Ha, you're pretty fucking funny," he said, setting the bottle back on the table. It clanged extra hard, which told me his faculties were off. He was probably high.

Just then I heard a snort, and I turned my head to see this twerp with his nose running across a glass plate, sucking in white powder.

"You stupid sonofa—" Terri grabbed the plate and dumped it on the floor, although I saw another bag of white powder next to Crack Daddy's chair.

One of the guys jumped on the mass of powder on the ground. "No, no, you can't throw it away."

Terri nudged him with her knee, her gun aimed right at his

head. "Back on the couch, shitface." He crawled back on the couch, next to his partner.

I glanced over at the guy at the money table. He wore black-rimmed glasses and had a ten-key machine at the edge of the table. He seemed a bit nerdy, with a neat, collared shirt and jeans that actually fit him. He spoke not a word.

I said, "While it's very enticing for us to focus on what we see before us—"

Terri jumped in. "I could probably come up with five or six felony charges without much thought."

"That's not our focus, not unless you want us to focus on that."

"I don't want to go to jail. I just need my coke, and I'm a happy man," the guy on the couch said.

"Stop being a bitch and act like a man," Finley said.

Terri motioned with her gun at the desperate guy on the couch, "Get up and get against the wall."

He began to whimper.

"Do it. Now."

He staggered to the wall and put his hands against it. I pulled out my gun as Terri holstered hers. She kicked his feet apart and proceeded to pat him down. Turning back to me, she said, "Clean."

He brought his hands to his back, mumbling words I couldn't understand.

"Get out of here."

"What? You're letting me go?" He turned and wiped his eyes, his face ashen.

"Yes. Leave this place and don't come back. Got it?"

"Yes sir. I mean, ma'am." He scooted past Terri and then nearly ran into me, his balance obviously skewed.

Terri pulled her gun back out as I checked to make sure the

man exited room 225. He did. I also noticed the couple was still doing their lip-lock thing in the corner bed.

"Okay, Finley, we need to talk. You want an audience?"

"What's the big secret?"

I looked at Terri, then back at Finley, who grabbed his bottle of champagne and took another gulp. His girl grabbed it from his hand and tipped her head back. Some of the liquid dribbled down her chin and onto her pink robe so sheer you could see her skin.

"A girl died two nights ago." I paused for a moment and watched his eyes shift upward to his girl. She didn't act like she heard me.

"The girl who died was one of your girls."

Now the girl looked my way. "What did you just say?"

"I said one of your boyfriend's girls died two nights ago."

Suddenly agitated, Finley tried to sit up, grabbing at his pants, and the girl fell to the floor. I leaned down to help her up while keeping an eye on Finley. He scooped his pants back on.

"Sit back down," Terri said, now aiming her Sig at him.

I found a bath towel over another chair and tossed it to the girl. "You got clothes?"

"They're around here somewhere. Anyone know where I put those clothes?"

Finley brought his hand to his head. He seemed annoyed, possibly at his girl, definitely at us. I noticed he had four gold rings on that hand.

"Over here." The nerd finally spoke, although he had a meek voice.

The girl wrapped the towel around herself, picked up her clothes, then stood behind the nerd and slipped a dress over her head.

"You can sit on the floor," Terri said to the girl. She complied, although her lower lip protruded, pouting. "Finley, we need information. If you don't give us what we want, then we shut down your entire operation."

"Don't call me Finley. You're going to ruin my street cred."

"We don't give a shit. Answer our questions and you might have a little street cred left."

He waved a hand at Terri, acting like he was dismissing her.

I took a chair from a table, turned it around, and sat, now eye to eye with the baddest guy around, or so we were to believe.

"Are you aware that one of your girls died?"

He scratched a few whiskers, his eyes on the cash. "I heard."

"What else did you hear?"

"Nothing," he said, turning his gaze to me. "I don't get involved in other people's business. I wish other people had the same courtesy." He cocked his head, his voice laced with attitude. I wondered if this was going to work on his turf. He believed he was untouchable. I had to bring him down to earth, to make him feel vulnerable.

I held my Glock in the air, then unlatched the clip of ammunition and slapped it back in. I had an audience. I threw my arm downward, slamming the metal gun into Finley's kneecap. He cried out and grabbed his knee.

"What the hell you go off and do that for, you—"

"Courtesy," Terri said.

"Fuck courtesy. I think this crazy woman just broke my kneecap. I used to be able to run a four-four forty with these knees."

I inched the chair closer, and I could smell his boozy breath.

"Listen, Jasper. I don't care about your four-four knees or your street cred. That was a shot across your bow—a last warning. Share everything you know, or we will make one call. Then it's all over. Your whole world will implode."

"Okay." He grimaced, showing off his single gold tooth.

"This girl, Pandora, she worked for me a bit. Off and on."

"Two nights ago. Do you remember seeing her?"

His eyes looked to the ceiling. "I don't know. Maybe. The days and nights kind of blur together. Know what I'm saying?"

"Think harder. Two nights ago. It's important."

"Shoopey, did you see her?" he asked his accountant, the man in the Celtics cap sitting at the cash table.

He shrugged his shoulders. "I can check, but I don't think she came in for any type of...exchange."

"What the hell is an exchange?" Terri asked.

Shoopey looked to his grand master, who flicked a hand and nodded. "It's when they give us a percentage of their proceeds, and we reciprocate the transaction with a nice bonus."

"Coke?" Terri asked.

"I don't want to implicate myself. I just count money."

I recalled Candy saying she saw Emma on the street. Either she was lying or she could have gotten her days mixed up.

I turned back to Finley. "Did you know her real name?"

He huffed out a breath, as if our conversation was taking years off his life. "I think it's Emma."

"She has two kids."

"So?"

"That doesn't mean anything to you?"

"I got kids in five states, at least the ones I claim." He rocked back in his chair, laughing hard at himself. No one else joined him. In fact, I looked at his girl, and she had her hands over her face.

"What's your name?" I asked her.

No response.

"Hey, she's asking you a question," Terri said.

The girl lifted her face to show off a pair of raccoon eyes, a trail of black tears streaming down her gaunt cheekbones.

"Misty. My name is Misty. And you guys are really freaking me out. It just hit me that you're not just giving CD a hard time. I think it's true, right?"

I nodded.

She squeezed her eyes shut. "I can't keep doing this, CD. I just can't. It's going to kill me, or I'm going to get picked up by some nut job who wants to get his jollies by killing us working girls."

Finley said, "You just need a couple of days to unwind. Why don't you get Shoopey here to give you an extra bonus for that work you did for me earlier. Then you can go to one of those fancy spas in Back Bay. Go ahead, Shoopey, give her a few bills."

"I don't want your fucking money. I just need to sober up and stop taking chances with my life, dammit." She clawed at the carpet as a new round of tears fell from her face, then she moved to her knees. "Can I go now?" she asked me and Terri.

"Did you know Pandora...Emma?"

She shook her head. "No. I usually work only by request through CD or Shoopey, then I go to where the customer is. I guess you could say I'm higher end."

CD only nodded, as if she were affirming his business model.

I turned back to him. "So you're not sure if you saw Emma two nights ago. What about her typical customers? Do you guys know who they are?"

"Some. Why?"

I nodded at Terri, who had already pulled out her phone and flipped to Vince's mug. I took it from her and showed it to CD, then over to Shoopey, and even Misty. The other guy on the couch had his eyes shut.

"Hard to say. Kind of looks like a lot of customers," Finley said.

Terri handed out her business card and told everyone to call her if they remembered anything about Emma, her whereabouts two nights ago or her customers.

"We're taking the coke with us," I declared.

"I would put up a fight, but it's not going to do me much good, is it?" Finley asked.

"Nope. But I know you'll get your hands on more drugs within a day or two."

He smiled, and his gold tooth sparkled from a nearby lamp.

Terri and I turned to leave.

"Hold up. One quick thing," Finley said, lifting from his chair.

We turned. He was about my height, maybe shorter. Kevin Hart came to mind, minus the easy smile.

"If you ask around, you might hear a couple of folks saying me and Emma got into an…argument."

"We're listening," Terri said.

"It was a few days ago. Maybe a week. I don't know, but it wasn't two days ago. Anyway, she owed me money. I'd given her a loan of some product, just to keep her from going nuts, and she hadn't repaid it. So I got on her. She kind of went ballistic on me, tried clawing my eyes out. She's got daggers for nails, man."

"Did you beat her like you did that other girl?"

He gave me a blank stare. "I didn't touch her. But I did call her every name in the book. I don't like it when people cheat me out of my money, even if they got a habit they can't kick."

I wanted to give this asshole a lecture, but it wouldn't do any good and certainly wouldn't help us find Emma's killer.

"Thanks. Let us know if you remember anything else."

He nodded, and we left with the bag of coke hidden inside my jacket. On the way down the stairs, Terri read her phone. "Search warrant finally came back."

"Judge approved it?"

"Yep. Want to make it an all-nighter?"

"If we can keep Tripuka off the streets, I'm game," I said. "I can't say for certain he's our killer, but something about him is off."

Twenty-Two

Miss Lucille stood just off her back porch wrapped in a blanket, as red, white, and blue lights flashed across her angst-ridden face. It was obvious she wasn't enjoying any aspect of the late-night search of her garage apartment, the home of her tenant, Vince Tripuka.

I paused for a second to let a woman wearing a CSI jacket walk past me. She was carrying a black plastic chest that undoubtedly was filled with all sorts of tools to collect evidence: bindle paper, electrostatic dust lifter, glass vials, acetate sheet protectors, a flashlight for oblique lighting, all sizes of tweezers, and evidence bags. She probably had a hundred other tools back in her van.

Gravel crunched under my shoes as I made my way over to Miss Lucille. I nodded, but she hardly paid me much attention, her gaze on the people coming in and out of the garage apartment. We'd already spoken a bit earlier, when I woke her in the middle of the night to let her know we were going to be conducting a search. She proceeded to shed a few tears, then gave us the spare keys to the apartment.

Between cops, CSI personnel, and SMEs (subject matter experts) from the FBI whom I'd brought in to support the

Somerville team, there were about fifteen people on site. So far, not a single person had complained about the crazy hours—it was now almost five a.m. As a point of emphasis, once all the teams were on site, Terri had gathered everyone together and given them a pep talk, her message succinct: the suspect, Vince Tripuka, would likely walk if the team didn't find and process evidence connecting him to either of the two murders, Emma or Gloria Lopez from ten years earlier. But, she reminded them, if anyone had the notion of planting evidence, she would personally testify at their trial to ensure a conviction.

While I inwardly questioned her timing and even her approach, that woman had a pair on her that would rival anyone from the football team for which she used to cheer. The CSI team had been moving nonstop for a good three hours.

"Do you think he did it?"

I glanced to my left to see Miss Lucille still staring at the movement in and around the apartment. The entire area around the garage looked like the setting for a breaking-news media scene with all the spotlights the Sommerville officers had set up. The floodlight attached to the garage was still not working— Miss Lucille had mentioned that light being out when she'd let her dog back in the house, the night of Emma's death. "That's why we're here, to gather evidence that allows us to make that conclusion."

"I understand. But do you, Agent Troutt, think he killed that poor girl?"

I paused, considering my response. "I don't know. I've learned over the years that guessing and hoping doesn't do us any good at all. We use every legal means possible to gather facts, then sift through everything to determine what is truly evidence, not an opinion or even an assumption. Once we stack up enough of the evidence cards, it points us in the right direction."

"Doesn't that take a while to do, especially when you don't have an eyewitness or the actual murder weapon?"

I turned my head slightly to her. She knew just enough of the process to be dangerous, probably from watching too many of those CSI TV shows. "It can, yes."

"But didn't I hear your partner say that you only had a few hours until Vince would be let out of jail?"

I knew Terri's pep talk had been ill-timed. "We're really not at liberty to discuss the details of the case."

"But don't you think I should know if a potential killer is going to be let loose in just a few hours, especially since this is probably where he'll show up after he's released? It's a safety issue."

A moment later, I heard a few sniffles. I put my arm around her and said, "Miss Lucille, I can understand how traumatic this is on you. You will be safe, even if we have to assign an officer or agent to watch your home."

She released a choppy breath. "Maybe I'm naïve, but I just don't think Vince would hurt me, even if he is the awful person you think he is. More than anything, I'm ashamed of myself."

"Why?"

"Because of Arthur," she said, quickly grabbing a tissue from her robe pocket and bringing it to her mouth. "I've shamed his good name by having all of this going on." She waved a blanket-covered hand in the direction of the garage. "While he was very compassionate and I've tried to carry on in the same manner, it's just plain stupid for me to rent an apartment to a murderer."

"I wouldn't blame yourself, Miss Lucille. How could you have known? And right now we don't know for certain that he's done anything of that sort."

"Right. Follow the evidence," she said behind a few more sniffles.

I saw Terri emerge from the apartment, wearing blue nitrile gloves. She was speaking to another cop. She glanced down at me and nodded. My heart skipped a beat.

"We'll talk again before we leave, Miss Lucille." I walked over to the garage, shuffled around two CSI people holding large plastic bags, then made my way up the wooden set of stairs.

"Did you find the murder weapon?" I asked the moment I hit the landing, my eyes already peeking inside.

"No lead-in question or introduction?" Terri asked, moving to her left to allow another cop to get by. "You just go straight for the home run."

I shrugged my shoulders.

"I guess I would have done the same."

I put my hand on her shoulder. "You would have yelled at me from across the yard." I winked, then stepped just inside the apartment. While I'd taken a brief look inside when we used Miss Lucille's keys to open the door, I'd quickly exited to give the real pros more time to do their work.

"Gotta admit, you have me pegged, Alex." She moved up next to me as we watched the rest of the team continue the search process.

"Excuse me," a lady said, coming out of the bedroom holding a monitor and a cable. Just behind her a man carried one of those tower computers.

Terri said, "That's either ten years old, or it's one of those new-age computers that can be built at home, which means Vince is a real gadget guy."

The computer guy looked our way. "I think it's about nine years old and has less processing power than my two-year-old phone."

"We don't care if he was trying to fly a rocket ship to Mars. We only care if it has valuable information on it. How long will it take to search through the files and let us know if there is anything noteworthy?"

"Eh. On a computer this old, there's only so much security that can be loaded. Not long. I'm guessing within a few hours."

"Cool, thanks." I felt a burst of energy, knowing we might finally get a true perspective of Tripuka's private life, where he spent his time, his hobbies…what his passions were—and wondering if those passions stretched into the sick and twisted kind.

"By the way," the man said, stopping briefly at the door, "we might find more jewels on his hidden tablet."

Terri stuck out a hand. "Hidden? Where?"

"We found it under the pillow top of his mattress."

Without wasting another second, I led the way to the bedroom where we found a woman placing a tablet inside an evidence bag.

"Nice catch," Terri said.

"Thanks." A redhead wearing gold-rimmed glasses sounded all business. She picked up her own tablet and typed on it, likely logging the piece of evidence.

"Can you show me where he had it hidden?" I asked.

She walked to the foot of the bed, lifted a brown and orange floral comforter, then the sheet, and pointed at a small slit between the pillow top and the actual mattress.

"Anything else in there?"

"Nope. Just big enough for the tablet."

An FBI agent was on the other side of the bed, carefully peeling back the matted, stained carpet in the corner. "Did you see anything that makes you think Tripuka has stashed something under this top-notch carpet?" I asked him.

"No. Just being thorough. Plus, if he hid his tablet in his mattress, he's got the mindset to conceal personal property. I guess not everyone who does that is a murderer though."

"True. But they usually have a significant other or someone they're hiding it from."

I turned back as the CSI person started to walk out of the door with Tripuka's tablet.

"How long until—"

"I was waiting for you to ask. This is a new model, and they're difficult to hack. Maybe he knew that when he bought it…maybe he didn't. Even with your SMEs helping us out, it's hard to make promises on the unpredictable. Could take us two hours to get in—"

"We'll take that," Terri said while sifting through clothes hanging in the closet.

Red shook her head, a brief look of exasperation. "I was about to say, it could just as easily be two days, maybe more. And that's with us working nonstop, which I'm willing to do."

"Have at it, and let me know when you find something," Terri said.

"Will do," she said, adjusting her glasses. "For what it's worth, I really hope we find the evidence we need. There is something about this that really sticks with me. And I think it's because Tripuka, or whoever killed those girls, preyed on women in their most desperate state—addicts who are hooking just to pay for that next fix. Sometimes I don't know how we can think that humanity has really evolved, not with psychos like Tripuka out in the world. Well, I'll stop pontificating and get on this."

She walked out of the room.

I ambled over to Terri, as Red's words rattled in my mind. "I guess there's no weapon then?"

She tried to smile, but her nose wrinkled. "Not a single gun on the premise. Even his knife set was dull and old."

"His red pickup. I didn't see it outside," I said.

"We had it impounded the moment the warrant was approved. It's already in our garage with another three-person team poring over it. I just talked to them before you came up. No weapon in the car either. But they are looking for trace evidence. Maybe we'll get lucky."

"If we're thorough enough, we won't need luck. But I know it's not easy, especially with this clock ticking in the back of our minds."

Terri and I finished sifting through Tripuka's few sets of clothes in his bedroom closet when we both heard a technician saying, "...logged into our evidence database. And this piece of evidence might be significant."

I quickly walked into the living room area, the eyes of a mounted deer head staring me down from the opposite wall. I turned my back to the dead animal as a technician slid a tablet under his arm.

"What did you find?" I could feel Terri right behind me.

"A few strands of hair in the corner of this tiny closet here."

"Good. Let's get it analyzed. Although DNA analysis might take a while."

"True, but in my years of doing this, I'd bet my reputation those are female hairs."

Terri and I locked eyes and she said, "But do we have enough time to prove it before he's released?"

Unfortunately, I knew the answer to that question.

Twenty-Three

Whoever came up with the phrase Keystone Cops must have foreshadowed the scene I was witnessing. Stuffed into a small conference room with four chairs were nine people. One comment couldn't be finished without another person jumping in to counter that point and offer up another idea. Multiply that by four, then add in someone new popping into the room to give us updates every couple of minutes. In addition to the lack of effectiveness of the group, the air had become stagnant and humid. A waft of BO had just invaded my personal space, and I quickly stopped breathing through my nose.

Nick, who'd taken an Uber over to the Sommerville police station to join Terri and me for this last-minute evidence-review session, nudged my arm, whispering in my ear. "Too many cooks in the kitchen."

I raised an eyebrow, then gulped another mouthful of lukewarm coffee, the only thing keeping my sleep-deprived brain functioning at the moment.

"My grandfather used to say that when he was watching all his sisters bicker over how to cook the Thanksgiving turkey. He'd try to put in his two cents, but they never listened. So he'd turn around, walk to the bar, and pour himself a scotch. I would be standing right at the doorway. He'd pat my hand a couple of times and mutter that phrase under his breath on his way to his chair in the living room. Then he wouldn't move until dinner was ready."

For a brief second I could feel a familiar yearning for having those typical family moments growing up. I couldn't recall anything like that. I never had a lot of family around.

I shifted my eyes to Nick for a second. "All the cooks haven't stopped the pot from boiling over. Everyone is in CYA mode."

Nick gave me a fist bump on that one. Not that we at the FBI were immune to clusterfuck meetings, but usually, rank or the alpha of the group would win out, and the rest would follow. I glanced at Terri sitting in one of the few chairs. She'd just brought her hands to her head as two men stood and argued above her—the lead of the CSI unit, a portly fellow named Kerr, and her detective lieutenant, a beast of a man who must have stood six-six and went by the name of either Sir, Lute, or just plain old Jackson.

The door swung open, and everyone stopped talking midsentence. A uniform who looked like he hadn't started shaving yet stammered to get the words out.

"Come on, spit it out, man," Jackson barked.

The kid swallowed once. "Tripuka's lawyer, Winston Wise, has already posted bail. Tripuka is being processed right now, and then he'll be released on the terms that he'll check in with his parole officer once a day."

"Can't we lose his paperwork or something?" Longfellow, one of Terri's detectives, leaned over my shoulder and palmed the table where there were dozens of preliminary reports and pictures. "What are we running here, a bed and breakfast? We can have a say when these known felons are being released to the public. We may not be able to stop it—at least not like we could in the good old days—but we can damn well make it as tough as possible."

A few grunts in the room, apparently no one willing to talk in detail about the good old days.

The kid spoke up. "Does that mean I should tell the boys downstairs to purposely lose Tripuka's file or figure out another way to purposely delay his release?"

"Kid, don't be so blatant about it, but yes, figure something out to keep this maniac behind bars."

"Okay, Detective Longfellow."

Jackson wiped a hand across his face, the loose skin so rubbery it appeared the bags under his eyes had been pulled below his nose. "Hold on." He took a glimpse over at Nick and me before returning his glare to the kid and Longfellow. "We'll have no such thing. That's not how a professional law enforcement department works, and both of you know that. Follow the law, just like we have every other time. Understood?"

The kid said, "Yes sir," and then shut the door behind him.

Terri, meanwhile, gave the evil eye to Longfellow.

"We might have ten, fifteen minutes before he's released. A killer walking the streets." Jackson actually tugged on his face this time. It was like watching a cartoon character. He slowly turned his exaggerated face to his counterpart from the CSI team, Kerr.

"Everyone in here is working their tails off. If your team had pulled its weight..." His eyes dropped to look at Kerr's sizable tire around his waist. He rolled his eyes as he lifted his sights back up. "Then we could have saved a life, maybe more."

"You're fucking insane, Jackson. Oxygen levels aren't the same at your level apparently."

I felt like I'd just witnessed a middle-school hazing incident. The maturity level of this outfit had reached an all-time low. I couldn't take any more, even if I couldn't make evidence appear out of thin air like Jackson desired.

I stood up just as the door swung back open. It was Red, the CSI technician who'd found the tablet.

"Do you have any good news for us?" I asked before anyone else.

She touched the rims of her glasses. "I'm afraid not. We—"

"Well, there you go. We get screwed up the ass again," Longfellow said, throwing his hands to the ceiling.

I could almost see spears shooting out of Terri's eyes as she glared at Longfellow, who was now standing next to me. I ignored the excuse of a detective and turned to Red. "Please continue."

"I was just going to say that we've got preliminary results back on both the tower computer and his tablet."

All heads turned in her direction. Then not a single person moved.

"The computer was completely clean. A few documents and spreadsheets, but most of those had to do with his prior incarcerations. We found a few other grocery lists, fantasy football documents. Nothing prominent."

Terri spoke up. "So no pictures of women?"

"Nope."

"Browser history?"

"Typical stuff: news, weather, sports sites. Raciest one we found was the *Sports Illustrated Swimsuit Issue* website. Pretty typical guy stuff."

"But you were able to penetrate the security on the tablet? What did you find there?"

She turned to me, nodding. "Not sure why he had it hidden in his mattress, frankly."

"Why?" Jackson asked.

"Again, nothing real special stood out. Apps from Facebook, ESPN, Angry Birds and a few other games."

"Dammit!" Jackson pounded a fist into his opposite hand.

"The only thing that was a little strange were a few pictures we found on there."

"Pictures of prostitutes in the act, or just naked women, or what?" Longfellow said. He apparently hadn't felt the vibes from just about everyone in the room to shut his trap, although I was keenly interested in the answer.

"Heck no, nothing like that. Just random things." She poked a finger inside her thick head of red hair and scratched her scalp. "I don't know, pictures of little figurines, dolls, medals of some kind. A bunch of stuff like that. Very random and not very interesting to our case."

Jackson barked at her. "So you're saying you couldn't find any real evidence that connects Tripuka to the murder of our vic, Emma Katic." He swatted a hand toward me and Nick. "And definitely nothing on the FBI cold case. A complete strikeout, right?"

"I…uh," she stammered.

"Lay off, Jackson." Kerr poked a finger into the lieutenant's arm. Jackson looked down at Kerr's finger, then glared at him. Kerr didn't stop there. "You can't find evidence if it doesn't exist, unless you're in the business of evidence tampering."

Jackson tightened his shoulders as his lips spread apart, showing off a set of yellow teeth. I assumed he smoked.

Kerr was on a roll. "Have you thought about looking in the mirror? Your team of so-called detectives identified Tripuka as the only real suspect in this murder. And what did it give us? Squat—that's what it gave us. Even if Tripuka is the perp, your team focused on his apartment and truck. So we found nothing. That's because there was nothing to find. Get us the right suspect, or put us at a location where an actual crime was committed, and my team will find the evidence if it's there."

Jackson growled between his teeth as Kerr reached to the table and gathered up a notebook and a few loose papers.

"Sir, there is one more thing. The hair," Red said.

"Oh, right." Kerr straightened back up. "Is that our smoking gun?" he asked.

"Who knows? But one of the veterans on the team swears the strands of hair are female, you know, based on his experience and all."

A few mumbles.

"That would hold up in court thirty years ago, maybe," I said. "It's going to take DNA analysis."

"We've sent off a sample, and even though we've ordered a rush job on it, it's still going to take upwards of a week, five days if we're really lucky."

"That's what I thought. Thank you for the information."

She huffed out a tired breath and left the room. As the door shut, another cloud of BO passed by me. It almost brought tears to my eyes.

Jackson addressed the team for another five minutes, trying to save face and put a positive spin on the case. We all knew he was blowing smoke up our collective asses. It was a huge disappointment. The meeting broke up, and we spilled into the detective cube farm, where I finally took in fresh air.

"This place, sometimes, is so damn..." Terri's lips drew a straight line as she walked up to me and Gimpy, otherwise known as Nick on crutches.

"Frustrating?" Nick offered.

"Disturbingly inefficient?" I countered, tossing my coffee into a trash can.

"Both, times ten." She tried to smile as she walked to her

desk. I padded behind Nick, whose speed on crutches was sloth-like.

I emptied my lungs, my body already sucking fumes. I pressed my fingers against the bridge of my nose, reminding myself that sleep wasn't optional if I expected to pull this investigation out of the ditch and find incriminating evidence on Tripuka—or whomever the culprit was.

"You look like shit," Nick said to me.

I cocked my head to the side. "I haven't slept in thirty-six hours, and you just toss that grenade in the room? Tell me something I don't know."

Terri, on the other hand, barely had a wrinkle in her suit. Somehow her makeup had remained intact, and her hair had an easy flow to it, where it didn't look like she'd just rolled out of bed.

My simplistic, perhaps carnal thoughts, went from a bed to Brad. Dammit, I'd forgotten to reply to his text. I put that on my mental to-do list as soon as I had a spare moment.

"You really know how to charm the girls, Nick," Terri said.

Nick and I instantly looked at each other. We held straight faces for about two seconds, then we both erupted into laughter. The kind of laughter that pulled tears from your eyes.

"Damn, what got into you guys?" Terri said with a perplexed smile.

Nick was red from laughing so hard. Well, his pale skin could turn red with a cool breeze, but right then, he could have led Santa's sleigh with his glowing head.

"It's...nothing." He almost lost his balance and tumbled to the floor.

I thumbed moisture from under my eyes, knowing my face was a hot mess by now. Terri didn't know our little secret—about Nick being gay. He and his significant other, Antonio, had been together for more years than any straight couple I knew.

"Okay, so you guys still see me as an outsider. I get it," she said, acting as if she'd been reduced to some type of law enforcement subclass.

"It's not that, I promise you. When this is all over, we'll grab a drink somewhere, and when the alcohol is flowing, who knows what secrets I'll tell?" I winked.

Nick shrugged his shoulders and found a chair to sit in. He propped his crutches against a desk. "You two need some sleep. What can I do while you get some shut-eye?"

I knew he was right. "Well, check in with Gretchen and see if she's made any progress on Tripuka's past."

"The cellmate angle? Because I can tell you that as of last night she'd yet to make any progress. Just getting the list of his cellmates is proving to take an act of Congress. If and when we talk to anyone who knew Tripuka, I'm not sure we'll get anyone to talk, not unless there's an incentive. Guys like that don't like ratting on anyone unless there's something in it for them."

"Good point. While she keeps an eye on the past, you focus on the present, or at least the recent past. We still don't know if Tripuka left his apartment two nights ago during the time the ME believed Emma was murdered."

"Right. I'll see what I can think of on that front. What else?" He grabbed a sticky note and a pen off Terri's desk and started writing a few illegible words.

"Two other things come to mind. First, find Susan Miller."

"The girl Tripuka assaulted when she was just sixteen," Nick said.

"According to him, it was only statutory because she was under age by a week and thought they were in love. He said she only went along with the charge because her father forced her to. But her father has a much different story. We need to know the *real* story."

Terri chimed in. "Not sure what Nick can do. The parents aren't going to give us her contact information. They're trying to protect her."

I looked at Nick. "I'm too tired to think, but I know you'll figure it out."

He nodded. "Next?"

"Get me those pictures that were on Tripuka's tablet."

"Those silly things?"

"They're part of his profile. Silly to you and me might mean something entirely different to a guy who kills women and cuts out their eyes."

Nick jotted down another note. "Damn, he's a sick sonofabitch."

An idea popped into my mind, and I was out the door in no time flat.

Twenty-Four

As I stared at the shoddy repair work on the ceiling in the reception area at Dr. Dunn's office, I heard the pop of bubble gum and then a sucking noise. I glanced down at Ashling, who was trying to blot the gum remnants off her face with the bigger wad from her mouth.

"Taste good?" The scent of wild berry filled up our space.

"Eh," she said, still working on the gum cleanup, reminding me of our cat, Pumpkin, licking his paws to clean his face.

Ashling appeared remarkably relaxed, considering the assault and resulting fight for our lives at the hands of her Neanderthal ex-boyfriend just a couple of days earlier. Then again, she always seemed calm. Now that I knew she'd been involved with an abusive guy, her inner turmoil had probably been off the charts. I wouldn't be surprised if she had an ulcer.

"When is the ceiling going to be fixed?"

She shrugged her shoulders while bulging out her dark-rimmed eyes. "Could be a while. I heard Dr. Dunn on the phone with the insurance company. Seems they don't want to pay up for his trigger finger. He wasn't happy. So I think we're at a standstill."

A moment later, Dr. Dunn opened the door to the back.

"Come on in, Alex."

"I appreciate you fitting me in for a few minutes." I followed him through the door and down the hallway.

"As long as you don't mind watching me clean out the fridge. I think we could fossilize a few of the items in there." He chuckled as we walked into a small breakroom where a white fridge sat in the corner.

"What's that noise?" It sounded like an animal dying within the bowels of the fridge's gurgling motor.

He waddled to the side of the clunker. "Twenty-three years. It's the most reliable thing we've got around here."

I nodded and smiled.

"Now if I can just get Dr. Swift to not leave his wife's lasagna in here for months at a time, we could avoid an outbreak of mold."

"Dr. Swift?"

"Yes, he's my part-time partner. Sees a few patients three days a week. Semi-retired, but likes to keep his mind sharp."

The moment he opened the fridge door, I had to hold my hand over my face. He swatted his arm a couple of times. "Damn, this might be the worst yet."

He removed a couple of dishes that had wrinkled plastic wrap covering only a small part of each. Another wave of something foul hit my nose, and I quickly dug through my purse until I found a tube of Carmex lip balm. I removed the cap and hovered it just in front of my nose, setting up my best line of olfactory defenses.

"On your voicemail to me, you said you had something from your professional life to discuss." He lifted what looked like a piece of chocolate cake. His bushy mustache twitched a couple of times before he dumped the remnants in the garbage.

"First of all, this is confidential, correct?"

"If you want it that way, sure," he said.

"More than anything, I just need to bounce a few things off you, someone who's educated in the study of psychology but isn't jaded like me by a never-ending interaction with killers."

With his head still stuck in the fridge, he said, "We're all impacted by our environments, whether we're killers or accountants, or accountants who have killed."

I paused for a second. The doc's statement was a simple observation—rather obvious—yet it was good for me to hear it said out loud. I moved on to my main topic. "What do you think would motivate a man to kill a prostitute?"

"A prostitute. That's a complex question. We could probably sit down over dinner and discuss it for two, three hours."

He looked up from his fridge task and smiled. Was he essentially asking me out on a date? I didn't want to go there, not with my shrink, and not with him. I just needed Dr. Dunn to keep being Dr. Dunn, not my love doctor. I had Brad to fill that role. Crap...I'd once again forgotten to send him a simple text. He was, after all, the man I cared about. After this appointment, I would send him a message. I couldn't be that self-absorbed.

"Alex, are you with me?"

"Sorry, just thinking through this crazy case I'm working...well, two cases actually."

He went back to digging though the fridge. It appeared that he'd understood my non-response about his hint of a dinner—it was not happening.

"You see, Alex, murderers of any kind are rarely one-dimensional people. Like others in society, they have their own unique set of interests and desires, disappointments and pleasures. They can even have customary goals and dreams."

"Which is why they can be so damn hard to find."

"Indeed. Just think, it can be anyone you bump shoulders

with while you're walking through a packed mall. The person might be carrying a package from the shoe store and rushing to meet a friend for drinks. Seemingly normal behavior."

He turned back around to face me. "During my graduate studies, I had the opportunity to interview a man who'd killed three people. It was something I'll never forget." A shake of the head, and then he hunched lower and started sifting through one of the bins. "One thing really stood out during that interview."

"What was that?"

"His humanity. It was really quite striking. For instance, I found out that he cried himself to sleep every night."

It sounded unstable, but also very human, as the doctor noted. Who hasn't lived thirty, forty years on this earth and not experienced trauma of some kind?

"While there are exceptions, killers are rarely categorized as monsters. To them, there's really no such thing as a senseless killing."

I nodded, recalling some of the same information from my FBI training back in Quantico, although Dr. Dunn seemed to communicate it in a different way. Maybe I was sensing his compassion. It had been a good thirteen years since my time back at the academy.

"Make no mistake, though, murderers, especially those who are considered serial killers, are profoundly damaged people who are driven by a history of devastating trauma."

I nodded, letting his perspective resonate in my mind. Another sickening waft drifted by, and I realized my arm holding the lip balm had dropped to my side. I took in a whiff of the Carmex and exhaled. "I've heard various theories about those trigger events that can lead people to kill years later. Do you think it's a singular event, or a number of events piled on top of each other?"

He had just dumped a jar of something purple and gooey into the trash can.

"What the hell was that?"

His eyes got wide. "Homemade jelly from Mrs. Swift, I think. Lordy, this is like changing the diapers of my twins when they were babies. That smell could have knocked over a horse."

"My Erin was probably worse in that department than her brother. But raising twins at any age must have been challenging for you."

"You see this head of gray hair?" He pointed at his head, careful to keep his stained fingers out of his hair, which was beginning to thin. He was looking more and more like Albert Einstein.

I chuckled, and he continued tackling the natural disaster in the fridge.

"Now, to answer your question, it really depends, Alex. We're all so different, as is our ability to deal with trauma. How we internalize events, how it manifests itself in our behavior, our self-esteem...it's a complexity I'm not sure we'll ever truly figure out. But I will say this: more and more studies are showing that continuous trauma over a period of time can have a longer-lasting effect, even if it's not outwardly visible. It might be someone who was in an abusive home for years on end or was constantly exposed to violence at school. Or it could even be a person who suffers tremendous emotional abuse over a long period of time. That's what I've heard called the waterboarding effect. It can really screw with a person."

"I think you're trying to say that the killer's prostitute focus may not have anything directly to do with women in that line of work."

"How we as human beings express our feelings, including resentment or rage, a lack of self-esteem or torment, can be as different as the proverbial snowflake. So it may or may not have any direct association with actual women in that line of work. In the world of psychology, we don't deal with absolutes."

The fridge's motor sputtered twice, and Dr. Dunn used a fist to pound the side, which instantly quieted the unsettling noise.

"Why don't you get Ashling to do these types of tasks for you?"

"She's not really into working a whole lot, if you know what I mean."

I shrugged, a little perplexed with his inability to get Ashling to actually work for her pay.

"She pretty much just likes to sit in one spot, read her book, speak a few words, and if I'm lucky, she'll answer the phone and generally provide a human presence out front. You know, just something to at least pretend we have a real business." He winked at me.

A fictitious life. I wondered how much trouble Tripuka, or whoever had killed those girls, had taken to hide their twisted obsessions in order to blend in with the rest of society. Without purposely going there, I'd allowed my mind to strongly consider someone other than Tripuka committing these murders. But why? Before I took another few seconds to ponder my mind's deductive process, Dr. Dunn said it was time for his next appointment, and we retraced our steps down the hallway. My phone buzzed, and I started digging through my purse. I found the edge of the phone and pulled it out as the doctor opened the door. It was a text from Erin.

Mrs. Harris said I have to actually do art that I am researching. That means I have to paint something in Impressionism style...by TOMORROW. Help!!

I could feel her stress through the phone. It was another one of those teenage, end-of-the-world moments. At least it had to do with schoolwork and not some type of mean-girl drama. I rubbed my temple, thinking through our options, given her looming deadline to complete her homework, my lack of knowledge to provide any help whatsoever, and, of course, the fact that we might have just allowed a killer to walk out of jail. Would Tripuka kill again? Did he even kill Emma and our cold-case vic, Gloria Lopez, or was the killer stalking his next victim a thousand miles away?

"Alex, do you mind moving out of the doorway so my next patient can get through?"

I glanced up and saw the elderly woman from the other day standing there, her nose angled above my head, even though she was a couple of inches shorter.

"Pardon me." Mrs. Carano pulled gloves off each hand and placed them in her purse. It looked like a Dolce & Gabbana, and I momentarily lost my train of thought.

"Alex? Hey."

A familiar voice broke me out of my trance. "Oh. Hi, Colin."

"You look troubled. Everything okay?"

Just as I was about to respond, I heard—and even felt—a sneeze just behind my head.

"Mr. Brewer, are you ready for your appointment?"

I flipped around while touching the back of my hair to see a portly man stretching a suede vest to its limits. His nose was red and his eyes puffy.

I pointed at him. "Dr. Swift?" He gave me a passing "yes," then looked beyond me to Colin.

"Oh, you see Dr. Swift, not Dr. Dunn," I said to Colin.

He gave me a polite nod. "Usually, yes."

Then Mrs. Carano practically pushed me out of the way. "Will people ever learn it's not always about them?" she said to Dr. Dunn. He smiled politely and held the door open as Mrs.

Carano shuffled by Dr. Swift and into the back. Dr. Dunn held up a hand and whispered, "Sorry," then he disappeared behind his patient.

"Time on task, Mr. Brewer," Dr. Swift said through a nasally voice.

Colin held up a finger. "Just one moment, doctor." He gently touched my elbow, and we moved a few steps to the side.

"Everything okay?" He wore a tweed sport coat over a blue, collared shirt and looked more like a literary professor—a handsome one at that. His pleasant nature was a welcome relief from the stressed-out text from Erin, not to mention the pursuit of a killer.

"I'm okay."

His eyes shifted to Dr. Swift, and then I realized he was probably referring to my mental health.

"Oh, nothing like that. More of a professional visit with Dr. Dunn than anything else."

His almond-shaped eyes sparkled off the overhead lights as he offered a curious grin.

Dr. Swift coughed into a handkerchief, then cleared his throat for a good ten seconds. Just as he ceased with the noise-making, Ashling blew a basketball-sized bubble, which burst once again across her face, even catching a bit of her hair this time.

I turned back to Colin, trying not to laugh. "Wow, this place has all kinds of entertainment." This time I was drawn to touch his elbow.

"Are you in a rush to rid Boston of every criminal on the loose?" he joked.

"Funny you mention that."

"Why?"

"Well, nothing for you to worry about. Right now, I need to go rescue my daughter."

"Erin okay?"

I held up my phone. "Well, from the latest text she sent me, she's a bit anxious. She supposedly just learned from her teacher today that she actually has to do a painting herself. And it needs to be in the same style as her project."

"Impressionism," Colin said with a smile. His teeth were white and straight, the opposite of Vince Tripuka's grill. Why I went there, I had no idea.

"I need to rush home, pick her up from school, and I guess we'll go to the art store and see what we can figure out."

"I don't think that's a wise move."

"I'm sorry, what?" Was he questioning my parenting skills? That came out of nowhere.

"This is my area of specialty, and I would love to help you guys out."

"Seriously? Don't you have important things to do?"

He smirked. "It's my passion. We all have one, right?"

"I guess so." I thought about my kids and Brad. I just couldn't include my FBI work in the passion department.

A sudden, guttural, throat-clearing sound almost caused me to jump out of my small heels. I turned and saw Dr. Swift blowing his nose.

"Ignore him," Colin whispered as Dr. Swift honked twice more.

I nodded.

He continued at a normal voice level. "I won't be long here. Why don't you and Erin meet me at my loft? I have a little paint studio there, and we can get right to work."

I debated the offer, then quickly realized it was the only legitimate chance Erin had to make this happen on short notice.

"I don't want to inconvenience you. You must let me pay you back."

"We can talk about that later." He patted his coat, then pulled out a pen and a business card and wrote on the back.

"This is my address," he said, handing me his card.

"Looks familiar."

"It's in the Leather District, you know, on the south side, right by South Station. It's really kind of cool. It's a nineteenth-century brick warehouse that has been refurbished into loft apartments. By the time you go pick up Erin, I'm sure I'll be home. Call me on my cell if you can't find me." He pointed at the number on his card.

"Okay," I said, my voice still apprehensive.

"Listen, this is fine. It will be fun. I'll order in some food, and we'll make sure Erin has the best painting in her class before we're done."

With a reassuring wink, he disappeared into the back. I could have sworn that Dr. Swift rolled his eyes as he closed the door. I quickly started typing a text response to Erin.

"You know he likes you, right?"

Lifting my eyes from the tiny screen, I saw Ashling chomping on her gum. Then she blew another bubble.

"You're talking to me?" I glanced around the room.

"You can pretend you don't notice it, but it's obvious to me. He thinks you're cute."

I could feel warmth under my hair at my neckline. Was I actually blushing? "It's just two adults talking in a friendly way, that's all. He's a very nice man, very kind."

As I typed in another couple of words, I could feel her stare, and I glanced up again. She popped an eyebrow. "I'm just saying he's digging your chili, that's all. What you do with it or him is your business. Although, if you ask me—"

I held up a hand. "I didn't ask your advice, Ashling. He's just a friend."

"Right." She smacked her gum a few more times, then sat back in her chair, propping her open book on her desk. I finished the text to Erin and then pocketed my phone. As I walked past Ashling's desk, I noticed the title of the book she was reading: *Friends With Benefits*.

I pushed Ashling's ridiculous notion aside and darted off to Salem.

Twenty-Five

Classical music played in the background as I sipped chardonnay from my wine glass, let it roll down the back of my throat, and exhaled. A moment of peace. While I'd been going nonstop for almost two days straight, staying awake on one caffeine fix after another, I relished the few minutes of calm. I strolled over to the corner of Colin's apartment, looking through floor-to-ceiling windows, and took in the Boston skyline just as the sun was setting behind a nearby downtown hotel. Through a sheen of thin clouds, I could make out the arc of a rainbow. It calmed my nerves that much more.

It only lasted a few seconds. Guilt plowed right through my plot of serenity, and all of the uncertainties about our two unsolved murder cases crammed my mind.

A giggle from Erin disrupted my thoughts. I backpedaled a step and looked across the expansive apartment. My daughter held a paintbrush in front of a canvas. A computer monitor was perched to the left. Colin was pointing at the monitor, then over to the canvas, where there were shades of blue smeared across it. She was actually having a blast learning about this stuff. It would have bored me to tears when I was a teen, both the subject matter as well as the activity. I was far too hyper to have the patience to sit in one spot and intricately create a painting from my imagination, or even from a picture.

I took another sip of wine and walked in their direction, passing a white leather sofa and a glass coffee table that had two picture books on top, one featuring colonial Boston and the other focused on French art. Go figure.

"Just tell your teacher…"

"Mrs. Harris," Erin said as I pulled up next to a steel pillar outside of Colin's makeshift studio.

"Right, Mrs. Harris. Make sure you tell her that you used a size 4 black hog brush filbert. She'll really think you know what you're talking about then. You never know, she might give you some extra credit for your knowledge."

"Cool," she said, then she tilted her head closer to Colin, her voice quieter. "Don't tell Mom, but even though we're just a couple weeks into the school year, I've got a C in this class. So anything I can do to bring my grade up would be totes."

Being positioned next to the pillar, I was apparently not visible from her vantage point.

"Erin, you have no worries. Combined with your research paper, and how you've already started this piece of work, I think your grade will be the envy of everyone in your class."

She squealed, which in itself shocked me. She seemed so happy to have Colin helping her. His knowledge and enthusiasm about art was infectious, and he was easy on the eyes. Well, easy on my thirty-nine-year-old eyes anyway.

"So for this cobalt-blue hue, I think it's best if we go with this size 8 round synthetic brush. That will help with the arc on the waves," Colin said.

As I continued my stroll around the apartment, I took out my phone and looked for updates from the team. Nothing. Silence on the text toy. I knew they all had their assignments and would report back the moment they came across anything important. It was rather apparent that Tripuka hadn't left any obvious smoking guns lying around, but that didn't mean there wasn't something right before our very eyes that we had yet to notice, or at least understand its significance to our case or the murdered girls. After our search of his apartment, our best hope rested on the hairs that were found. The DNA testing would take a minimum of five days. My mind had already started counting the hours, but I had this strange sensation that something would happen before we ever got the chance to read the results.

The doorbell rang.

"Hey, Alex, do you mind getting that? It's probably our Chinese food delivery," Colin called out.

"Sure thing." I set my wineglass on his concrete bar, then walked to my purse to retrieve some cash.

"By the way, I already paid for it with my credit card, so you can put up your wallet."

I turned around and heard him laugh. "How did you know I was—"

"Because I know you. If it's Chen, give him a good tip. He's trying to pay for college."

"Got it." I waltzed over to the large metal door and pulled it open.

A young guy with an acne problem was smiling while holding two plastic bags. "Where is Mr. Colin?"

"He's busy painting. I'm his friend. Are you Chen?"

"Yes ma'am. Mr. Colin is a good painter. I've seen some of his work."

I thought for a moment. I hadn't seen anything with his name on it hanging in the apartment.

"Here's the food. More than his usual," Chen said.

I took the bags and placed them on a table by the door.

"And if you could sign here." He handed me a credit card slip on a small clipboard along with a pen, but I couldn't see it very well. I tried angling the clipboard.

"Oh, sorry, let me help you." He grabbed the door frame and hopped his feet onto the other side, then shimmied up toward the ceiling, reaching for a recessed lightbulb just above the doorway in the hallway. He screwed it to the right, and just like that we had more light.

"Thanks," I said as he hopped down. "Are you sure it's okay if I sign his name?"

"Of course, his lady friends do this all the time."

I paused a second, caught off guard by his comment. But why should I be surprised? Colin was an educated, attractive, apparently well-off, single, straight man. Well, I couldn't vouch for the straight part, but Ashling's comment about his innocent flirtation had resonated a bit. Yeah...I knew he was as hetero as they got.

"Hold on a second." I ran over and stuck the small clipboard around the pillar with my eyes closed and asked Colin to sign his name.

"Oh, Alex, you could have signed it. You're such a fuddy duddy."

I ran back and handed Chen the clipboard. "Wow, thank you, Miss..."

"Ms. Troutt. Have a good night."

I shut the door and brought the bags of food over to the kitchen area. My stomach growled at the smell of kung pao, as well as lobster rangoon and wasabi and other spices I couldn't identify.

"Thanks, Alex," Colin said. "Give us a few more minutes, and then we might have something for you to look at."

I took the opportunity to check my phone one more time. The

screen was blank. I went ahead and set up a conference call and sent out the invite to the team for later tonight. I figured that would give them a few more hours to try to wrangle their contacts for more information, as well as let them have dinner in peace. Pocketing my phone, I picked up my glass of wine and continued walking around Colin's place, taking a closer eye at the creator of each painting that hung from the wall. While many of the artists' names were probably noteworthy, I didn't recognize a single one. And not a single painting by Colin.

An Asian-style room divider caught my attention. The three panels were positioned near the wall by the living area. I approached it and noticed the edge of a small canvas on the other side. I peered around the other side of the divider and found a number of paintings leaning against the wall. I glanced over at Colin and Erin, who were still focused on her school project. I'd really never seen Erin so engaged with another person who wasn't one of her teenage friends. She seemed to care enough to slow down and listen, take in the guidance of someone with immense knowledge about the subject of art—his passion, as he called it. He was an absolute savior, and I owed him big time.

My curiosity was piqued, so I crouched lower and looked closely at the first canvas in the pile. It was a painting of a field with a pond, with brilliant shades of green and cobalt blue. It was done in the Impressionist style and even had Colin's name on the bottom, signed C. Brewer.

I then pulled back the first painting to reveal the next one. I was taken aback, initially because of the style—it was painted with precise detail. It was a portrait of a woman, a very striking woman, with chestnut hair as shiny as a thoroughbred's coat. Sitting at a forty-five-degree angle, she revealed a sensuous amount of skin with an off-the-shoulder chiffon dress, an aqua blue that accentuated her radiant eyes. Her beauty was only outmatched by an aura of quiet confidence. This woman had substance. Kind of like Colin. I instantly wondered if she was a friend or nothing more than a picture from a book or magazine.

I flipped to the next canvas. Another portrait of a beautiful woman with Colin's signature in the lower right corner. She wore a reserved smile, as if she were in mid-conversation and someone had just told a witty joke. A simple, blue blouse opened to show a powder-blue camisole. The clothing style, along with her natural curls, gave her a youthful appearance. Her brown eyes were kind and unafraid.

On to the next one, where a woman wore a stunning, black-sequin dress that showed off nearly all of her taut back. Golden waves of hair draped over her shoulders, like trailing branches of a weeping willow. There was a small scar just under her left eye, the only flaw on a face with perfect bone structure. Her eyes looked like orange stars.

"You found my stash."

I flinched, nearly spilling my glass of wine. "Oh, Colin, you startled me."

"Sorry, didn't mean to scare you."

"I'm starving," I heard Erin say from the kitchen area, followed by her riffling through the Chinese food.

I moved to my feet and headed in that direction. Colin picked up the bottle of wine from the nearby bar area and held it up. "One more glass, just to ensure you stay relaxed for another hour?"

I held up my hand. "No thanks. While this has been nice, if I drink any more, I might end up face down on your couch."

He gave me a subtle wink. "We can't have that, can we?"

I quickly changed the topic and extended a hand to his paintings. "Your work is remarkable."

"Thank you, Alex. That really means a lot."

His response seemed overly effusive, especially considering my eye for artwork was contained to dozens of stick figure drawings by the kids to a single Thomas Kincade painting of Lombard Street in San Francisco. I recalled Mark saying over and over again that he planned on taking me there for one of our anniversaries. It never happened, but for whatever reason, I never took down the painting. Something about the lighting, the amazing view high atop the hill, mesmerized me. Somewhat like the women in Colin's paintings.

"These women are stunning, Colin. Are they models, or did you draw them from pictures?"

He chuckled just once while setting out cloth napkins for each of us. "They're just friends."

I waited for more information, but it never came. Perhaps they were relationships that had gone bad, and he didn't want to think about them. I could relate to keeping the past just where it belonged.

While I tried to peek at Erin's work, Colin insisted that we wait until after dinner, saying the vibe of the painting would change as it dried a bit. We gathered around his table, and each of us, including Erin, tried a little of all the dishes, including Peking duck and stir-fry vegetables.

"This is the best Chinese food I've ever had," she said as chow mein noodles hung off her lips. "Oops." She giggled while corralling the noodles with her chopsticks and stuffing them back into her mouth.

"China King has the best food in all of Chinatown, even though it's this tiny place with bright red walls."

"Red walls. What were they thinking?" Erin said.

Interesting to see Erin have an opinion about the décor. Maybe she had a knack for color and design after all. Probably not from her mother's side.

"About how to make the best Chinese food in the city," Colin joked.

As Colin cleaned up the dishes, the last of the sun fell out of sight, leaving the city lights to illuminate most of his apartment. "You've got a heck of a view."

"And I pay for it every month."

I wondered what Colin did for a living, to be able to afford this place, his high-end furnishings, all of the artwork. While his business card basically stated he was a jack-of-all-trades, it didn't relay his main source of income. I was interested, but not nosy, so I decided not to inquire further. It was his life and not for me to judge.

"And now for the unveiling," Colin said, waving his arms upward in a flourish as he headed toward his mini-studio. "Erin, would you like the honors?"

"Why thank you, Colin."

I couldn't help but laugh at how Erin played along.

She walked over and stood in front of the easel that held her painting, while I blocked my vision with my hand just to make sure I didn't sneak a peek. "Mom, while I know we had a few issues during our vacation back in your hometown of Port Isabel, hanging out at the beach made a big impression on me—the roar of the waves, the seagulls running on the shore. So, I give to you my painting. I call it 'Summer Vacay.'"

She stepped aside, and my jaw hit the floor. I glanced at Colin, who smiled and shrugged his shoulders. "The waves seem so real. I can practically feel the spray from the water. Erin, are you sure you painted this yourself, without any help from...?" I pointed at Colin.

"He was a big help," Erin said. "I didn't have a clue about where to start."

Colin put his arm around her. "But every stroke on that

canvas was hers. Erin has quite the flair. And I'm not just saying that."

She stuck her hands in her jeans pockets, shuffling her shoes against the concrete floor. "Thanks."

I checked the time on my phone and knew we had to get home. I wanted to say goodnight to Luke before he went to bed, and it was a school night for both kids. As we made our way to the door, I found myself still caught on the image of Colin with his arm around Erin, like a proud father almost. A stepdad? What was I thinking? If I cared for Brad, why did I go there with Colin? Was I still seeking a so-called normal relationship with someone whom I didn't have to worry about being mistaken for a son or younger brother?

It wasn't until I was behind the wheel heading north to Salem that two realizations hit me like a ton of bricks: I was so tired that my eyes burned from the inside out, and I'd been so wrapped up in Colin's world and Erin's project that I'd forgotten to text or call Brad. I was a bad girlfriend.

Twenty-Six

Fifteen years ago

Junior peered out the screen door in the kitchen, beads of sweat still clinging to his eyebrows as he admired his progress on the back fence. He'd spent the last six hours removing the old, rotted planks, pouring concrete, and setting the metal poles for the new fence he would start later in the afternoon. Using his T-shirt, he wiped his face clean, then sipped iced lemonade, one of his mother's signature recipes. It cooled his inner core. He opened the fridge and poured himself a second glass, then downed half of it in just a few seconds, appreciating the balance of citrus and sugar.

He heard voices from the front of the house. Mom's visitors were still lingering, no doubt talking about important subjects like last week's game of bridge or the latest gossip about who was screwing the milkman, although he'd never heard his mother use a foul word in his life.

He shuffled closer to the entrance of the dining room, but paused there, knowing Mom wouldn't be happy if he were to track his filth across the nice Persian rug. Still, though, he was curious, wondering what these women really spoke about when they thought they were in private.

He tiptoed by the oval table and glanced to his right, where a picture of him and his mom stood proudly on the buffet. He was young and was missing his four front teeth. But what he recalled most from that photo was right after it was taken, when all he wanted to do was run outside and play kickball with the boys down the street. But his mom wouldn't allow it. She said he had to continue to find ways to enhance all facets of his life, his knowledge of the world, and how he acted around others. She'd insisted that he study his Latin lessons for an hour, then practice the piano for another hour.

He pushed those early memories out of his frontal lobe and walked a few more steps through the dining room. Ice jingled against the side of his glass, and he stopped in his tracks. He'd forgotten he was carrying the beverage. He looked around for a place to set it down. But everything was an antique, and he couldn't ruin one of Mom's treasured pieces, so he was forced to stay put and simply turn his ear toward the living room, hoping he could hear the chatter.

"Dear God, if Bill asks me to…you-know-what one more time, I think I'm going to gag."

"Eww, Mary, do you have to be so crude? We are in our forties, you know. This isn't high school," his mother said. "Besides, it's all about mutual respect…and, of course, reciprocation." The ladies giggled.

"Reciprocation," Mary repeated. "That word might have too many syllables for my Bill. I might have to dumb it down for him. What do you think, Heather? You're the schoolteacher."

Junior leaned forward until he could see Heather's legs. With her skirt well above her knees, he was able to get the full picture of her endless, toned legs. He began to feel a new line of perspiration along his spine. Heather was not much older than he was and had that All-American athletic type of body. The fact that she was also a teacher turned him on even more.

But his mom would never allow such heresy...dating another woman from the neighborhood. And he knew he had a lot more on his mind than going to the movies and then grabbing a late-night dessert at the local diner. Things his mom had probably never heard of.

"Heather, is this conversation suddenly making you shy? You're the single one in the group. You should be leading us down the raunchy path, not the other way around," Mary hooted again.

"Ladies, might I remind you that my son is out back working," his mother said. "This is not the type of conversation he should be hearing."

He rolled his eyes, wondering again if his mother realized he was no longer a little kid.

"He's twenty-five years old, Doris," Heather said. "Do you know what most twenty-five-year-old young men are doing these days? I'll tell you. They're not outside in the heat of the summer replacing their momma's fence."

Junior saw Heather adjust her bra strap. His pants grew tighter.

"Oh my, Heather, are you—" Mary started to ask but didn't finish.

"Am I what?"

"Am I sensing that you'd like to pop Junior's cherry?" Mary howled with laughter, drowning out Mother and Heather. Junior should have been embarrassed, but her question went right along with his thoughts. He envisioned seeing Heather in a tight, pink cardigan sweater while preparing food in front of her kitchen window. Junior would march right across her yard, hop up two concrete steps, and then kick in the door. In seconds, he'd rip off her clothes and...

"Ladies, do I have to remind you that I'm his mother and I'm sitting right here? For the love of God." Mother, as usual, was the ultimate buzzkill.

The room became quiet, then Junior could hear a ring clink the side of a glass.

"Now, I'm very proud of my son. He's a handsome gentleman. I've worked hard for him to become the man he is today."

He rolled his eyes so far back in his head that he gave himself a headache. He took a quiet sip of his lemonade—the ice had melted—and glanced out the dining room window where shadows in the form of tree branches seemingly clawed at the neighbor's window. The sun had begun to dip in the sky, and he knew there wasn't much daylight left if he hoped to get the first few panels of the fence up. He scooted slowly backward through the dining room, keeping his noise pollution practically nonexistent.

"Mary, Heather, I think it's time you know why I've been so determined to ensure my boy was raised with the proper manners, a broad array of intellectual stimulation, and the kind of moral fiber that could only be compared to someone like Gandhi."

"Gandhi. Oh dear," Mary said, her voice tinged with doubt. "Doris, yes, please share. Frankly, we're dying to better understand your obsession in continuing to...uh, work on Junior."

Junior stopped moving. His mother had never really addressed this topic with him. He'd asked a few times as a kid why she drove him so hard, and she'd said one of two things: "because you have great potential" or "because I said so."

"Well..." His mother sounded stressed.

He could feel his heart pumping against his chest. He held his breath for a moment, eager—actually craving—to hear his mother's explanation for her decisions regarding his life.

Her voice dropped a half-octave and so did her volume. "I'm swearing both of you to secrecy. Promise?"

"Promise," the other two ladies said with a bit too much enthusiasm.

"My son is…not really my son."

Did he just hear what he thought he heard? His sights drifted across the dining room until they landed on that picture of him with his snaggletooth smile and his mom.

"What do you mean he's not your son? Whose son is he?" Mary asked.

"He's adopted."

"Adopted? But I've seen pictures of you holding him when he was barely the size of your two hands," Mary exclaimed.

"He was a preemie."

"And look what he's turned into now," Heather said with a provocative tone. But Junior didn't have the same blood surge as before. His mother's words were still pinging the outer edges of his mind.

"Don't mind Miss Horny Toad over there," Mary said. "How big was he, Doris?"

"Just four pounds, six ounces, if you can believe it." His mother chuckled. "He was just two days old. It was all very quick, and we only had a couple of hours to make the decision."

"Do you know anything about the parents?" Heather asked.

"That's the thing. We know why he was so small at birth. His mom was a heroin addict. She made her living as a whore."

He could hear a flutter of gasps as oxygen flooded his brain, his balance suddenly rocky. His thoughts turned inside out, as he tried to understand who he really was…who he was meant to be.

His breaths came out in shallow bursts, as a ball of anxiety formed in the pit of his gut. The more he thought about his real mom, the more his knot began to twist and turn, faster and faster, spinning wildly out of control like a tornado. He could feel a venomous rage take root in the eye of the inner storm, feeding off the frenzied emotions of inadequacy and abandonment. It grew like a cancerous growth, and there wasn't a damn thing he could do about it.

A moment passed, and his brain began to finally resume control, bringing him back to the dining room. His clothes were soaked with perspiration, his mouth so parched he could barely swallow. Using his shirt to wipe his face, he exhaled and stared at the same picture on the buffet. But he wasn't studying himself or his adopted mother, Doris.

A calm washed over his body, his mind now profoundly aware of his purpose on earth.

Twenty-Seven

I pulled out my earbuds and set the dangling wires on the kitchen bar. Wiping my eyes for a moment, I was tempted to lay my head down and fall asleep on my laptop keyboard. I didn't even have the energy to close the darn thing, let alone make my way upstairs to the bedroom.

"Are you finally off that darn call?"

I peeked through my fingers and saw Ezzy shuffling into the kitchen. She wore her pink robe and matching slippers that looked like she'd walked across the country in them. They were that old.

"I'm done, yes." My voice sounded like I'd smoked a pack of cigarettes in the last hour alone.

"I don't know why you do this to yourself, Dr. Alex. It's just insanity." Ezzy released an exhaustive breath as she filled up the coffeepot. No doubt, she was getting ready for the morning stampede.

Not thrilled with the lecture, I counted to three. My eyelids shut, and I came within a blink of falling asleep and out of the barstool. Damn, I was a hot mess.

"If you don't mind me saying, you're a hot mess."

I always suspected she could read minds. I released a sigh

that lasted at least ten seconds.

"I know, I know. I need to get to sleep. I'm just frustrated as hell that we haven't been able to find that first domino that will finally make sense of all this shit."

She arched an eyebrow on her way over to the cabinet, where she retrieved the dark roast coffee and measured out six scoops for the coffeemaker. "I'm sure you'll figure it out," she said.

"We're not making progress. Tripuka looked guilty as hell the day we chased him down, but now it's like he's made of steel. Nothing sticks."

"Maybe it's because you're so darn tired you have no hope of being able to piece the evidence together. Have you thought about that?"

"It crossed my mind, but I was too tired to give it any thought."

We stared blankly at each other, then broke out in laughter at the exact same moment. After a few seconds, Ezzy calmed back down, but I had moved on to the tear-laughing stage. "Oh my," I said, grabbing a napkin and dabbing my eyes. I took in another tired breath. "I need to make better decisions with my life, don't I?"

"You said it, so I don't need to repeat the obvious."

She shuffled to the other side of the kitchen. "This old lady is going to bed now. And you?"

"I just want to review these pictures that Terri sent over, and then I'm off to bed. In fact, in the morning you might want to make sure I'm alive if I'm still asleep past eight."

She smiled and waved over her head, mumbling something as she shuffled away.

I downed a full glass of water, the round of heartfelt laughter with Ezzy infusing my body with another dose of energy. My second wind.

I clicked on the zipped file that Terri had sent containing the photos from Tripuka's tablet. As the photos downloaded to my laptop, I almost chuckled at my ability to sugarcoat my own well-being. Second wind? Who was I kidding? I was probably on my seventh or eighth wind by now. And I knew the clock was ticking before invisible weights would pull my eyelids shut.

I opened the first file and looked at a picture of a small Santa Claus figurine. He had those rosy red cheeks, with a bagful of toys hoisted over his shoulder. On to the next jpeg. Another figurine, this one of three carolers dressed in suits with red or green vests and top hats. Reminded me of the Charles Dickens classics from the late 1800's. The attention to detail on the figurines was rather impressive—from their mustached faces to the texture on their vests. I knew a number of ladies in the neighborhood who took great pride in their collections, usually with a Christmas theme, but others branched out to other holidays, including Halloween, Thanksgiving, and even Easter.

I clicked through another twenty or so pictures of varying figurines, all of which were in the Christmas bucket: a Georgia-style home outlined with lights, a one-horse sleigh with kids in the back, ice skaters, and a few of Rudolph and his fellow reindeer.

"Hey, Mom."

I nearly choked on my own spit. "Hey, Erin. What are you doing up so late?"

"I fell asleep and dreamed that I forgot to turn in my art project essay." She opened the fridge and scoped out the options. A clip in the shape of a fat cat held her chestnut hair on top of her head. She had on an old T-shirt and plaid boxer shorts. "How can you forget to turn in homework, especially such a big project?"

She turned and gave me one of those "you got me" smiles. "Let's just say I don't want it to happen again. So I got out of bed and started reviewing my paper. I made a few changes, but nothing drastic. I felt better about it when I finished, so I guess that's a good thing, huh?"

"Sure is. Did you print it?"

"No, I was going to actually give Mrs. Harris my laptop. Hello...of course I printed it."

Teenage sarcasm. Her tone wasn't harsh, so I let it ride. I'd learned that counting to ten, or any other coping mechanism I could think of, had allowed Erin and me to coexist a little more peacefully. And that had led to a few mother-daughter moments that I cherished.

She pulled a can of Coke from the fridge and held it up to her cute face, almost like she was a product model.

"Uh...no."

"But Mom, I won't be able to go back to sleep anyway. I can study for next week's chemistry test."

I rubbed my ear, wondering if I had heard her correctly. "You're going to study for a test that's not until next week?"

"Yeah." She paused. "Well, I'll be online, listening to some tunes, maybe Skyping with Trish at the same time. But we study good together. We actually challenge each other."

"Nice try."

"Does that mean yes?"

I chuckled. "You're pretty relentless."

"Okay." She put the can back in the fridge and walked over to me.

"Speaking of sleep...I thought you'd be dead asleep by now."

"Just finishing up some work, and then I'm headed in that direction."

She perched her chin on my shoulder. I leaned my head against hers and then gently tapped her cheek.

"Thinking about starting one of those Christmas

collections?"

We were looking at a picture of three kids in a snowball fight. "Eh, maybe. But these pictures are related to a case I'm working."

"Right, the same one that has kept you working for over two days straight with no sleep."

I opened my mouth, ready to justify my actions. But what was the point?

"I guess so."

I clicked again and found the picture of one of those American Girl dolls. Erin giggled. She had always shied away from anything that was viewed as overly feminine, or too girly-girl, as she would say.

"You don't like that dress?"

"I don't like any dresses. But a pink dress with lace and white tights…you couldn't pay me enough to wear that." She crossed her arms and stuck out her hip.

"Someday," I said with a smile.

"Okay. Maybe someday far, far in the future."

"Like Star Wars. You do kind of remind me of that tomboy in that latest Star Wars movie. What's her name?"

She brought a hand to her face and snorted out a giggle. "First of all, Mom, Star Wars isn't set in the future. It's in the past. And her name is Rey."

I nodded. "You like her?"

"She's pretty cool, yeah."

Shifting my eyes back to the laptop, I pondered why Tripuka would have a picture of a doll, albeit one that probably cost north of two hundred bucks. I strummed my fingers on the granite counters. The figurines could have been for any female friend, but the doll made me think about girls…young girls.

My thoughts took me back to his conviction of statutory rape.

I recalled his recollection of his relationship with Susan Miller, and then the exact opposite perspective from her father. Both were convincing in their own right. While I couldn't necessarily accept Tripuka's take on his relationship with Susan, I'd yet to completely dismiss it. One thing I'd learned was not to be too quick to shut a door all the way. I couldn't be like that one figurine I'd just seen a picture of—a horse wearing blinders, which are designed to keep the animal focused straight ahead, ignoring any distractions. I needed to be just the opposite—open to all possibilities around me, so that I could find that sometimes-elusive connection between perpetrator and victim.

As a yawn escaped my lips, I clicked to the next image. I saw a picture of what looked like a gold medal from the Olympics—1984 in Los Angeles. It was probably a fake, but it looked authentic.

"Where did you get these pictures?" Erin asked while picking at her nails.

I stretched my arms and glanced out the kitchen window into the backyard. A quick flicker of light. Or was that a reflection from the corner street light?

"Uh…" I turned back to the laptop screen, wondering if Tripuka's criminal footprint also included theft, possibly related to selling imitations of real items in some type of online black market. The Dark Web. "Just the case I'm working on, sweetie."

Erin's nail-picking continued. I looked at her. "Is there something wrong?"

"No, no, everything's cool."

I went back to the screen.

A rumbling thud from outside.

I quickly turned toward the backyard, then jumped out of my seat to get a better view by prying open the blinds.

"What was that, Mom?"

I scanned the yard as well as our neighbor's, the Dunkleburgers, whose garage and driveway were on the left, bordered by a row of hedges. "I don't know."

"A dog maybe?" she suggested.

I glanced over my shoulder and saw her still picking at her nails. "That's a bad habit, Erin. I should know. What's got you all worked up?"

She didn't respond, but I could see her veins popping out around her temples. Did her eyes just glance at the computer screen?

I looked at the screen, then was drawn to take another glance into the backyard. A shadow flashed behind a tree.

"Erin, take my phone." I reached into my purse and held it out for her.

"I already have mine." She reached around to the small of her back and produced her phone. *Some folks hide guns; my daughter has a hidden place for her weapon of choice, a cell phone.*

"That's even better." I removed my Glock out of a side pocket, then reached over and pulled the blinds shut.

"Mother, what's going on?"

"I'm going to queue up a text." I typed: *call 911*

"If I tap the send button, you then need to call nine-one-one. Okay?"

"What the fuck, Mom?"

I ignored her language and took hold of her arm. "Erin, it will be okay. I'm going outside to make sure we don't have an unwanted visitor."

"But you could get hurt," she said as I marched across the kitchen to the back door, my pulse doing double-time. I reloaded my ammo and put a hand on the doorknob. "I'll be fine. Stay back from the windows and watch your phone. If you don't hear from me in ten minutes, get Ezzy and call nine-one-one."

"You're scaring me, Mom."

"You just haven't seen this side of me very often. Honey, I'm trained for this kind of situation. If anyone is out there, they probably aren't trained. I like my odds. Be alert, but don't panic. You good?"

She blew out a breath and held up her phone. "I'm good."

Twenty-Eight

As I swung the door open, I paused at the threshold and scanned the area, my eyes adjusting to the darkness. No one in sight, which wasn't surprising.

The Glock was at my waist, my fingers comforted by the familiar steel grip. A lazy breeze fluttered limbs on the higher part of the trees. Spindly shadows danced across the yard and the rooftop of the detached garage about forty feet in front of me. That garage was an easy hiding spot, and a dangerous one—too many nooks and crannies in which to hide. I'd get to it in due time. For now, I had to ensure the yard and surrounding area were clear.

I stepped out and shifted to my left, the changing angle slowly offering a different perspective of the yard, especially behind the large tree trunks. I quickly glanced at the Dunkleburger's property, my eyes focusing on the thick row of hedges standing about three feet high. Swinging my sights back to our yard, I crouched down until my hand reached the soft grass, a moist dew already settling on top. Now on my knees, I lowered my head to about six inches off the ground and then scanned the thinned-out lower area of the shrubs. I looked up and down the hedge. No sign of feet or legs. All clear.

As I pushed off the ground to lift to a standing position, my knuckle popped. I stopped breathing. I quickly scoured the yard, searching for any movement. Nothing except the shifting branches and now the soft tingle of an outdoor chime. A gust of air made my eyes water, and I realized I hadn't allowed myself to blink.

Releasing a quiet breath, I continued my search, taking each step as if I might step on a land mine. I walked the outer rim of the yard, making my way toward the back. Another breeze dropped a strand of hair in my face. For an early fall night in New England, the weather could be considered ideal for a late-night stroll or even just standing in a backyard to take in the crisp air. I was almost halfway around the perimeter and not even a squirrel had shown its face. Everyone was asleep...except those of us who had issues setting boundaries for work, apparently. I was beginning to wonder if my sleep deprivation might have created a hallucination when I'd looked through the blinds into the backyard.

I advanced three more steps and then stopped, my pulse thumping like a rabbit's foot. I was staring at the area on the other side of the garage where Luke had once again set up his make-believe world of an NFL football game. He would use anything he could find out of the garage as players, including the large plastic garbage containers. One was lying on its side right on top of the narrow sidewalk, with two trash bags sprawled just outside the rim. The plastic top was about fifteen away, next to a root of a tree.

I replayed the sound that had gotten my attention earlier when I was in the kitchen. It connected to the image before me—someone had knocked over one of the garbage bins.

Who was it? And were they still on the property? Another quick survey of the grounds and I came up empty. That left the garage.

With my Glock near eye level, I pulled my phone out of my front pocket and tapped until the flashlight cast a cone of light on the area around me. Moving around the garage toward the side door, I could see the soft yellow light seeping through the blinds in the kitchen. I'd given Erin a ten-minute window, and then she was to call the cops. I guessed that I'd used up a good six or seven minutes.

A high-pitched squeal just to my right caused me to swing my arms in that direction, my finger on the trigger. Two squirrels raced down a tree trunk, and I released a lungful of air. It appeared one of the critters was running for its life, away from the other one. They scampered across the grass and up another tree. More squeals, then they made three rotations around the tree as they ascended high into the branches.

Given the state of the trash container, I'd say our unwanted visitor wasn't nearly as agile as the squirrels.

I made my way to the southwest edge of the garage, the door just around the corner. I knew my phone's flashlight would give my presence away, but I had to risk it. I had no idea what was in there. I took in a breath, again wondering who this could be. Someone I knew, or just a nomadic stranger passing through town? Or maybe it was a kid from Erin's high school. I hoped not—for that kid's sake.

I turned the corner and found a closed door, just the way I'd left it when I got home earlier. I put the phone in my mouth and slowly twisted the knob. As expected, the door squeaked when it reached a foot ajar. I pushed it all the way open, the light picking up the front corner of my FBI-issued Impala. Dust danced in the beam of my flashlight. I didn't say a word, but scanned the space. Crap was everywhere. The garage had become our family dumping ground for anything and everything we didn't want in the house. Piles of old toys, metal cabinets, tools, lawn equipment. Elevated about ten feet off the floor was a ledge that ran along two walls. Most of that space was covered by bins and crates of Mark's old stuff. I couldn't stand having it in the house, but I also couldn't bring myself to give it away. So it remained at the edge of our existence—the garage. Luke could probably find about twenty places to hide in here.

I reached up and flipped on the overhead light.

Nothing happened.

Crap. Another lightbulb had blown. We probably had five dead lightbulbs in the house right now, including two in my bathroom. I walked down one side of the garage, constantly looking in between crevices of boxes and tall metal shelves for something human. I made my way around to the back end of the car—no sign of life, human or rodent. I wondered if this was a big waste of time. Who hid out in a garage after knocking over a trash bin? Wouldn't it make more sense for the perp to simply run away?

Gears cranked, and I literally jumped in the air, my heart stuck in my throat.

Behind me, the automatic garage door slowly began to rise, the noise cutting through the still air. I backpedaled to the opposite side of the car, waiting to see if the perp would slide out from underneath and try to escape through the garage door opening, which fed into the side street.

The door moved as slowly as a snail. Before it reached its apex, I cupped a hand against the car's window. No one was inside. I backed up near the wall, as close as possible given the mound of stuff in my way, trying to get a better angle to look under the car. Out of the corner of my eye, I saw a golf ball bounce out from the rear and roll down the driveway.

"What the…?"

Movement to my right. I jerked the light and my gun in that direction, just as someone raced out the side door.

"Stop!" I bolted out of my spot, but tripped over a hula hoop. I quickly regained my balance, but then my next step landed squarely on a skateboard.

"Shit!" I somehow stayed upright until the skateboard rolled to a stop against a giant blue bin. I jumped off and ran for the door. Just as I got there, I realized his likely path was to run around the garage, through the gate, and onto the side street. I could cut him off if I was quick enough. I pushed off my back foot and scooted around the car, glancing down to ensure I didn't step on any more toy traps. A few more toe steps and I was on the driveway. I jogged into the road where I could see the gate to our backyard. It was shut. And no one was running down the street.

The only other way out of the property was through my other neighbor's yard or...

The house!

Avoiding the death-pit garage, I raced to the side. Through the gate in a split-second, I hit full speed in ten strides and took the corner with my arms pumping.

A person straight ahead at forty feet. I jumped to a stop just as I brought up my gun. "Stop or I'll shoot."

The person stumbled into the one upright trash bin and fell to the ground. It was not a man. "Ezzy?"

She rolled over on the grass as I dropped to my knees. "What are you doing out here? Are you okay?"

"Yes, I'm fine," she said with a frustrated tone.

I took her by the elbow, but she jerked her arm away. "I said I'm fine. You did scare the shit out of me though."

"Sorry. What are you doing out here?"

"Looking for you, of course. Erin was worried. She woke me up."

Sirens echoed in the distance.

"Erin must have called the cops. You should have called them before you came outside on your own." She sat up, her arms on her knees.

"Ezzy, you of all people should know that I'm trained for this situation. Waiting wasn't going to help. And by the way, you could have gotten really hurt by coming outside."

"Erin was getting upset. She kept shouting that she thought you might have been attacked and were lying on the ground dying. So I came out looking for you."

I'd broken out in a sweat. I swiped my arm across my forehead, then looked across the yard. "I'm sorry, Ezzy. Sorry to have worried you and caused Erin to be upset."

She followed my gaze and looked toward the neighbor's yard. "I think I saw the bastard," she said.

"What?"

"Actually, I know I did. At first, though, I wondered if it was you."

"Tell me more."

"I came around the garage toward the gate, then I heard someone running across the yard, so I hustled back around. I didn't see anything at first. Then, out of nowhere, a man jumps up from the neighbor's driveway and takes off running. Then you hollered. It almost gave me a heart attack and I ran into the trash bin."

I knew she was on heart medication. "Is your ticker okay?"

She gave me a straight-lipped smile. "I'm not a china doll. Of course I'm okay."

I jumped to my feet and jogged over to the line of hedges. Usually manicured by Mr. Dunkleburger to perfection, I found a gaping hole at the top third of one bush.

Ezzy plodded over next to me. "You think he tripped while

trying to leap over the bushes?"

"That's the way it appears."

Dogs barked a few yards down. A quick rush of adrenaline, my mind consumed with catching this asshole. But then I thought about Erin inside the house.

I turned to Ezzy. "Can you describe the man you saw?"

She twisted her lips while tapping a finger to her chin. "Just had a little bit of light, maybe from the moon, I guess. I could only tell that it was a man. Or at least the person had a boxy shape like a man."

"Hair color or length?"

She shook her head. "Don't think it was very long. So it must have been a man."

"Did you see what he was wearing?"

"Pretty sure it was a long-sleeve shirt and pants. It was like I was looking at a silhouette."

I could hear cars screech to a stop out front. I took Ezzy by the arm and guided her toward the back door.

"One more thing, Alex. I know he wore athletic shoes. I could hear the rubber soles shuffling on the pavement."

"Good to know. Thanks."

Once inside, Erin buried her head in my arms. She didn't leave my side the entire time the police were there.

After telling Ezzy not to wake me in the morning, my head finally hit the pillow and I was out. It was just after four a.m.

It turned out to be nothing more than a long nap.

Twenty-Nine

$\mathbf{A}$ man with a beard that touched his chest quickly lifted a tray of steaming coffees over a gaggle of shorter women. They were talking so much they didn't notice. To avoid a collision, he bumped my shoulder, which spun me around, my cell phone at my ear. At the same time, a mother walked in with her son, who proceeded to break loose from her grip on his hand. He ran into me and kept my momentum going, allowing me to complete a full pirouette.

"You should try out for the Boston Ballet." Terri had a smirk on her face as she tried to wait patiently for her name to be called so she could grab our lattes.

"I think that's the first dance move I've ever completed in my life." I put the phone back to my ear.

"You don't know how to dance, do you, Alex?" Nick said on the other end of the line.

"I was always working on my tennis footwork." I heard a man yell out Terri's name. "If I don't gulp down my coffee the moment Terri gives it to me, I might just collapse."

"You're welcome," he said.

"Sorry if I didn't say thank you for pulling this together."

"As your partner, I used to bring your coffee to you. This

time, I arranged for *you* to be brought to your coffee."

Nick had come through in a huge way. He had not only located Susan Miller, the victim in Tripuka's statutory rape crime, but he'd also convinced her to talk to me and Terri during her first break this morning.

"Tell me, Nick, how did you persuade Susan to talk to us?"

"It wasn't that difficult. I mainly just told her that the only way more women will get hurt is if people stay quiet. And then I asked her if she still let her daddy control her life."

"You took the gamble that she wanted to be independent and make her own decisions. Nice."

"Let me know what you find out. Gretchen just got in, and she whispered to me that she's close to sharing some new data on Tripuka. Catch you later."

I shoved my phone in my purse just as Terri handed over my lifeline. I blew into the cup to try to cool it off, then I took my first sip. I repeated that routine about ten times, until I had my first full hit of caffeine.

We found a small table in the corner, and a few minutes later, a woman walked in our direction. After brief introductions, she pulled her red apron over her head and draped it across her chair before she sat down. She wore no makeup, and her hair was in a simple ponytail, but it was her plump cheeks that stood out most.

She took in a heavy breath before saying a word. "Agent Radowski told me I wouldn't have to testify, but you needed to ask me a few questions about…back then."

Terri spoke up. "We realize that the last thing you probably wanted to do was relive those memories. But it is important."

"It's Vince. He's in trouble again, huh?" Her hands were clasped on the table, but her thumbs were in constant movement.

"This much we can tell you. He's currently not in custody. He's actually out on probation right now, after being charged with a parole violation and attempted assault of a peace officer."

Susan's eyes went from Terri to me. "But if that was everything, you probably wouldn't be talking to me. Am I right?"

She might work at a coffee shop, but this girl was sharp.

"More than anything, we just need to know the real story about what happened eight years ago." I slurped another mouthful of coffee. Waited. She was thinking. I added, "I'm sure your experience was quite difficult, especially as a teenager."

"You have..." She brought a hand to her face and swallowed back some emotion. "You have no idea."

She pulled a napkin from its holder and dotted the corners of her eyes.

Not one for any type of warm-up, Terri placed a hand on the table and got right to it. "Did you have a relationship with Tripuka, or was he truly a predator?"

She sighed. "It's complicated. And with Vince, it was even more complicated."

"How so?" As Terri clasped her hands, I noticed her flawless manicure. Wearing another tailored suit that accentuated all the right curves, everything in the appearance department seemed easy for her. She was aggressive as hell, but she could somehow roll out of bed and still look like a million bucks. I, on the other hand, was sure I saw another "fine line" creeping out from the corner of my eye this morning. I needed a day at the spa....no, more like a month.

"I'm twenty-four now, so I see things a little bit differently than I did back then."

Terri nodded and finally let Susan think a bit more without throwing another fastball at her.

It paid off. Susan said, "Vince was charming. He knew what a sixteen-year-old girl wanted out of life. At least *this* sixteen-year-old." She pointed to herself.

I jumped in. "Did you actually have a relationship, or was it all about him?"

"We actually had a real relationship. Well, as real as you can get at sixteen. We both had that fascination with Star Wars. And he was actually pretty worldly. Well read, knew a lot about things outside of my little high school world. I found him very interesting. Sometimes we would stay up and talk on the phone until one or two in the morning."

Her eyes found a generic picture on the wall of a couple holding hands "Honestly, I think I would have called him my best friend. But I..."

She paused and scrunched up the napkin in her hand.

A few seconds passed, and I could see Terri open her mouth. I subtly touched her hand and closed my eyes for a brief second.

"I know what I did was wrong," Susan said, her eyes swelling with tears.

"What do you think you did wrong?' I asked.

"I turned my back on Vince just because my dad found out."

"I'm confused," Terri said, with one eye on me. "Earlier, you acted like this thing with Vince wasn't a normal relationship."

Susan took in a sniffled breath. "I'm not very good at communicating all the things in my head back then. And my heart. So many emotions, and then my parents came down on me so hard, especially my dad. He's a bit old school."

That wasn't entirely surprising to hear, but then again, I couldn't imagine the range of emotions I'd have if Erin got involved with a guy in his twenties. And then add sex on top of that. The mere thought made the coffee churn in my stomach.

"Are you saying your dad did influenced your story?"

"Yes."

Terri turned and looked at me with an expression of *now what?*

Shifting my eyes over to Susan, I made another attempt to better understand the events so many years earlier. "Can you help us with a few gaps?"

"Sure. That's why I'm here, right?"

I nodded just once. "You felt like Vince was a good friend, and you connected with him."

"Right."

"But then you had sex. And your dad caught you or maybe just heard about it."

"Caught Vince going out the window. It wasn't a pretty scene. Dad was trying to pull him back in, and Vince was trying to get away. He ended up jumping into a rose bush. He looked like he'd been in a cat fight when he finally crawled out of there." A brief smile washed over Susan, accentuating her cheeks, now a cherry red.

"And then your dad threatened to remove you from the family will, and that's when you altered your story to say that it was not consensual sex."

She hissed out a breath between her teeth. "Dad was such an ass. I was a bit of a rebel, but he made me think he wasn't *just* threatening to remove me from the will, but to excommunicate me from the family. I wouldn't be able to see my aunts, uncles, cousins, no one. And when he said Vince would go to prison regardless, I began to really feel alone. I kind of felt like I didn't have much of a choice. Accept his conditions or be exiled forever. And when you're sixteen, a week can seem like forever."

"Where does the complicated part come into play?" Terri asked, strumming her fingers along the side of her cup of latte.

"I did a lot of soul searching after that. Wondering about who I was, why a guy that much older than me would want to hang out with me, find me interesting. And—"

"Is it true that you also dated a twenty-seven-year-old before

Vince?"

Terri was having a difficult time letting the game come to her. Much more, and I was going to have to ask her to chill.

Susan turned her head, then held up a finger. "You talked to Vince, didn't you?"

Terri didn't respond.

"Okay. Yeah, Ray and I 'dated,' if that's what you want to call it."

"I'm just saying, I'm not sure I understand the dynamics of your relationship with Vince, you know, with being swept off your feet, if you'd already gone down that road with another older guy."

"I get your question. To tell you succinctly, it was purely physical. I was at a college party, and this guy gave me the eye. Then I overheard two other guys talking about using this powder to put in this girl's drink. I stole it from them and used it on the dreamy guy, Ray."

"So you drugged him so you could have sex with him?"

"I was a virgin, and I wanted my cherry popped in the worst way. He was the hottest guy I'd ever laid eyes on. But it was a one-night thing. Nothing more."

There was a moment of awkward silence at the table. "I'm assuming your dad never knew."

"He would have killed that guy and then disowned me," she said without hesitation. The mom-son combination from before walked by. The kid bumped my shoulder and then Susan's arm. We didn't say anything as he took off again and the mother chased him down.

Susan's eyes shifted between Terri and me. "You both think I was a teenage slut, don't you? And once a slut, always a slut. Isn't that what everyone thinks?"

Terri jumped in before I could respond. "It's not that, Susan.

We're women. Both Alex and I understand there is a double standard that exists in society. If a boy had done what you did, he'd be a legend with his friends."

"Absolutely," I said. "But—"

"Thanks for understanding. I'm not ashamed of any part of my life. I didn't always make the best decisions, but it helped make me who I am today. Flawed, yes, but a little more mature and maybe a little wiser too."

I smiled, and then continued. "But as we look at all the evidence, including this new information, we're trying to draw some conclusions about Tripuka. It's not black and white, I get it."

She chewed at the inside of her cheek. "I remember talking to Vince about how magical I thought Christmas was, but that at our house, Dad was such an old-fashioned curmudgeon it was usually such a downer. Dad would make us sit around, hold hands, and chant some kind of religious crap over and over again. He basically made me feel guilty for getting excited about receiving gifts for Christmas."

A quick image of my mom flashed through my mind. A half-decorated Christmas tree in the corner of the room and Mom sitting on the hearth while she held a cross and chanted Bible verses. I was watching her from the edge of the room until Dad came up and touched my back. Mom saw us and then she called us over. I had to sit there and try to recount her sayings, but they all seemed so negative, and I got this feeling that I was such a bad person.

Terri nudged my arm. "Alex, are you lost in Christmas memories?"

"Uh, just thinking everything through," I said, trying to refocus my thoughts back to Susan's comment. "What made you think about Christmas and your dad?"

"It was Vince."

"What about him?"

"He got me this Christmas figurine. Two happy snowmen dressed up in red and white, ice- skating across an outdoor rink." A smile came over her face. "I thought it was the sweetest thing."

"You guys were really pretty close, then. I guess it made it that much harder to not defend him when you talked to the police."

She nodded, but her cheek sucked inward. "There's something I haven't told anyone before."

Terri inched up in her seat. "Yes, Susan?"

Her eyes drifted away from the table.

"Susan, we're not here to judge you. We told you that earlier," Terri said with urgency in her voice.

A quick shake of her head. "I don't know why I've allowed myself to carry this burden around for so long. I guess I thought it was all meant to be. I justified it."

"Justified what?"

"My decision to rat out Vince. It really had nothing to do with Dad's threats. Not the promise of money or him separating me from the family. I was young, naïve, and idealistic. I didn't really care about any of that crap."

"Then what was your reasoning?" I asked, the cobwebs in my brain suddenly clearing.

Her big, round eyes looked straight into mine. "My best friend…my only real girlfriend, Penny. Vince slept with her."

Terri narrowed her eyes. "You're saying that all these years you never told anyone?"

"No one that mattered. Penny and I had a discussion about her…behavior. I felt so betrayed. It was the last time I ever talked to her."

She wiped a tear from the corner of her eye.

My thoughts suddenly shifted in another direction. "And what about Tripuka? Was he aware that you knew?"

"Hell yes. We had it out at the park. He gave me this bullshit that he thought we were over and that Penny was there to be a friend and comfort him."

It sounded like a typical response from someone who was digging his way out of a bald-faced lie. But I was more interested in getting a read on Tripuka's underlying pattern of behavior.

"Vince never told anyone about Penny?" I asked.

"Of course not. He knew he already had one statutory rape count to deal with. And while it was consensual, a second one wouldn't look good."

"How old was Penny?" Terri asked.

"Fifteen."

Both of Terri's palms smacked the table. "Fifteen? Did Tripuka know how young she was?"

"Of course he did. So while I definitely wanted him to pay for cheating on me, I've had a lot of time to think since then, and grow up. And a few years ago, I came to a final conclusion."

"What's that, Susan?" I asked.

"Despite how he treated me, talked to me, gave me gifts…he was, plain and simple, one thing—a child predator."

Terri's phone rang, but she didn't immediately reach for her purse. I broke the three-way stare-down and saw her eyes almost in a catatonic daze. I nudged her arm.

"It's Jackson," she said as she looked at the phone screen. She quickly lifted from her chair and walked toward a corner with fewer people, leaving Susan and me alone.

"How have you kept this inside all these years?"

"It hasn't been easy. I feel like I've been to hell and back." She stopped talking, her eyes staring into nothing. I could only imagine her mind reliving the torment she'd apparently felt. "So many raw emotions, especially when everything blew up." She wiped her hand across her face, clearing a few wayward tears. "As time passed, and all the anger and hurt finally faded away, I started to listen to my inner self." She patted her chest.

"You did some soul searching. Traumatic events can bring out the best or worst in people. Sounds like you got the better of it. That's pretty cool."

"On one hand it is, but I heard a few months ago that Vince had gotten out of prison, and for some reason, I felt guilty for not opening up and telling everyone about him and Penny and my suspicions of him being a child predator."

"Guilt is a debilitating condition. I highly recommend avoiding it. Take action, deal with it, or wipe it from your brain."

Her lips cracked a brief grin. "Sounds like you have experience."

I could see Terri walking up. "Life doesn't offer free gifts, but it's how we respond that ultimately decides our happiness."

"Thank you. I'll remember that."

"Alex, we gotta run," Terri said, grabbing her purse.

Her direct tone matched her rigid facial expression. "What's up?" I asked, grabbing my coffee and standing.

She gave me a cold stare. Without her saying a word, I knew that look: there had been another murder.

Thirty

A distinct smell of Chinese food invaded my senses, distracting my attention from the series of disturbing images attached to the whiteboard.

I turned and saw a twenty-something kid in a white shirt and tie shoveling in some type of noodles while walking over to Gretchen at the main conference table in the FBI war room.

"Who's he?" I asked Nick, who was hobbling up on just one of his crutches. I assumed just using one crutch was his way of convincing himself he'd made significant progress in his recovery from his sprained ankle. He grunted with each pained step. When he finally finished his twenty-foot hike, he huffed out a breath and looked for something to anchor his weight. I moved over, and he took hold of my shoulder.

"Thanks."

"No problem. Isn't that what partners are for?"

He gave a straight-lipped smile, but didn't respond. That was code for only one thing: he thought I was cheating on him by partnering with Terri on this crazy "eye killer" case. He'd basically said as much when I was forced to work with a CIA operative named Archie a few months earlier. Nick was a funny guy, but if my husband had been half as loyal as Nick, he might be alive and I might still have my family intact.

"That's Brandon. He's another SOS, on the same team with Gretchen."

"She's been heads down pounding that keyboard like it's nobody's business. Is he working with her?"

"I think so. But I also think he's kind of got a thing for her," Nick said with a wink as both of us peered over at the unlikely couple. Standing at least six-three, Brandon was all arms and legs. His belt was so cinched that it looped around to his back. Meanwhile, Gretchen's tiny feet couldn't reach the floor when she sat in a chair. But it wasn't their polar-opposite body types that stood out most. It was their age difference.

"Gretchen couldn't rope in Brad, so now she goes even younger, and dopier," Nick said. "I might be gay, but I still don't get women."

Almost instantly, my neck grew stiff. I tried stretching it both ways. I tried too hard.

"What's wrong?" Nick asked, looking at my face as I kneaded my neck.

"I think I just got the mother of all cricks."

"Is that some type of cougar joke? Mother...?" he said with a wry smile.

Just when I thought I was finally comfortable with the age gap between me and Brad, Nick shot off his mouth.

"Gretchen is lonely, I think. Maybe she and Brandon actually have that special connection."

"Are you serious? The Alex I know would have hit me with a raunchy joke."

"Let's just focus on the case."

He gave me an odd look, and then we both turned to stare at the gruesome images from the crime scene along the rocky, tree-lined shore of the Mystic River, the second in the last three days.

While the similarities between this homicide and Emma Katic's murder were eerily similar—a single gunshot wound in her forehead, and her eyeballs cut out—there was one noticeable difference: I knew this victim.

The victim was Candy, the hooker Terri and I had questioned the other night from the back of our car.

"Do we have her estimated time of death yet?"

"No, but I did just get her bio information. Full name is Candace Sandberg. She was twenty-seven."

I shook my head as the door to the war room popped open. In the background, Jerry, my SSA, gave me and Nick a wave. That was his signal for handing off the visitors walking toward us—Terri and Lieutenant Jackson from the Somerville Police Department.

After it was confirmed this morning that Candy's eyes had been surgically removed like the other two victims, Jerry had made a few phone calls. The FBI would no longer play second chair to the Somerville Police Department. We were officially in charge, yet I knew we needed their help, particularly my spirited counterpart, Terri. Perhaps as a career-saving move, Jackson pushed to be included in our war-room session. I was less than enthusiastic, but Jerry had said it was required to maintain an ongoing working relationship with Somerville and other local police departments who might hear about the FBI's enhanced role.

"Any updates?" Terri asked, pulling up next to Nick.

"Not really. Nick verified her full name and age," I said. "She was only twenty-seven."

Terri shook her head. "Twenty-seven going on forty-seven. She'd lived a hard life."

Jackson wiped his big mitt across his rubbery face, then locked his arms across his chest. He just stared at the photos, not uttering a word.

"She was sitting in the back of my car, dammit," Terri said, further examining the photos.

"And we offered to help her, remember?" I reminded her, though I didn't feel any better than she did about Candy's death. "Unless we lock up every girl walking the streets, no questions asked, then they're basically signing up to play Russian roulette with all the perverts out there."

Terri raked her fingers through her thick, long hair. "With Candy's death, I'll bet there's going to be an abrupt exodus of girls walking the streets, at least in the short term."

"Numbers will be lower, that's for certain," I said. "But there are too many strung-out, desperate girls for the entire lot to disappear. And with the eye killer striking twice in the last few days, it means we're dealing with a guy who is completely unhinged."

Nick plucked a photo off the board, the one that showed the bullet entrance wound in her forehead. "I keep wondering if it's the same guy. Ten years is a long time to wait. Plus, the cause of death is so different. Yet we know the surgical removal of the eyes is not exactly a well-practiced skill."

"Can't rule out a copycat killer, albeit one with a great deal of skill or practice."

A few seconds of silence. While we'd tossed around the idea of the killer being a surgeon, current or former, a new thought pinged my mind: what if this mysterious person was someone who cut on people once they'd died—a medical examiner?

"We did bring some data about Candy," Terri said. "Time of death, based on rigor mortis, was estimated by the ME at between ten p.m. and midnight."

"About the same time as Emma. Nick, do you remember the time of death for our cold-case vic?"

"It's on my laptop. Let me go check." He put the picture back under the magnet on the whiteboard and turned to hobble off, but Jackson's enormous body was in the way. He didn't even seem to notice Nick, his eyes fixated on the death images.

"We need to bring in Tripuka. And I mean now," Jackson said. "This crazy, fucking thing should have never happened. We had him locked up. This death is on us!" he barked, his legs shuffling like he had to use the bathroom.

Terri and I locked eyes. Jackson was her boss, but he was on FBI turf.

"Lieutenant, no one feels worse about Candy's death than Terri does. But we can't create evidence out of thin air."

He kept his sights looking straight ahead and scratched his leathery skin. It sounded as if he was buffing an old saddle. "Now that we know the estimated time of death, we need to find out Tripuka's whereabouts during that window."

"Tripuka didn't have a phone when he was released yesterday," Terri said, her eyes shifting to Jackson for a quick moment.

"I'll put in a call to his lawyer," Nick said.

"And I'll call Miss Lucille," I said, pulling my phone out of my pocket. "I've been wanting to drop by her place one more time anyway." I tapped the screen a couple of times, then paused a moment before I dialed her number. "One thing I need to share with everyone, just to be transparent. It's about last night."

I gave the group a brief rundown of the incident with the man in my backyard.

"And your nanny couldn't say if it was Tripuka?" Jackson asked, a balled-up fist buried into the palm of his opposite hand.

"Lighting was poor. She's rather certain the intruder was male and wore athletic shoes."

Nick hobbled a step closer. "What does your gut tell you,

Alex? Was it Tripuka?"

All eyes were on me. "Honestly, something about Tripuka doesn't sit right. And it mainly has to do with what Terri and I learned this morning from Susan Miller. She wasn't the only underage girl he targeted."

Terri jumped in and provided the detail on Susan's friend hooking up with Tripuka, and Susan's belief that he was a child predator.

"I guess it's possible for people like that to be rehabilitated," Nick said. "But even if he's still a predator, how does that jive with a serial killer with a fetish for cutting out his victim's eyes?"

"Precisely. My exact thoughts ever since we left the coffee shop," I said.

"Tripuka's our guy. I can feel it in my old bones," Jackson said.

For obvious reasons, Jackson's comment immediately lessened my belief that Tripuka could be the eye killer. "He might be, might not be. I'm sure I don't have to remind everyone that we need proof." I looked at Nick. "Let's start by seeing if he has an alibi for last night. But we need the DNA analysis on the hair completed. If that comes back with a high probability of being Emma's hair, we have enough to arrest him again and get him off the streets."

Nick brushed by Jackson's shoulder as he tottered back to the table.

"One more thing, Nick. Have Gretchen run a check on recently fired MEs or coroners in the area. Actually, go back ten years."

He swung his head around, and his crutch caught the leg of a chair. He started to fall, but quickly caught himself on the arm of the chair, then twisted his body into the seat, almost as if it were a planned dismount. He was huffing and puffing.

"Smooth," I said.

He let his crutch crash to the floor. "Where's Brad when you need him?"

With the mention of Brad's name, I felt my heart skip a beat. Nick splayed his arms, and for a moment I wondered if his question was something more than rhetorical. I was just about to conjure up a response when he continued. "I'll figure something out here with Gretchen." As he turned to talk to her, I could see her nodding, but her fingers never slowed down. She took multitasking to a whole new level.

I stepped to the side and called Miss Lucille, while Terri told Nick she would go ahead and call Wise Ass herself. Miss Lucille almost sounded happy to hear my voice. When I asked if Tripuka had come back to his apartment since he was released yesterday, she said she didn't believe so. I then told her I needed to swing by, and she welcomed my visit.

I pocketed my phone and turned back to the whiteboard. Terri was doing the same, and Jackson stood in the middle of the room as if he were the main cog in our investigation. Unfortunately, I viewed him as more of a wayward wrench on the verge of derailing the investigation completely.

"His lawyer—Wise Ass—did he give you anything?" I asked Terri.

"You kidding? He just used it as another opportunity to remind me that we're harassing his client with no proof. And he said if I continue to... How did he say it?" She grabbed the bridge of her nose for a brief moment. "Ah, I remember. If we continue to treat Vince Tripuka like he's John Wayne Gacy, then he will not only file a lawsuit against the Somerville Police Department and FBI, but he will then solicit every interview he can across the media and start naming the main harassers. He then said my name and yours." Terri pointed at me.

"He's nothing but an ass hat."

Terri snorted out a chuckle as Jackson just stood in silence, brooding like a little kid. Well, a little kid whose nickname could have been "manster."

I felt another headache coming on, most likely a combination of three hours of sleep over three nights and a complete lack of replenishment from anything remotely healthy.

"You don't look good," Terri said, her strained expression almost making her look unattractive. And that was saying something...about her and me.

"You know how much women love hearing that," I said, rubbing the area under my eyes, then taking a glance at my outfit. I must have been a walking zombie when I'd gotten dressed earlier. What was I thinking? A lime-green shirt to go with my blue blazer and khakis?

"But it's woman to woman, so it's not as bad," Terri said.

I shifted my eyes upward and saw Jackson still scratching and staring. He had to know that he was the elephant in the room, in more ways than one.

Motioning for Terri to follow me, I walked over to the main table and picked up my purse. "We're heading over to Miss Lucille's house. See if we missed anything."

"You think you can find a piece of evidence that an entire CSI team might have overlooked?" The gangly friend of Gretchen's had a big smile on his face as he munched on his Chinese noodles while sitting on the edge of the table. "Dude, what a dis!"

I glanced at Terri, Nick, and then Gretchen, whose hands stopped moving as she turned a nice shade of pink.

"Dude," I said, trying mightily to not roll my eyes. "Barney, is it?"

"Brandon." He squirmed to his feet. "I, uh, you know, was

just wondering about your strategy and all."

"Here's my strategy: chase every lead we can possibly come up with as fast as we can. And then double-check to make sure we didn't miss anything. It's called being thorough. If you want to be part of the solution and not the problem, you'll help Nick and Gretchen here with anything they need."

He looked down at Gretchen, let a grin sneak out, then he brought himself to attention, sticking out his scrawny chest. "Yes ma'am."

"I'm not your principal. Don't use that term, please. Just be professional and helpful."

I threw my purse over my shoulder and gave Terri a nod of my head, indicating it was time for us to leave.

"Hey," Nick said without looking up from his computer. "For starters, our cold-case vic, Gloria Lopez, had an estimated time of death at the exact window, ten p.m. to midnight."

"Thanks, Nick. Feel free to call or shoot a text if you or Gretchen find anything else."

"You know me. I'm not bashful, especially when I find something," Gretchen said.

"Great. No pressure, but we've got to have something, and quickly," I said, turning to head toward the door.

"By the way," Nick said. "I've got a bunch of those protein smoothies in the breakroom fridge. You're welcome to take one."

"Thanks." I grabbed two on the way out.

Thirty-One

Chugging the last of a strawberry smoothie, I maintained an even gaze over the back third of Miss Lucille's property, the garage apartment dead center of my focus. A gust of wind blew a lock of hair in my face, but I let it dangle for a moment as my eyes studied the façade and the stairs leading up to Tripuka's residence. I could already feel a surge of organic energy pumping blood through my system—a very different feeling than one propelled by caffeine.

I could hear the distant chatter of Terri and Miss Lucille, mainly Miss Lucille going on about something. And then a high-pitched yelp. I knew that bark to be Harry, her Yorkshire terrier. And it was quickly moving closer.

Flipping my head around, I first saw a squirrel zigging and zagging as it scampered right between my legs, heading toward the big oak in the backyard. A split second later, Harry took the corner at the front of the house so fast his back paws fishtailed on the driveway, but his legs didn't stop, and he barreled across the flat pavement and into the backyard. It was a race to the tree.

"Harry, you little shit. If you don't leave that poor animal alone, then you get no treat tonight. Do you hear me?" Miss Lucille said, her arms flailing above her head as she clipped forward in tiny steps on a pair of flats. Terri was alongside her, clearly disinterested in the dog-squirrel chasing game.

As the two ladies pulled up next to me, the squirrel started his ascent up the tree, but Harry refused to stop. He pumped his little legs as hard as he could and scurried up the trunk, taking a snip at the squirrel's tail just before gravity got the best of him. He tumbled into the grass and then quickly got back on all fours and restarted his barking barrage.

"Harry, Harry, you're embarrassing me," Miss Lucille said, waddling over to the dog's location and scooping him up in her arms.

Terri rolled her eyes as Miss Lucille scolded Harry as if he were a child. "Now that I have him under control, I can finally have an adult conversation," she said with a slight giggle. I'd bet she knew her interaction with the dog was a bit over the top, but that didn't mean she didn't enjoy the entertainment.

"You told me on the phone that you haven't seen Tripuka since he was released yesterday?"

"That's right."

"How about his red truck?"

"Well…"

"Oh," Terri interrupted. "Forgot to mention that, as of earlier this morning, Tripuka had yet to claim his truck."

I nodded and realized Harry hadn't barked since he was rebuked by his master.

Miss Lucille scratched just behind Harry's ear. "I forgot to ask, does this mean that Vince is innocent of those horrible crimes?"

"Not necessarily," Terri said. "We're still in evidence-gathering mode."

Miss Lucille nodded and then toyed with a gold hoop earring as she stared at the dog. A moment passed. "I guess that's why you called me up and wanted to come over."

"Yes, I'd like to take another look inside his apartment," I said. "You also said you had something you wanted to share."

"It's something that's kind of been tugging at me ever since all of those police and FBI cars showed up and did that search on Vince's apartment." Harry suddenly squirmed. "Oh, jumping junipers..." She nearly dropped him, but was able to keep her arm on him long enough to set him gently on the ground. "Go do your business, now."

The little furball trotted toward the pavement.

"Does he have some kind of treasure he likes to find in the yard?" Terri asked.

"It's not quite that...cute," she said, her nose wrinkling.

I turned and watched the dog slow down near the garage door, his wet nose sniffing the ground.

"Something inside the garage?" I asked, starting to move in that direction. As I shuffled closer, I began to wonder what was behind the double garage doors, the area directly underneath Tripuka's apartment.

"Just a bunch of old junk, including Arthur's old car—a baby-blue Ford Fairlane. They don't make them like that anymore."

"When's the last time you've been in the garage?"

"I can't recall. A while, I suppose. I used to try to do some gardening, but my old knees can't take that kind of bending and twisting. And with a few extra pounds on me, it takes a crane to get me back on my feet," she said with a giggle.

I found the handle and tugged, nearly pulling a muscle in my back. The door didn't budge an inch.

"That door typically gets stuck," Miss Lucille said, padding up next to me. "I think the foundation moves a bit during the seasons. But you can walk around to the other side and see if the padlock is still on the side door. Frankly, I can't recall seeing it there or not."

I walked parallel to the garage, my eyes drawn to where the door met the frame. They appeared to fit right against each other. Seemed like Miss Lucille knew what she was talking about.

"Look out!" Terri yelled.

I stopped in my tracks and looked straight down.

"Harry!" Miss Lucille shook her head. "Do you really have no self-respect? My God, dog."

The little shit was doing just that a few inches from my shoes. He looked up at me, and I could have sworn I saw a grin under that snout.

"I'm so sorry. This is very odd... I guess you'd call it his fetish. Whenever I used to let him out at night and the spotlight was on here at the garage, he would like to do his business right in the middle of the beam of light."

Acting as if my feet practically were cast in concrete, I looked over at Terri, who was rolling her eyes again.

"Would you mind running over to the back porch and grabbing my pooper scooper?" Miss Lucille turned to Terri as she said this. Terri looked at me. I shrugged my shoulders, and she shrugged hers, then she jogged over to the porch.

"Are you talking about this small trowel?" Terri held it up.

"That and the brown bag next to it, sweetie."

Terri brought it over and handed it to Miss Lucille just as Harry stepped away.

"One of his parents must have been a St. Bernard," Terri said, her eyes as big as saucers. "By the way, Alex, you're not standing on a land mine. You can move now."

"Thanks for the guidance." I took a few careful steps backward. "I guess I'm more used to a cat. They contain everything to a box."

As Miss Lucille lingered near the poop, maybe wondering if we would help her scoop up the heap of mess, I glanced up at the lightbulb, which was partially covered by an antiquated, glass light fixture.

"Did you ever get this light fixed, Miss Lucille?"

"I knew it would take a ladder, and I'm not strong enough to drag that out. Vince used to do a few things like that to help me around here. But now I guess I'm on my own."

She gave me a pitiful smile.

"Let me do that for you," I said as I took the trowel from her.

I wasn't just being nice. I had an ulterior motive. I finished the job and handed the bag to Terri to toss into the trash can at the far corner of the garage.

"Terri, give me a boost, will you?"

"For what?"

"I want to check something. I'm curious. Just hold out your hands."

"Okay, I guess, since you're shorter." She gave me a wink and lowered her center of gravity. "Just don't step where Harry did his business."

"Roger that." I put one foot into her interlocked fingers and pushed my body up while using the garage door to maintain my balance.

"Okay, hold it for just a couple of seconds." Up close, the light didn't look blown. I wrapped my fingers around the bulb. It felt loose. I turned it clockwise, and it rotated at least a full turn.

"I'm good."

Terri let me drop to the ground. I patted her on the shoulder. "Thanks, partner."

"Don't let Nick hear you say that," she said with a raised eyebrow.

"Just a figure of speech."

I turned to Miss Lucille. "Does this light only come on when it gets dark?"

"Well, I do have a switch just inside the porch." She smiled and looked at Terri again.

"No problem, I'll go flip the switch. After all, I made detective so I could become an errand girl," she muttered as she jogged back over to the porch. She opened the door, leaned inside, and moved her arm upward.

The light popped on.

A moment later, she had jogged back my way, pointing at the light. "How did you know?"

"I didn't. But I've seen it done recently. And I just wondered…"

"Do you know what this means?" she asked.

"What? What does that mean?" Miss Lucille bounced her focus between Terri and me.

"There's a good chance that Vince purposely unscrewed the bulb so that you couldn't determine if he was home or not the night that Emma Katic was murdered."

"Oh…" She brought a hand to her open mouth. After a couple of deep breaths, she began to shake her head. "That no good sonofa—" She closed her lips and put a hand over them. Another deep breath. "A real lady can't speak that way."

"This isn't a smoking gun, but the scale is definitely leaning in that direction, don't you think?" Terri asked me.

"Possibly. I'm still not sold. We really need to get the DNA results back on the hair found in Vince's apartment."

Miss Lucille cleared her throat.

I turned to looked at her. "Yes?"

She glanced down, her eyes following a sniffing Harry around the driveway. "I've been a bit stressed since you brought all those technicians over and picked apart Vince's apartment."

"Why were you stressed?" Terri asked.

That sounded a bit harsh, so I added, "Beyond the normal stress of having your property searched to determine if you had a killer living here."

She gave me a half-smile, her lips still moving as if she were trying to determine what to say. "I've been meaning to tell you that…"

Another distracting glance at the dog, who for once, wasn't doing anything wrong.

"Yes?"

"Well, I recently had a few things go missing from the house. And, you know, I just didn't know who could have taken them. I have a cleaning lady who comes in once a week, but I've known Dawn for fifteen years. She couldn't tell a lie if it was the key to her winning the lottery."

"You thought Tripuka broke into your house and stole your things?"

"I suspected it, yes."

"Did you do anything about it?"

She closed her eyes briefly. "I'm not proud of myself, but I waited until Vince left for work about a week ago, and used my extra key to get into his apartment and search for my stuff."

Terri gave me a quick look, then turned back to Miss Lucille. "Did you find anything?"

"I searched everywhere, but no. I didn't find even one of my missing items. On the one hand, I was relieved, but on the other, I was even more stressed wondering who could have taken my things. And then I thought maybe I'd just misplaced them."

I watched Harry sniff around my shoes, hoping he wouldn't hike his leg, then I said to Terri, "The hair evidence. It could be hers."

She nodded.

Miss Lucille put a hand to her chest. "Did I mess up? Oh, I think I did. I'm so sorry."

"It's not your fault. You were just doing what you thought was right, to protect your home," I said.

"I suppose." She snuffed out a tear just before it was ready to roll down her face. I went over and put my arm around her. "It's just been all so alarming. I wonder what Arthur would think of all this, of me," she said, her voice emotional.

"He'd think you're a strong woman who's trying to do the right thing."

She looked up at me and smiled. "Thank you."

"Hey, Alex."

Terri was standing at the corner, pointing at the side of the garage. I walked that way.

"What's up?" I asked in a soft voice.

"Lookee here. The padlock is unlocked." She raised an eyebrow.

"I'm going to check it out, quietly, without an audience," I said.

"Before you go in there, we've got to figure out what all this means. The lightbulb probably means Tripuka wasn't in his apartment at the time of Emma's murder like he said he was. So he lied about that. But on the other hand, that hair evidence could very well be Miss Lucille's. Nothing else turned up in his apartment. He's obviously a pro if we didn't find anything except that tablet."

"Right on both accounts. So we keep digging, starting with this garage."

Thirty-Two

I turned and opened the wooden door. It slammed back at me before I was even a full step in. Peering inside, I saw a stack of bins just on the other side of the doorway. I put my shoulder into it, but they wouldn't budge. I then squeezed through the narrow opening. Spears of sunlight sliced through gaps in the woodwork, casting just enough light to see that the garage was almost busting at the edges. It made my garage look organized.

I pulled out my phone, opened the flashlight app, and began shuffling through the garage, my shoes creating sandpaper sounds on the gritty floor. It smelled musty, like old furniture, maybe rotting newspapers. Boxes and bins were piled as high as ten feet in some places, and each one had been sealed with duct tape. I ran my fingers across a few, picking up a heavy layer of dirt and dust. This crap hadn't been touched in years.

Terri poked her head through the door. "Find anything?"

"Nothing. Just a bunch of storage. And I'm not peeling back duct tape on fifty boxes. Who knows what I'll find that used to belong to dear old Arthur?"

Making my way around their old classic Fairlane—its baby-blue color now coated with a layer of grime—I could hear Miss Lucille ask Terri a question, and my partner pulled back outside.

"You've had better days," I said out loud to the car, noticing at least two flat tires. I'd made my way through most of the garage, and it was obvious this place hadn't been inhabited in years. Well, I was sure a few rats and squirrels had taken up home somewhere in the labyrinth of boxes and storage bins.

I brushed against the back of what appeared to be a headboard, and I felt a rip at my pocket, like I'd snagged it on a screw or nail. Shining my phone flashlight on the side of my khakis, I saw the pocket was ripped from the seam.

"Nice, Alex." I blew out a frustrated breath. "I'm done with the dirty work."

I aimed my phone in front of me and maneuvered through the maze, careful not to touch anything. As I sidestepped past an old bicycle, my phone illuminated the side of the car. Something didn't look right. I backpedaled and focused the flashlight on the rear passenger door.

A handprint on the window.

Leaning over, I could see the outline of thick fingers, the size of the handprint almost double mine. Without touching the glass, I glanced inside. The filthy windows refracted my light, making it difficult to see much, but I was pretty sure I noticed boxes inside.

Through inspecting the door handle, it seemed more polished than the others, as if it had been used recently. I didn't want to ruin a possible fingerprint, so I walked to the other side of the car, and noticed that the handles and windows on this side had a full layer of coated filth on them. I pulled open the door and at first glance found three sacks and two untapped boxes. They looked and felt relatively new. I pulled back the edges of one and had to blink to ensure I wasn't hallucinating. I saw box after box of those figurines, many with a Christmas theme, a few in some type of Halloween colors, and a few more with Easter or

Thanksgiving themes. Inside the sacks on the floorboard, I found dolls dressed in various outfits. One with blond hair had on a pink outfit, while a brunette doll was wearing a T-shirt with the peace symbol on it. Putting my knee on the seat, I leaned across and pulled open the far box.

"Paintings?"

Very odd. It was the last thing I expected to find. I thumbed through each frame and found scenes of the countryside and the city. A few of them had people; others didn't. One was a portrait of a woman who looked like she was a cousin to Mona Lisa. Not a pretty face, with a frown almost. The quality of the work on each of the paintings seemed pretty good, at least to my untrained eyes. The name of the artist was different on each, and of course, I didn't recognize a single one.

Maybe Erin can educate me some day. Part of me wanted to call in the FBI Evidence Response Team at that very moment. But what would that accomplish? This haul had Tripuka's name written all over it, especially after what we'd learned from Susan Miller earlier in the day.

I closed the car door and scooted out of the garage without further damage to my clothes.

"What happened to you?" Miss Lucille said as she eyeballed my dangling pocket.

"A screw or nail of some kind. I'll live. Just needs a little sewing work, and they will be fine." I dusted myself off.

Harry made a beeline toward the tree again, doing his barking routine at the squirrels, and Miss Lucille chased after him.

"You were in there a while," Terri said. "What did you find?"

I coughed, some of the filth catching in my throat.

"You need me to do a Heimlich on you?" Terri quipped, putting a hand on my shoulder.

I hacked out another couple of coughs, my face turning red, and then caught my breath.

"I'm fine," I said, wishing I had a bottled water to down. After a couple of deep breaths, I gave Terri the scoop on everything I'd found.

"I'm calling our CSI team back out here. Not sure how this connects to the killings, but Tripuka is probably baiting girls with all these gifts, like he did with Susan Miller." She pulled her phone out of her pocket.

"Hold on." The words produced a cough that doubled me over.

"Agent Troutt, would you like some water?" Miss Lucille said from over by the tree. She still hadn't corralled Harry, instead letting him work off the energy, I assumed.

"That would be great, thank you," I shouted over Harry's yelps.

"Can you watch Harry while I'm inside? Thanks." She was already halfway to the back porch by the time I could say yes or no.

Terri and I glanced at each other, then walked in the direction of the dog known as "little shit," but who produced quite the opposite.

"Careful," I said. "You don't want to step in any of his horse-sized crap."

Terri held up her phone. "Now? I don't understand why we're waiting. He probably stole some of that from Miss Lucille. We can at least get him for burglary and B&E."

"But is that what we really want?"

She paused, dropping her phone to the side.

Trying to ignore Harry's incessant barking, I continued. "Tripuka is slime. But we don't know what kind of slime. Every day, even every hour, it swings between possible serial killer, child predator, or rapist. If he's guilty, I want to nail him on all three. But I can't send him to prison for killing someone if he didn't do it."

"And you think I would?" Her mouth hung open. I may have offended her.

"Not saying that, Terri. I know you only want to bring the right people to justice. I'm just stating the obvious, I guess."

"What's next then?"

I looked above us, into the dense set of branches and leaves of the oak tree. "I'd ask Nick, but he can't even walk."

Arching her neck backward, she cupped her hand from the sunlight that had found a crack in the thick canopy. "I can't imagine why you want me to prune her tree."

I almost laughed, but I coughed instead. Miss Lucille had just opened the door, carrying a bottle of water. I met her halfway, said thanks, and then chugged it as fast as it would pour out of the bottle.

"Better now?" Miss Lucille asked, already doting over her little Harry.

"Yes." I wiped my mouth with my sleeve, finally able to inhale without having the instant urge to cough.

Terri walked up to me. "It finally hit me. You want me to hide in the tree on some type of surveillance gig, and then wait and see if Tripuka comes back to retrieve any of his toys he uses as bait. Am I getting warm?"

"Hot as Ezzy's homemade salsa."

"Sounds tasty. I'll have to try it out sometime."

We reviewed our plan with Miss Lucille, who seemed comforted to have Terri's company for the evening. Terri would hang out inside until just before dark—or as long as she could tolerate the love tandem of Miss Lucille and Harry—and then would summon her inner Tarzan and ascend into the tree with me and half of the Somerville police force on speed dial.

On my way to the car, I called Nick and gave him the rundown of the evidence we'd found: the lightbulb and the items hidden in the garage. I told him about Terri "volunteering" for tree duty at Miss Lucille's house. He laughed, and then went on to tell me that Gretchen was in the process of sifting through an endless array of video footage from cameras across the city, including a number of businesses that voluntarily allowed access for law enforcement. She was using a new program that could digitally search for a match to Tripuka's mug shot. The software had about a ninety-five-percent success rate, but it also combed through the video files at a much faster speed than any human, or team of them, could.

As I pulled onto the two-lane road, another call beeped through. I quickly told Nick I would work from home the rest of the afternoon and for him to call or text when they had news to share. I tapped the green button and then executed a right turn, passing a mom on the right who was pulling two kids in a red wagon.

With my eyes on the road, I answered the call.

"Alex, did I catch you at a bad time?"

"Dr. Dunn?"

"Oh, yes, I thought you knew it was me."

"Too busy multitasking, sorry. How can I help you?"

He chuckled. "It's really more about how I can help you."

"Don't tell me I missed an appointment."

"Nothing like that, Alex. I know you've been very stressed lately working this case involving this killer who is targeting prostitutes, and I was wondering how you're handling everything."

I tensed up, which I realized was the opposite a person should feel when meeting with a shrink. "I'm fine. No problems."

"Ah, come on, Alex. I know you. Your brain never stops, and you usually don't sleep or eat worth a damn during one of your high-profile cases. Be honest with me now." He chuckled again.

While he had nailed my MO, it didn't make me feel any better. In fact, it felt odd to be discussing a case outside of his office.

"I had a protein smoothie earlier," I said, not really knowing how else to respond.

He chuckled again, and I imagined his glasses slipping down his nose, and then him corralling loose strands of his crazy Einstein hair. I spotted a sign that said Salem was just three miles away.

"Tell you what, Alex. My last two appointments canceled on me. I've got nothing better to do. Why don't we meet at an eclectic watering hole on the North Shore...you know, at least in the direction of where you live."

I hadn't thought about it, but of course he had my address on file.

"You're not saying anything, so I know you want to. Just a little break in the day, and I'll let you pick my brain on any topic you like. What do you say?"

My phone dinged, and I took a quick peek to see a text from Erin.

Mom -- can you help me finish my art project? Pleasssssseeee!!!!

I smiled, knowing exactly where I needed to be. "Sorry, doctor, but I have plans. Gotta run."

I tapped the line dead, eager to see Erin. But something nibbled at the back of my mind as I turned onto our road and spotted our house in the distance. The doctor had admitted that he interacted with some very disturbed people...people who killed for the most bizarre reasons. Maybe he thought we were kindred spirits because of my own brush with crazy killers.

Luke was shooting hoops in the driveway as I turned in. He tried showing off with some type of behind-the-back dribble, but it bounced off his knee. Needed some work. I waved, pulled into the garage, and shut off the engine. I could hear the nonstop pounding of the ball on the pavement behind me. *Maybe I could help him with his game.* What was I thinking? Brad was the bomb on the court. He would want to help Luke. If he would only come back from New York. I'd felt a little off ever since he left, and I thought I knew why. Brad hadn't been there to be my anchor every day. I missed him. I missed our little intimate moments.

I fired off a quick text to the man I cared about.

Miss you. Come back soon.

I wanted to tell him that I loved him. I felt it, but I couldn't get it out of me. Too many other things were tied to that four-letter word.

I got out, waved again at Luke, and walked toward the house, thinking about two men: the one I wanted to hold me, and the one who had just creeped me out...my shrink.

Thirty-Three

With the tendrils of sleep tugging on my extremities. I found it difficult to lift my arm to prop it on Erin's desk, let alone stay awake long enough to read the last paragraph of her paper on Impressionism.

"What do you think, Mom?" She brought both hands together at her face, as if she really valued my opinion.

"It's great, Erin. You put a lot of work into this," I said, grunting a bit as I pushed out of the chair.

She quickly slid into the seat, her hands already on the laptop keyboard. "I just thought of a new way to end the paper. Let me change this last sentence a bit."

I took my phone from my pocket and saw a blank screen. Nothing from the team, and nothing from Brad. Perhaps he'd grown tired of my lack of long-distance interaction. Perhaps he had moved on. A sadness seeped through my body. I huffed out an exhausted breath and toddled around Erin's room, admiring all of her pictures of friends and little mementos from school events, even a few trophies from youth soccer.

I realized I was tired as hell, and I was overreacting about Brad. He was probably working late or maybe enjoying a dinner out with his New York colleagues. Rounding Erin's bed, I saw something hanging off the bedpost.

"What's this, Erin?" As I pulled the red and blue strap over the post, my sleepy demeanor was replaced by utter shock, my pulse sounding like an internal drum roll. "Erin, did you hear me?" I held up what looked like a gold medal from the 1984 Summer Olympics in Los Angeles.

She turned and instantly hunched over, draping an arm across her face.

"Oh God," she said, suddenly breathing like she was hyperventilating.

"Erin, answer me."

"It's nothing. Well, it's something, but I learned from it. I just need to throw it in the trash and move on." She lifted her face, her red-rimmed instantly eyes pooling tears.

My veins bulged so much I thought my head might burst. "Who did you get this from?"

"A boy."

"What's his name?"

"Vinny. I think."

Vinny...Vince. Oh shit!

"Tell me you didn't—"

"Mom, hell no. I'm still a virgin, all right?" She jumped out of her chair and walked over to her window, her arms crossed.

I allowed a breath to escape my lips, although my heart was pumping like it was pulling oil from a mile underground. "Okay, Erin. I believe you," I said in a calmer voice. "Now tell me everything that happened. Don't leave out a single detail. It's important."

She turned back around, lifted her long hair off her neck, and fanned herself. I waited for her to speak. She took in a breath. "I'm sorry, Mom. I just...you know. I was curious," she said as her jittery hand wiped away a tear.

"I'm not going to judge you as a person, but I need to know what happened, and then we'll talk about the repercussions."

"Okay. It's pretty simple. I met this guy online, in one of the gaming chat rooms. Seemed cool and was really nice to me. This went on for two, three weeks. We'd then leave private messages for each other, and we started talking a little deeper, you know."

I tried like hell to avoid the snippy retorts. I licked my dry lips. "And then what happened?"

"We shared more about our personal lives and stuff. I guess I told him about one of my dreams."

"Which is?"

"To win an Olympic medal playing tennis."

"Really?" I knew she had started to enjoy tennis, but I didn't know she was that dedicated.

"Really." She set her feet, stopped fidgeting. It was like I was looking at twenty-year-old Erin, focused and resolute.

But I wouldn't be distracted from what was important right now. "So that's when he got you this medal?"

"Yes."

"Did you know how old he was before you met him? And where did you meet him?" I asked, my voice laced with anger, not at her, but at that fucking asshole, Tripuka.

"He told me he was twenty-two. But I never saw him, so I couldn't tell you."

"How did you get this?"

"He asked me to meet him at the mall. Trish's mom dropped us off one day after school a week or so ago, and I thought I'd finally get to see him. But some girl walks up and hands me this bag and said a guy gave it to her and asked her to give it to me."

I rubbed my temple. "Did you talk to him again?"

"I wondered what the hell happened, why he got cold feet. When I got home and started chatting with him, he told me I had beautiful eyes. And then he asked me why I'd brought my friend along. I started thinking about it later, and it kind of creeped me out. He was looking at me from somewhere in the mall, but he was too chicken to talk to me in person."

I ran my fingers through my hair. "So you're sure you never hung out with him or met him anywhere?"

"I'm telling you the truth, okay?"

I walked over and put my arm around my daughter. She rested her head against my chest and started bawling. "It's okay, Erin. We all make mistakes. I just don't want you to make one that keeps you from coming home at night."

"I know. It was stupid. I realize I'm still pretty naïve about the world."

I rubbed her back as she slowly calmed down. "Have you talked to him since?"

She sniffled and then said, "He tried messaging me, but I gave him the Heisman." She looked up and smiled.

"That's my girl. Why don't you get some sleep, okay? I'm going to do a couple of work things, then hopefully I'll do the same."

"Thanks for understanding, Mom."

I could feel my phone buzzing against my leg, but I ignored it for now.

"I get it. I'll think about how I'm going to respond to this. Give me until tomorrow."

I took hold of the doorknob, but she had something else on her mind. "You know that pickup line about my eyes? It was more funny than anything."

"Forget that guy. In fact, you don't need a guy to tell you that you're a pretty fifteen-year-old girl. Just believe in yourself, Erin, and let life happen at the pace that was meant to be. And by the way, your eyes are very pretty."

"Thanks." She forced out a giggle.

"What's so funny?"

"You know, when Mr. Colin showed us his artwork, I started thinking about the comment Vinny made."

"Why is that?"

"Well, one of his portraits wasn't finished. The only thing missing were the eyes."

A zap of electricity pierced the base of my skull. "I don't recall seeing anything like that."

She looked to the corner. "Oh, right. I guess that was when I went to the bathroom. I needed more toilet paper, so I looked inside this closet, and behind a hamper was this painting of a woman. She was beautiful...well, kind of, but she didn't have any eyes. Two blank areas on the canvas where her eyes should be."

A minute later, I was on the phone with Nick and Gretchen.

"Big news, Alex. You won't believe what Gretchen found," Nick said.

"In a minute. Gretchen, I need you to put everything else aside and find everything you can on a man named Colin Brewer. Background, financials, how he makes his money, and of course, his criminal history, family background. The works."

As expected, they pinged me with numerous questions, and I gave them what I knew.

"Are you concerned that Erin interacted with this guy?" Gretchen said.

"Fortunately, I was there the only time they'd actually met. At the same time, I don't know anything about Colin. Not really. As for Erin, she's lucky she's alive for a whole other reason."

I then gave them the scoop about Vinny and the medal. I suggested pulling Brandon in to do the technical legwork to find a connection between Vinny and Vince Tripuka, if it existed.

"I think that will be reasonably quick," Gretchen said. "I just got a hit on my search for Tripuka in the miles of video footage. Found him entering a car dealership down in the South Shore."

"I knew he wasn't bashful in the art of burglary, so now he's stepping up his game and stealing cars?"

"Nothing like that, Alex. He sat down in their Internet café, where they have computers set up for their customers to use."

"That's it!" I exclaimed. "That's how he's been reaching out to these girls."

"I'll hand this off to Brandon. Tracking that IP to Erin's computer probably won't take him long. He's a frickin' technical genius."

"Coming from you, Gretchen, that's high praise."

"Alex, I think we need to put a tail on Tripuka. We've got so much on this guy, we can't risk him meeting up with another underage girl," Nick said.

"Of course, makes sense," I rubbed my eyes as I walked down the stairs and past Ezzy. She just shook her head and didn't say a word. She didn't have to, but I knew what she was thinking: Alex was once again jumping off the work cliff. But this time was different. It had touched Erin. And I knew Ezzy would be urging me to catch the bastard, or bastards, once I told her what was going on. "Nick, shoot Terri a text, catch her up on what we've learned. I don't want her hanging out in a tree if we're able to catch him in the act. Once Brandon has evidence, we need to arrest Tripuka."

"But what if he's also the eye killer? We don't have the DNA analysis back yet. Other things could turn up as Brandon digs into his digital footprint."

"If we find real evidence that connects him to the killings, I'm all for it. But we can't afford to wait to find something that may not exist. Tripuka is scum, and we need him off the streets, away from any girl. Away from my daughter."

"Do you think our favorite lieutenant detective would agree?"

"Screw Jackson. It's not his decision."

"Well, we took over the eye killer case, but technically Tripuka's new crimes would fall to the local agency first and then—"

"Nick, I'm not taking a vote. No offense."

He chuckled. "I was waiting for that definitive answer. Works for me."

"One other thing," I said as I opened my laptop on the kitchen counter. "Whoever has time first, I have one more person for you to research. And—"

"I know. It's important," Nick said. "Everything is priority one."

"This one will be a Dr. Dave Dunn. Same routine on him as you're doing for Brewer."

"Do you have suspicions he could be our eye killer? If so, are you sure he shouldn't go at the top of Gretchen's list?"

I closed my eyes and focused on all the conversations and interactions I'd had in the last few days, everything concerning Tripuka, Colin, and Dr. Dunn. When it came down to it, I couldn't be certain, but Dr. Dunn seemed to be more of a threat to me than the case itself. At least I hoped.

"Stick with the same order. Dunn comes after Colin Brewer."

My phone buzzed again, and I checked the screen. I knew that number. I hung up with the team and took the other call. "Crack Daddy. If you're calling me, something must be wrong. Speak to me."

Thirty-Four

Ten years ago

With the stimulating smell of blood looming in the air, the man filled his lungs and steadied his hand. Using a thin, black marker, on a piece of masking tape affixed to the side of a reused glass jar, he wrote: *Gloria eyes.*

He added formaldehyde into the jar and then screwed the top on the jar.

Feet swished and squeaked off the rubber exam table behind him. It was Gloria, becoming more lucid by the moment. He didn't bother turning her way. He angled the jar just so, and the eyeballs glimmered off the portable spotlight in the corner of the room, particularly the irises. Gloria's eyes reminded him of gold masked by a rushing stream. Technically, they were brown, but the voluminous amount of liquid somehow altered the color, morphing her eyes from honey brown into a sparkling gold. They were almost like a mood ring, changed by the elements around them.

He glanced over his shoulder, a derisive scowl replacing a satisfied smile. "These eyes, Gloria, they're the best of you. But at least you have *something* to give to mankind. Some aren't even that lucky."

The sound of his voice created a stir, and her body lurched, putting a strain on the belts that held her arms and legs to the table. He'd tested the belts long before this event had started. She wasn't going anywhere. Not until he was ready.

He gazed at the jar that held her eyes and then back to his latest victim. "I realized a long time ago that a person's eyes are a reflection of who they really are. There are some women in the world who deserve the set of eyes they were born with. You're not one of them. You're a disgrace to women, to humanity even. I did what was required. It's really that simple."

She began to mumble and cry out.

"What are you trying to say, Gloria?" He leaned his ear closer to her mouth. "You need to enunciate if you expect me to understand you."

Another surge, this one more violent. She bent her wrists, scratching and clawing at the straps with broken fingernails. She flung her head back and forth, and drops of blood whipped just past the man's shoulder. Then she cleared her throat and spat in his face.

He flinched and jerked away from the table, the pungent goo clinging to his chin. Finding a towel from the supply cupboard, he wiped himself clean. "Even when the end is near, Gloria, your true colors shine through. You don't have an ounce of class in you. Nothing. You've ravaged your body and your soul, allowing anyone with twenty dollars and four wheels to use you like a blow-up doll."

He tossed the soiled towel on the pile with the others coated in blood, then took a moment to look around, admire his ingenuity. He had outlined the entire windowless room with clear plastic to create his very own, private surgical facility. It was sterile...mostly. He had all the equipment any surgeon could ask for, at least for his specialty—eye extraction.

Even though he'd spent countless hours studying medicinal practices from across the globe, he admitted that his best training had been actually performing the artwork on other mammals. He would normally have categorized them as animals with lesser intelligence, but after what he'd witnessed, it was difficult to accept that description. Sometimes, whether it be because of environment or DNA, humans simply were not human.

And then there he was, at the opposite end of the intelligence spectrum—perhaps he was an extreme example of that theory.

He pushed that thought out of his mind. It was unproductive, and at this stage of his life, he knew it was pointless to go there. He'd finally come to terms with who he really was and how he could best utilize his skills to accomplish his mission.

He'd found a place of peace, where he could exist in the real world and not have to continuously fabricate to cover up the meaning of his life. He'd been able to create an entirely separate life, one that satisfied a compulsion he'd had since he was a young tike. While his new hobby had infused him with a fresh sense of satisfaction and accomplishment, it had also served as an outlet for the peaks and valleys of his emotions.

The blue booties that covered his leather wingtips shuffled against the plastic on the old wooden floor as he brought his tools to the sink and washed them, taking care not to cut himself. When he completed cleaning each one, he held it up and admired the quality of the instrument. He had once dreamed of becoming a world-renowned heart surgeon. He knew he had the aptitude and his hands were the most precious tools he possessed. His mom said he would become the great healer, influencing the world like no person since Gandhi. She had been the one to give him the desire to learn, using a well-rounded education in math, sciences, literature, and the arts to make him into a great human being.

But what about his soul?

His mom. Deep down, he acknowledged that Doris was really his adoptive mom, a fact he hadn't known until his twenties. After dealing with a rush of emotion upon learning the news that his real mother had been nothing more than a five-dollar slut, his respect for the woman who raised him increased dramatically. Perhaps realizing that the odds of making something of his life were stacked against him just by pure genetics, Doris had taken it upon herself to nurture his mind and his pride for as long as he could recall. Despite all of the opportunities for her to berate him for the missteps in his life, she instead directed her focus on educating him about how to treat women, how to exude confidence, and how to have manners and be classy.

Everything his real mother was not.

She was nothing more than a crack-head prostitute.

Doris knew he deserved better, and she had proved that every day of his life right up until she passed away three months earlier.

He glanced around the old home and realized her gift would be put to good use for many years after her heart had given out. And he gave her thanks on a daily basis, in particular on days like this.

"Okay, Gloria, we're about ready to wrap up the first phase of our little date."

She began to squirm, screaming incoherent statement, her face in a ball of anguish.

He shook his head and said, "I was open to having a sane, adult conversation, but if you're going to act like a petulant child, then I'll just leave the operating theatre and let you wallow in your sweat and blood until you calm down."

Her lurching ceased, and she took in huge gulps of air, hissing up phlegm when she exhaled. She was disgusting. As her chest lifted with each labored breath, he noticed her exposed breast. It sagged like a deflated water balloon. The previous night she'd cupped her hand around that same breast as she leaned into the open window of his car, her eyes bloodshot and her nose begging for more blow. She thought she was enticing him to fork over his money to have sex with her. Instead, she had exposed herself for being a strung-out, gutter whore.

Then Gloria screamed until the cords of her neck looked like they might burst through her skin.

"Oh dear, Gloria. I might have to seek the services of an exorcist." He chuckled as he shed his body of his surgical mask and gown. He wadded them up and tossed them by the mess of towels.

Then it hit him. "You actually think you can get someone's attention by screaming, don't you? Well, I've got news for you, Gloria. In this neighborhood, if anyone happened to hear you, they wouldn't give it a second thought. In this neighborhood, it's a good day when you don't get mugged. So consider yourself lucky. I didn't take a dime of your slut money."

She gritted her teeth and grunted. Cautiously, he pulled himself closer, anxious to hear if she could actually formulate real words.

She could.

"You cut out my fucking eyes. You are the devil reincarnated, and you will rot in hell! Do you hear me?"

He couldn't dispute anything she had just said. He finished the clean-up and then injected her with a sedative that would keep her motionless during their road trip.

He picked her up and walked out the back door. She mumbled something as her lips quivered before not moving at all.

"Gloria, it's time to connect with nature." He knew he had to throw out the trash and let the sun drop below the horizon for the last time in her pathetic life.

Thirty-Five

I held the phone away from my ear, but his voice still echoed throughout the kitchen.

Crack Daddy, legally named Jasper Finley, asked the same question for the third time. "What happened to my mother-fucking Constitutional rights?"

I could hear the fire in his voice. He might as well have been standing on the steps of the Supreme Court with an American flag waving in the breeze behind him.

"Finley—"

"Don't talk down to me. I'm sick and tired of everyone messing with me and my business. I'm an entrepreneur, no different than the punks who come out of MIT or Harvard and get backed by some type of fancy fund to create a start-up. I created a business from the ground up, and I didn't get any type of million-dollar seed money. It's just me, Crack Daddy, doing what I can to put food on the table and create job opportunities for men and women in my community."

He paused, and all I could hear was his panting breath.

"Are you finished giving your 'woe is me' speech?"

More panting. "I'm tired of this crap. It's discrimination."

"Discrimination of what?"

"Everyone likes to think they're the morality police, and then what happens? I'll tell you what. They get caught in the bathroom stall screwing the tollbooth operator, or taking money under the table to award a multimillion dollar contract to a so-called acquaintance."

His belligerent tone was starting to annoy me. Actually, it was starting to bore me. He wouldn't let me finish a sentence to find out why he'd actually called. I scrolled through my email as he continued flapping his gums.

"It's all bullshit! But because of my address, because I don't have that fancy degree, or wear the kind of clothes that make people think I'm connected and intelligent, everyone wants to point fingers. Point all you want, but stop fucking taking my girls away from me!"

He barked twice, which actually woke me from my daze.

"Did you just say something about someone taking your girls away?"

"Yeah, aren't you listening, Agent Troutt?"

I bit my tongue and stayed on point. "Who's missing? When did this happen?"

"Tricia, one of my best. Usually one of my high-end girls. Brings in top dollar. She usually doesn't work the streets, but I didn't have any rich clients for her, so she decided to spin the wheel on the streets."

"How do you know someone took her? Isn't that really what you want, for someone to pick her up?

"Are you hard of hearing, FBI?"

"The name is Special Agent Troutt."

"Troutt mouth, whatever. Tricia is a savvy businesswoman. She's not some strung-out junkie with no self-respect. She knows what she's doing. And besides, my boy Romeo here saw it all go down. He saw the man reach over and grab her wrist, pull her into his car, and then take off. Practically dragged her down the street. She was screaming bloody murder."

This wasn't happening...again. "Crap. You're telling me the truth."

"Really, Sherlock?"

"Do you have a picture of her?"

"Of course. How else do you think I sell her services? Damn, woman..."

"Send it to me, and I'll have my team contact all the local police departments. They'll put out local APBs for her. What's her last name?"

"Rompola. Tricia Rompola."

"Is that her real name?"

"I don't do W-9 forms."

Not surprising. Crack Daddy shouted at his boy, Romeo, to send him the photo of Tricia.

"It's on the way," he said to me. "I don't get too attached to my contractors, but with Candy being killed and all, do you think Tricia's going to be okay?"

He sounded like a different person. More like a Jasper Finley, less like a Crack Daddy.

"We'll do everything we can to find her."

"Alive," he insisted.

"I hope."

Thirty-Six

The wooden porch creaked in protest as Terri and I attempted to peek through windows.

"I'll look. You keep an eye on our backs," I said, knowing this neighborhood had the highest crime rate in New England.

"Who would live in this dump?" she asked from behind me.

"Look around. It blends in."

"I suppose. It's just hard to imagine the guy you described—educated, good-natured, well-dressed, charming, attractive—would live in this shithole."

"Maybe you didn't hear the entire story." I thought I saw something through a crack in the paisley curtains.

"No, I was stuck in the tree. While my ass and back are screaming at me now, it was worth it to watch that slimeball get caught with his hand in the cookie jar."

One hunch had paid off. Tripuka had returned to the garage with a sixteen-year-old girl at his side, apparently to pick up a doll stored inside the dusty old car. Terri called in the cavalry, and three black-and-whites were on the scene in five minutes. Not completely under his pheromone spell, the girl told them everything, including how he tried to convince her to have phone sex. Even with his Wise Ass attorney, Tripuka was in all likelihood going back to the big house where he would be someone's bitch for years to come.

"The scoop on Colin's dream pad?" Terri reminded me.

"According to Gretchen, this is a rental property. It used to be in his mother's maiden name, Doris Smith, and just recently was transferred to his name."

Jerry had sent agents Mason and Silvagni to Brewer's downtown loft. They got the condo manager to open the door, but they found no one inside and no sign of foul play.

I moved to the other window, cupping my hand against a pane of glass with a spiderweb of cracks. I could only see a single ottoman just beneath the windowsill.

"So, like I asked earlier, who would want to rent this dump?"

"Gretchen said it had been rented out to two men in the last year who were truck drivers."

"Which means they were rarely here."

I listened for any noise inside. All quiet. I asked Terri to go around back and let me know if she saw anything. A dog barked in the distance. It sounded angry and possibly hurt. I wondered how it was being treated.

My phone buzzed, and I answered Terri's call. "I only see the kitchen table from here," she said. "Kind of messy and dirty, but no sign of anything human. I think I saw a mouse."

I knocked on the door, and no one answered. I tried turning the knob, and as expected, it was locked. Same result from the back, she said. We were going in. I drew my Glock and used it to bust out a pane of glass next to the doorknob. I coiled my arm inside and unlocked the door.

Four steps in and I could hear Terri walking in the kitchen. "See anything?" I called out.

"Nothing back here."

With my senses on high alert, I stepped through the house. A single picture hung in the living room above the fireplace, some type of ugly contemporary art. It looked like a ten-dollar print from Walmart. A low-back chair with no seat cushion and a small side table were in the corner. Terri and I met in the dining room. There was a card table set up, the layer of vinyl sliced open, and a folding chair next to it.

"It's like dining at the Ritz," Terri said.

"I wouldn't know." I tilted my head back to the east side of the house and found a hallway. First door led to a bathroom. Toilet seat was up, so I knew a guy had used it last.

Second door was a bedroom. It had sheets, a brown cover, and a pillow. "Looks like someone slept in it recently," Terri said.

"Slept or was held hostage."

She nodded.

Third door was just a few more steps down the hallway. The door was on tracks and looked new. I met Terri's eyes, and she readied her gun at her side. I then slid it open, and she walked inside. It was dark, so I flipped on the light switch. Nothing happened. I took out my phone and shined my flashlight around the room. Terri did the same. We both zeroed in on what looked like a doctor's examination table. I walked closer, careful not to touch it.

"See anything?" Terri asked, walking up next to me.

"There." I pointed at a burgundy spot on the white wall. "Blood." Swinging my light around the room, I noticed a sink. It was clean, but I saw drops of water clinging to the side.

"Someone used this recently," I said.

"Check it out." Terri pointed her light at a small built-in bookcase in the corner of the room. A spotlight was clipped to the edge. At another corner of the room, two more spotlights were clipped to a two-by-four nailed at an angle to the wall.

I opened the cabinet above the sink, and bile shot into the

back of my throat.

Glass jars were lined up in a row. And they were looking at me.

Eyeballs.

Terry flinched, nearly knocking me in the head with her gun. "Holy shit."

I forced myself to look away. I couldn't dwell on the disturbing images. It would lead me to thinking about Erin, even if she didn't fit the profile of the victims—at least the ones we knew about. I took another glance at the shelf with the jars…too many to count.

On the shelf below, a row of scalpels sat on a paper towel. Gauze and other medical supplies were also in the cabinet.

Raking my fingers through my hair, I took a step back. "I thought Colin was one of the good guys. He helped me take down that ogre at Dr. Dunn's office. He was kind and gentle."

"To you. But he clearly has a beef against hookers. Why? I have no idea. He's just fucking sick, demented." She turned away from the cabinet.

"The question is: where is he? And is Tricia with him?" Moving to a crouching position, I swung around the room, pausing my flashlight every few seconds. I made it three hundred sixty degrees.

"Nothing." Just as I turned away, a sparkle caught my eye. "Hold on." I crawled under the table, reached across a support beam, and picked up a gold earring.

"Do you think it's Tricia's?" Terri asked, huddling over me.

I brought it a few inches from my face. It was a gold hoop with the letters TR in the middle. "I'd say yes." We locked eyes.

"Crap. We've got to figure out where they went."

Terri started opening every door and drawer she could find, and I jumped to my feet and followed suit. I moved to the bathroom, unsure what we could find that might give us a clue, or even a hint. I could hear doors slamming from the adjacent room. Under the sink I found a plunger and a container of disinfectant.

"Alex, in here. Quick!"

I ran out of the room and cut around the corner where I found Terri on her knees next to an armoire, both doors open. I could see colorful dresses and scarves hanging inside. But Terri's head was buried behind the dresses. She then stood up and pushed the dresses to the side.

"Shit." A painting of a woman faced me. She had long, dirty-blond hair that spilled over her shoulders. Her lips were full and moist. She wore a strapless gown, purple and gold. But none of that stood out. Not like the two dots of white canvas on either side of her nose. "No eyes."

I pulled out my phone and thumbed through a few photos to find the one Finley had sent me. I brought up Tricia's picture where Terri could see it over my shoulder. She had circles under her eyes in the phone image. Other than that, she was a match for the painting—the cheekbones, the shape of her ears, and the straw-colored hair.

Terri pulled the painting out and held it up.

"What is it?"

Her jaw began to quiver.

"Terri, do you know her or something?"

I could see her knuckles turn white, the painting shaking from her jittery arms.

"Terri..." I put my hand on her back. "Put the painting down," I said, knowing we needed to preserve the evidence. "What's triggering this reaction?"

Shaking her head, she set the canvas down, and it plopped against the armoire. She brought a hand to her face, now splotchy red. The first tear rolled off her cheek.

"You can tell me, Terri. What is it?"

"I know where this is," she gasped, as more tears escaped faster than she could wipe them away.

"That's great. Where is it?"

"North side of the Mystic River in an area of trees by the river. It's a reservation. You see the river there, in between those bushy trees?" She pointed at a dark blue area between the trees, and then a low, westerly sun cutting across the body of water.

"That's a pretty specific spot. Are you sure?"

She didn't respond. She just stared at the painting. Her gaze wasn't so much directed at Tricia, though, as it was the surrounding landscape. "Terri?"

She puffed out a breath, her eyes puffy and dripping mascara. "My sister..."

"Yes?"

"My little sister was abducted from that exact same location twelve years ago. The case was never solved, and I've lived with the torment of her disappearance, and most likely her death, for all these years. She's the reason I got into law enforcement."

"I'm so sorry, Terri. I had no idea."

She pressed her lips together and closed her eyes for a few seconds.

A thought entered my mind. "Is this location upstream from where they found the two previous bodies, Emma's and Candy's?"

She sniffled and thought for a moment. "Yeah. I guess it is."

"How fast can you get us there?"

Without taking the time to respond, Terri bolted out of the room. I was right on her heels.

Thirty-Seven

Choosing to forgo the cherry light and siren, Terri gunned it past a slower vehicle, then swung the car right to exit off Mystic Valley Parkway. A hundred yards later, she slammed on her brakes and fishtailed into a mostly empty parking lot.

A woman carrying a briefcase and a package loped to her car about fifty yards in front of us, but Terri still punched the gas, maneuvering around the few parked cars like a slalom skier. My hand smacked the roof as Terri cut to the left, just in front of the pedestrian, who grabbed her chest and fell back against the side of her car.

I didn't bother saying anything. Terri had seen her just like I had. She was on a mission, maybe one that included thoughts of her long-lost sibling. Terri gripped the wheel with everything she had, her shoulders stiff, her jaw locked. We soon reached the end of the parking lot, and we were still going hot. "Terri!"

"Hold on," she said, tapping the brakes for a split second. Then the car popped the curb at about thirty miles per hour.

My head bounced off the ceiling. "What are you doing?"

"Quickest path to our destination." She pounded her foot onto the brake and swerved the car to the right. The heavy branches of a twenty-foot evergreen flopped against the passenger-side window as if we were moving through a car wash.

The nose of the car ate dirt a few times after sailing over mounds of earth. Then she found the walking path, the frame of the car sticking out on both sides of the path.

"Can't turn on the lights. Might see us coming," she said.

In just the last couple of minutes, the sun had dipped below the horizon, and the farther we moved away from the street and parking lot, the less we could see.

She angled the car around a blind corner, both sides lined with a wall of trees and brush.

"Watch out!" A possum had darted in front of the car.

Terri jerked the car to the left and slammed the brakes, but the tires couldn't dig in against the dirt, and we mowed right over an evergreen.

I took a breath. The car had stopped, but I heard the engine whirring. I realized that Terri still had her foot on the accelerator. I touched her shoulder. "Your foot."

"Oh," she said, quickly removing it. I realized we were at an angle. We'd driven on top of the side of the tree.

Then I saw blood dripping onto the seat. Leaning forward, I could see red smeared across Terri's face and a cracked window. "Terri, you're hurt."

"I'm fine. Let's get out of here. It's just another quarter mile or more along this path, then off to the left."

I jumped out of the car as she scooted over to the passenger seat. She grabbed her head. "I think I'm going to throw up."

I looked around and, as expected, saw no one. "Crap." I took out my phone and swiped the screen.

"I'll call for backup," Terri said. "You go see if you can find him." Pacing, I ran fingers through my hair.

"Alex, go."

"Put your gun between your legs. I'm shutting the door and

locking it. Dial the number right now." I handed her my phone and took off running. I jogged alongside the path to soften the sound of my shoes hitting the ground. In and out of an S-curve, dodging trees, I tried to keep my eyes open for any sign of Brewer—or anyone else for that matter. A few birds rustled their wings as I clipped branches. The farther I went, the less I could see. While I was moving toward the west, where there should have been a bit more light, it felt like I was entering the mouth of a volcano, with dark, ominous trees standing guard around the border. Taking Terri's directions to heart, and recalling the painting itself, I veered away from the path at the next curve, then slowed to a walk, both hands on my Glock, my head on a swivel.

Twenty more steps and I had this surreal feeling wash over me, as if I'd been in this exact location before. Probably came from viewing the painting. It looked all too familiar, my feet now buried in ivy and a few leaves. A bird fluttered out of a tree. My heart skipped a beat, and I jerked my weapon up, watching for someone to come out of the dense vegetation. Nothing.

I could now hear the rushing water of the river somewhere nearby. A few crickets chirped, and a small flock of birds in a V-formation sailed overhead. The little remaining light cast a purple glow across the cloudless sky. It was just me and nature, yet I didn't feel settled. I felt like someone was watching me. Making a full rotation every few steps, I continued plodding forward. My foot tripped over a hidden log, and I threw out my hand just before I fell on my face. Now hunched lower, I took in the surrounding area, looking for any sign of a human, alive or dead. Some of the ivy must have been two feet deep, which made me realize that the log could have been a dead body, maybe Tricia's. I wondered if there was any hope she was still alive.

I stood up and backpedaled two steps to get my bearings.

"Alex, welcome to my own version of paradise."

My breath caught in my throat as I tried to figure out the location of the voice. Swinging left and then right. I saw no one, but I knew the voice. It was Colin Brewer's.

"Colin, let's talk this through. We're cool, right?"

No response. Had he heard me? Was he even still around?

I moved two more steps, squinting to pick up any movement in the murky woods.

"Tell you what, Colin. It's been a stressful week. Let's get out of here and go get a drink. We can talk over a couple of drinks, relax, and just shoot the breeze."

Leaves rustled at two o'clock, and I swung my pistol in that direction. Branches moved higher in the tree. *Probably caused by a gust of wind.* I didn't want to start shooting wildly. I couldn't, not without seeing at least a figure.

"I'm not one of your regular suspects, Alex. I'm probably the most intelligent person you've ever met, in fact."

And modest. "You are definitely one of the most unique and interesting people I've had the pleasure of knowing. But I'd like to get to know you more."

"Oh, how I wish that were true. You have a natural beauty, Alex. Just like your daughter."

I could feel my insides clench.

"Don't worry, I'm not some pervert who's into young girls. I love women...of all kinds."

As a drop of sweat trickled to the end of my nose, I turned to face the trees that lined the river, almost certain he was hiding in that area. I took one careful step and then another, wondering if he would allow me to move much closer.

"I kind of thought you were handsome."

"No need to stroke my ego, Alex. I know I'm the complete package. My mother told me as much since I was a little kid."

Now it seemed like his position had changed. I turned forty-five degrees and stepped southward.

"Do you have Tricia with you, Colin?" I hoped like hell she was still alive.

"Why would you care one damn bit about a person who had thrown her life away? She had no self-respect, treated her body like it was a piece of meat."

Another rustle right behind me. I twisted my neck so fast I felt a sharp jab in my shoulder blade. The return of the great crick. For now, I hardly noticed the pain.

"Colin, she's a woman just like me. She just had some bad luck. I know you see the good in people. Why don't you bring her to me and let's get her to a hospital?"

I waited for a response. A bird flapped its wings and then soared into the sky, the purple now engulfed by a gloomy darkness. I felt alone, like I was a million miles away from another sane human being. I wondered if that was how the women felt as they sat in this area and had their portraits painted. Alone. They had been chewed up and spit out by society and were on the verge of being killed by a lunatic.

"Alex, eyes are the windows to the soul—but only if you have one. Tricia did not have a soul. And neither did Emma or Gloria or any of the other women."

The back of my tongue burned from the return of acid. I thought about all those jars of eyeballs. How many had he killed?

"Colin, you can't keep doing this. Please—"

"My mother...my biological mother was a worthless hooker who spread her legs for anyone with five bucks or a shot of heroin. She had no self-respect. My birth certificate said unknown for father. We can't allow these so-called women to procreate. That's my gift to this world, Alex. I am the final judge, jury, and executioner."

This guy was completely off the rails. I took two more steps, although my eyes stayed on the cluster of trees by the river. Cicadas buzzed in the distance, and I wondered again if he'd left. I couldn't delay any longer. I blew out a breath and banked right toward the river.

Just as I turned, I ran straight into a brick wall—it was Colin.

"Funny running into you here."

I brought my gun up, but he quickly twisted my hands, snatched the gun from my grip, and tossed it into the weeds behind him. Besides his massive frame, all I could see were his white set of teeth.

I cocked an arm, but before I could throw a punch, he'd turned me around and twisted my arm behind my back. He dipped his head and breathed into my ear as he rubbed his body against my backside.

"I could snap your arm like a twig, so please don't be a pest." He inhaled and released a slight groan. "Oh, how you smell like a real woman. It could have been special, Alex. So special. We could have been the ultimate power couple. But now, I must say goodnight."

He moved behind me, his fingers fussing with something. I turned my head slightly to find a needle poised just above my shoulder. Without another thought, I swung my elbow into his gut and tried to spin away. He grunted, but pawed at my arm until he locked his fingers around my wrist. He then started laughing. I tugged with everything I had, but my arm was locked within his vice-like grip.

"Don't you think dusk is the most tantalizing time of any day? The cloak of darkness is so very close, but temptation looms in the air."

I momentarily stopped struggling, mesmerized by his words.

"Alex, has anyone ever told you that your eyes are to die

for?" He barked out a loud chuckle and brought the needle toward my arm.

A crackle echoed off the trees. Colin dropped the needle and grabbed his shoulder. He cried out as a look of intense anguish split his face. He'd been shot. I lunged backward and fell on my ass, then turned to see Terri walking in our direction, her gun raised.

"Down on the ground!" she barked.

He didn't respond.

"Down. Now!"

I jumped to my feet. "Colin, get down on the ground or she'll have to shoot you again."

No response. I could only hear Terri pumping out breath after breath. Finally, he angled his face to look into the sky.

"It was because of you, Mother. You made me the man I am today. Bitch." He dove to the side while swinging his arm around. Did he just grab a gun?

"Shoot him!"

Terri released three quick rounds. Brewer squirmed for a moment, then rocked to a stop, face up, his mouth agape. I ran over and kicked the gun out of his hands. Leaning down, all I could see were his eyes staring back at me. A window to his soul, or what was left of it.

The killing finally had ended.

Thirty-Eight

Water trickled out of nine holes, slowly cascading down an elaborate carved wall that served as a fountain on the outdoor patio of a well-known bar in Back Bay. As the water dropped into the well, I could feel wayward droplets soak my extended hand. The pitter-patter sound drowned out the murmur of voices all around me, including my table.

Terri walked up with a drink in her hand.

"How's it going?" I asked.

"Eh. Hanging in there. Received a commendation for taking down both Tripuka and Brewer on the same day."

"You deserve it. If you hadn't come along when you did in the woods, then I wouldn't be able to see you right now. Even worse, I might be dead."

"Well, if I hadn't been so out of control, then we both could have gone after Brewer and your life wouldn't have been threatened."

She sipped her clear drink, lime floating on top of the ice. Smelled like a vodka tonic.

"No one is perfect, Terri. You're one of the good ones. I was honored to work with you on this case."

She released her million-dollar smile. She reminded me of

some beautiful Hollywood star. I just couldn't put my finger on which one.

"Two cases," she said with a wink.

"But fourteen jars. I think that's what I recall the Evidence Response Team saying they'd confiscated. All local and federal agencies are digging through cold-case files to try to find possible matches to Brewer's vics," I said, gazing at the water display.

"It's been going on since his adoptive mom left that old home to Brewer in her will. The adoptive father died a few years earlier. It's just bizarre, how this guy was able to live a seemingly normal life, but at the same time possess this warped trait that had him killing young women who needed the most help."

"Judge, jury, and executioner—that's what he said. Whether it be from the way his adoptive mom raised him or it was just part of his DNA, he was mentally out to lunch. And he thought he was smarter than everyone else. Lethal combination."

Terri said nothing, just turned her sights to the water display, her lips slightly open.

Now more than ever I could sense the void she felt from losing her sister. Taking down two horrible men wouldn't stop the hurt. I thought about saying something, but I knew she would appreciate the quiet even more.

A moment passed, then Nick called out for us to join them at the table.

"Drinks are on me!" he exclaimed.

With one arm around Gretchen, Brandon then called to the waiter. "Tequila shots for everyone."

Terri and I both said, "No thanks."

"Every word you speak, you have to drink another shot," he declared. It suddenly felt like college and one of those classy drinking games.

The shots came, and I dumped mine in my water and continued drinking my margarita on the rocks.

Gretchen drank two shots, slammed the tiny glasses to the table, and received a high-five from her new boy toy.

"Hey, Alex, did I tell you what I learned about Dr. Dunn?"

She'd caught me mid-sip so I just shook my head slightly.

"He's currently being sued by two former patients for sexual harassment. One of them said in the filing that he tried to put her in a trance and then exposed himself to her."

"Nice. Guess it's time to find a new shrink."

"I'll drink to that." Brandon tilted his head and drained the shot glass, then leaned down and smooched Gretchen.

I whispered to Nick, "I guess they aren't afraid to come out of the PDA closet."

"Not sure that's a wise career move, if you ask me," he said, and then he turned to grab a waiter to order some appetizers.

I wasn't sure how to take that. Did he know about Brad and me? Frankly, at this point, I would have given anything for Brad to walk out to the patio, lean down, and give me a huge kiss on the lips right in front of everyone. Anything to end the secrecy and to allow me to feel like I wasn't a criminal for having a grown-up relationship with a man I cared about.

Appetizers were delivered, and everyone reached for something—a potato skin, nachos, or some fried calamari. Everyone except Terri, who seemed distant, her eyes looking around the area, watching all the fun and laughter.

"You okay?"

"I still think about her all the time, Alex. I wonder if there is any way she's still alive."

I thought about my mom and her death, still feeling it wasn't resolved because they never found the guy who'd killed her with his car. Her death was my reason for going to law school. Of course, at first, I hadn't linked my mother's death to my career choice, at least not until I'd worked my first year in the DA's office, a mind-numbing exercise of futility. And then I saw the opportunity with the FBI, and I took it and ran with it.

"I get it. You need closure."

She nodded. "Not sure I'll get what I want. Sounds like I might need to see a shrink to help me come to terms with what life has dished out."

I looked across the growing crowd as the sun set just beyond the brick wall. "It's certainly true when they say, 'Life is what happens to you while you're busy making other plans,'" I said.

She lifted a shapely brow.

"Just don't lose your barometer. It's obvious that you were meant to do this kind of work."

"You don't think I could have been the first fifty-year-old cheerleader?" We both cracked up, and everyone looked our way.

I nibbled on a nacho and sucked down melted ice from my glass.

"Another drink, Alex?" Nick asked.

A longing for family, for closeness had begun to take root.

"No thanks." I lifted from my chair. "I'm calling it a night."

"Gonna take a long, hot bath, read a book, and finally catch up on some sleep?"

I just smiled. I knew exactly what I needed to do.

Thirty-Nine

I walked in the back door, waved hello to Ezzy, and then went upstairs. I found Luke playing a game on his phone. I hugged him and squeezed him and rustled his hair.

"I love you, buddy."

"Back at ya, Mom. Can you stop squeezing me? It's kind of cramping my style."

Leaving him to do his thing, I walked across the hall to Erin's room. She was lying on the bed, writing in a small notebook.

"What are you doing?" I asked as I scooted up next to her.

"Writing in a journal. Just feels better when I can get all the crap out of my head and down on paper."

"I'm proud of you."

"Why?"

"Because you know when you've made a mistake, and you take responsibility. And now you're figuring out ways to enhance your life, to cope with all the hurdles that get in your way."

She let me hug her and kiss on her for few seconds, and then she went back to writing.

After leaving her to concentrate without further distractions from me, I went and packed a small bag of things, then made my way downstairs. Ezzy was on the couch, reading a magazine. I told her about my spontaneous plans.

"Go. Get out of here before you change your mind. And trust your heart."

We hugged, and I did just what she said.

I drove to the train station and jumped on the next train to New York City. I arrived just over three hours later, and even in the city that never sleeps, the streets were nearly desolate. I took a cab to a hotel in Brooklyn. The place was nice, but not extravagant. I asked to speak to the manager and just happened to have my FBI credentials out as he approached. His small, round eyes stared at the shield, and then he listened to my story and how I needed his help.

"I'm sorry, but that's against company policy. I'm afraid you'll need a warrant."

I took a moment, glancing at the revolving door into the hotel lobby...my mind, for once, interlocked with my heart. I'd come this far, and not just in distance. I couldn't let one roadblock stop this important next step in my life. I took in a deep breath, stored my credentials in my purse, and then explained everything in my life that had gotten me to this juncture. And I spoke with no filter.

With his little eyes as wide as he could get them, the manager blew out a breath and then cleared his throat. "Really? That's all happened in the last few months?"

I nodded. "But it's my life, and I've come to realize that I need to own it. So this is what I'm doing."

A moment later, he set a plastic keycard on the counter with his hand on top of it.

"Please don't let me regret doing this favor for you. I don't want to lose my job."

I told him thanks and gave him a wink, adding that if he heard reports of screaming from the room, he shouldn't worry. He blushed, slid the key to me, and quickly got back to work.

Up on the sixth floor, the elevator doors dinged open. I looked for room 648. A sign pointed me to the left. I walked down the quiet, carpeted hall, not a soul in sight. I took a right at the end and found the room. Holding the key just above the insert, I paused for a moment. One final little demon on my shoulder tried to shake my confidence, to question my intentions. "Own it, Alex," I whispered out loud.

I popped open the door, dropped my bag, shed every piece of clothing on my body, and crawled into bed with the man who would no longer be relegated as a secret relationship.

"Alex, what are you doing here?" Brad said through a cracked voice.

With all the passion I felt, I kissed his lips.

"Does this mean—"

"Shhh." I then moved on top of him.

For months, he had showered me with praise, been a kind, gentle man to me and my kids. He wanted me in every way possible. I would no longer push him away or pretend that our chemistry was nothing more than a passing flirtation. I knew deep down that he was *the* man, and I intended to prove it to him all night long. At last.

Forty

Four weeks later

The moment the man stuck one foot out of his truck, a gust of wind launched the car door forward, smacking the side of the vehicle parked to the left.

"Well, screw me a river," he growled. After a brief glance at the nearby vehicle, he quickly checked for damage along the red edge of his door. Since he'd recently forked over thirty grand on his new Silverado, he was relieved to spot only one small nick. He relaxed, thinking he'd dodged a bullet. Until his mutt, Barney, started barking.

"Ah, Barney, what do you think you see now?" He rubbed the ears of his faithful hunting dog and now focused on the beat-up truck next to him. A dent with a red line running through it was prominently displayed.

Other than the new red mark, the dent almost blended in with the litany of dings and discoloration. The old-model Ford F-150 was a reliable truck—about five presidents ago, he thought with a quiet chuckle.

"Okay, Barney, I'll roll down the windows so you can bark at all the folks walking by while I run inside to pick up a few things."

With Barney wagging his tail as he stuck his head out the open window, the man re-set his cap and felt the bitter wind chafing at his skin. "Early cold front," he said to himself.

He tipped his hat twice while saying hello to a couple of local ladies—a must-do in this small Blue Ridge town—and skittered inside the door of Grow 'N Go.

"Hiya, Sam." He gave a quick salute to the owner behind the front counter.

With a phone to his ear, an employee tugging on his shirt, and two customers watching him bag a few groceries, Sam was still able to respond. "What's up, big man? First cold front of the year just hit."

"It hit alright, just at the time I opened the door on my new Silverado."

"Ooo-wee, Jake, that's a beaut, big man," he exclaimed while glancing out the front windows. "Hey, you want to go huntin' this weekend?"

Before Jake could respond, Sam was pulled back to the employee at his side and customers pinging him with questions. All for the better, since Jake knew Sam could be a little long-winded. He rotated on his heels and surveyed the bustling store, on the lookout for who might be the owner of the old Ford F-150.

Lots of folks he recognized, and with each one he could associate a car from the lot. The blue Tundra, the black Ram, and two white Suburbans to go with the twins who'd once appeared in a Doublemint Gum commercial. Wearing matching red sweaters, Liz and Laney were giggling near the prophylactic section. Damn, they were a couple of lookers, he thought to himself.

"That hurts me."

"Let her go."

Two other female voices cut through the din of noise, and their tone was full of distress.

He walked over to the next aisle and found a grisly bear-looking man holding the hand of a teenage girl, while her mom was rebuking her husband. Jake wasn't good at confrontation so he just cleared his throat. All three heads turned in his direction.

"Hey, uh..." His eyes searched the space. "Oh, do you mind if I cut in front you to grab a roll of paper towels?"

"Sure, go right ahead," Grisly Bear said, starting to usher the two females away.

Sliding in front of the paper towels shelf, Jake studied the mother. She wore some type of bonnet that covered her silver hair, and he could now see she was a good twenty years older than the man, whose beard dropped to his stomach. Both females wore long, flowing skirts, while Grisly Bear had on boots and pants that would have been in style sixty years ago.

Mountain folks. That's what the locals called them. They lived from another era, not just in terms of technology and dress, but also in how they treated women.

Jake knew he couldn't change the entire colony, but he'd be damned if he was just going to watch this guy abuse the woman or her daughter.

"You guys know if Sam's gonna put these paper towels on sale?" Jake asked the trio.

The woman pulled away from her husband and started to approach him.

"Come on, let's go. No need to gab with folks you don't know," Grisly Bear said to her as he grabbed her wrist.

She swatted Grisly Bear's hand away and walked three more steps. "That's a good question, sir. We're always trying to save a few cents. Why don't I go up and ask Sam?"

"You want to take your daughter with you?" Jake asked.

When the woman quickly pulled the teen close to her, Grisly Bear's eyes almost popped out of his head.

"I'll grab one of these rolls so Sam can do a check on it." Then she leaned closer to Jake and whispered. "Thank you."

Jake looked into her eyes. She might be sixty-something, but her eyes were captivating. Yet, he also saw so many mixed emotions behind those eyes: a wearing pain, but also a strong resolve.

"You need me to call the cops?" he asked under his breath.

She paused for a split second, but it was long enough for him to detect that she needed help.

"There's a back door down the hall, just beyond the bathrooms. Go out that door and I'll meet you there. I can take you to a home for battered women and get the cops involved. Does that work?"

"Woman, we need to get out of here. You two got chores to do," Grisly Bear said.

The woman didn't respond. She gave a stiff nod of her head to Jake, grabbed the paper towels, and with the teen at her side, casually walked down the aisle toward the front.

Jake went the opposite direction, nonchalantly making his way toward the front the door to get to his truck. He wanted to make sure the lady and her younger friend could quickly hop into the Red Barron the moment they exited the back of the grocery building. From there, he and Barney could take care of everything.

With one hand on the front door, Jake's heart shot into the back of his throat. Grisly Bear was hightailing it down an adjoining aisle, his boots clopping off the concrete floors.

"Excuse us." One of the twins—was is Liz or Laney?—barreled into Jake with her arms full of grocery bags.

"Uh…" Jake shifted to move past the woman, but was

instantly met by her twin sister.

"Hey, Jake, any hope you can help us take our bags to our Suburbans?"

Just then, Grisly Bear had cut in front of the woman and her young friend, stopping them at the threshold of the hallway to the back door. They tried to go around him, but he wasn't letting them pass.

"Can you let me get by?" Jake pleaded with the twins.

"Why Jake Mathews, didn't your momma raise you the right way?" one of the twins said with her mouth agape.

"Oh, right. Sorry." He grabbed, three, four, five bags of groceries and followed the twins across the parking lot, while keeping one eye on the store.

"Let's see, the two in your left hand go in my Suburban, and the rest go in my sister's," one twin said.

"Wait, actually, I need the fruit bag in mine," the other one said.

"Hold on," the first one said, reaching into one of the bags. "Here we go. Need to have a piece of gum." She snickered along with her sister.

The second one then said, "Jake, the bag with all the meat is my sister's. She hasn't figured out how to become a vegetarian yet."

Jake tried to sort out their volleying orders—until the moment Grisly Bear stomped out the front door, his mammoth hands clasping the wrist of each woman. The trio was making a beeline toward the beat-up pickup. Jake let the groceries slip through his fingers and drop to the ground. As he jogged toward them, he could hear the Doublemint Twins calling out for him, but he didn't hear a single word. His eyes were trained on Grisly Bear and the two women he was pulling along.

"Hey," he called out, trying to slow them down at the same

time as doubling his speed.

No heads turned his way.

"Yo, I need to talk to you," he shouted.

Still no acknowledgement that they'd heard him. But he knew they had.

He planted his hands on the back of the old Ford a second after the doors shut and locks were engaged. Not ready to give up yet, he knocked on the driver's side window.

"Just want to ask you a question."

The F-150 started backing up.

"Yo, can you just stop and we can have a conversation? I want to make sure the ladies are okay."

Just then, the woman leaned forward and reached her hand toward him—but Grisly Bear smacked it away and kept backing up, running right over Jake's foot. But Jake was too focused on the well-being on the two women to notice.

"Hey, man, that's not how you treat a lady. You hear me? Stop this truck and get out, dammit."

Grisly Bear ignored him and the brakes whined as the truck slowed. Jake knew Grisly Bear was about to shift gears and take off, so he jumped on the hood. "Let the ladies leave this truck. I'm not screwing around!"

Grisly Bear smiled, then lifted his arm to show a hunting knife. He moved it within inches of the older woman. "None of your business, boy!" Grisly Bear shouted through the windshield.

"Okay, I get it. Just don't hurt her, okay?"

As Jake started to slide off the hood, Grisly Bear punched it, and Jake tumbled to the ground. When he looked up, all he saw was the woman staring at him.

And then only one word could now describe her eyes: fear.

John W. Mefford Bibliography

The Alex Troutt Thrillers (Redemption Thriller Collection)
AT BAY (Book 1)
AT LARGE (Book 2)
AT ONCE (Book 3)
AT DAWN (Book 4)
AT DUSK (Book 5)
AT LAST (Book 6)
AT STAKE (Book 7)
AT ANY COST (Book 8)
BACK AT YOU (Book 9)
AT EVERY TURN (Book 10)
AT DEATH'S DOOR (Book 11)
AT FULL TILT (Book 12)

The Ivy Nash Thrillers (Redemption Thriller Collection)
IN DEFIANCE (Book 1)
IN PURSUIT (Book 2)
IN DOUBT (Book 3)
BREAK IN (Book 4)
IN CONTROL (Book 5)
IN THE END (Book 6)

The Ozzie Novak Thrillers (Redemption Thriller Collection)
ON EDGE (Book 1)

GAME ON (Book 2)
ON THE ROCKS (Book 3)
SHAME ON YOU (Book 4)
ON FIRE (Book 5)
ON THE RUN (Book 6)

The Ball & Chain Thrillers
MERCY (Book 1)
FEAR (Book 2)
BURY (Book 3)
LURE (Book 4)
PREY (Book 5)
VANISH (Book 6)
ESCAPE (Book 7)
TRAP (Book 8)

The Booker Thrillers
BOOKER – Streets of Mayhem (Book 1)
BOOKER – Tap That (Book 2)
BOOKER – Hate City (Book 3)
BOOKER – Blood Ring (Book 4)
BOOKER – No Más (Book 5)
BOOKER – Dead Heat (Book 6)

The Greed Thrillers
FATAL GREED (Book 1)
LETHAL GREED (Book 2)
WICKED GREED (Book 3)
GREED MANIFESTO (Book 4)

To stay updated on John's latest releases, visit:
JohnWMefford.com

Made in the USA
Coppell, TX
03 January 2023

10242121R10173